MEN IN SUITS

British detectives confront a heinous crime

MARTYN TAYLOR

THE
BOOK
FOLKS

Published by The Book Folks

London, 2024

© Martyn Taylor

ISBN 978-1-80462-205-6

www.thebookfolks.com

MEN IN SUITS *is the second novel in a brand-new series
of crime fiction titles by Martyn Taylor.
Look out for the first book,* IN THE FAMILY, *available on Amazon.*

*Further details about Martyn Taylor's books
can be found at the back of this one.*

Prologue

The young man saw the girl standing beneath the lamp post, young, slender to the point of boyishness, honey-blonde hair curling down her shoulders, strawberries-and-cream complexion with dramatic purple-and-blue eyeshadow. Just what the doctor ordered. Then he had another look, closer. She wasn't the girl he'd ordered, but she'd do.

He stopped his black VW Golf beside her and wound down the window. "You waiting for me, sweetheart?"

She stared at him, put one hand on her hip and pumped it twice in time with the gum she was chewing. "That depends."

"Depends on what?"

She laughed, opened the passenger side door and climbed inside. His heart was pounding so hard he could hardly hear her laughter.

"Fasten your seat belt," he instructed. "Can't be too careful, you know."

Chapter One

Bev Ford rattled downstairs into her kitchen, brushing her hair, searching for her handbag, hoping it was on the work surface. It wasn't. Wayne sat at the table, eating cornflakes, a half-drunk glass of orange juice in front of him and a comic in his left hand, ignoring her. Not that she minded. He could be a lot worse than existing in his own world. He could be like his father, which he wasn't, even if he did share his features.

Bev was like her kitchen, neat and well-maintained but needing some money spent on new work clothes for her, new doors for it. The fridge-freezer was taller than herself and both doors were covered with multi-coloured Post-it notes reminding them all of things to do, places they had to be.

"Where's your sister?" she asked. "She's usually up by now." She had to be up when Bev left for work if she wanted a lift to school. "I said, *where's your sister?*" she said more loudly.

Wayne looked up, removing one earbud, allowing her to hear faint sounds of heavy rock music. "Am I my sister's keeper?" He replaced the earbud.

Bev went back to the bottom of the stairs and called, "Kimberley, will you get a move on! I can't be late today." No, even though she had only got in from work after eleven the evening before, she could not risk her boss's wrath by being late today. "Kimberley Anne!" She only used her daughter's full name when she wanted her to know that Mummy's patience had worn not so much thin as see-through. She went back into the kitchen and poured herself a glass of orange juice, which she gulped down even though she would have much preferred a mug of strong, black coffee, sipped very slowly while watching the shopping channel on the small TV hanging on the wall just over the door into the hallway. Taking her phone from her bag, she cursed under her breath, not wanting Wayne to hear, when she saw it was even later than she thought.

Running upstairs, she hammered on Kim's bedroom door with the heel of her hand. "Will you come along, child! We are going to be late!"

There was no reply.

"I am coming in," Bev called, "in three… two… one!" Still, she hesitated, then opened the door.

The tiny room was spick and span, showing that the child took after her mother. Everything had a place and was in it. The curtains were open, and the bed was made. Bev's heart thumped hard, painfully, twice. "Kim…" she whispered, then took out her phone and called her daughter's number.

The number you have dialled is not available.

Kimberley was like any thirteen-year-old girl, surgically attached to her phone.

She thundered downstairs. "Where is she? Her bed hasn't been slept in!"

Wayne looked up, shook his head, removed both earbuds and closed his comic. It was time for him to walk to his sixth-form college. "Didn't she say she was having a sleepover at Bella's?"

Disdain in his voice made it clear he did not approve of his sister's choice of friends. Bev wasn't sure she liked Bella either.

"On a school night?"

Wayne shrugged, got to his feet and picked up his bag. He said nothing about his mother not being home for Kim to ask about a school-night sleepover, well aware of his mother's situation at work. He didn't like the way she was exploited, but there was nothing he could do about it, and saying anything would not make it any easier for her. He sat down again as Bev called Bella's mother.

"Hi, Sonja, this is Bev Ford ... Yes, Kim's mother. Was Kim staying with Bella last night?" The furrows in her brow deepened even further with concern as she listened. "Thank you, yes…" She shook her head and ended the call. "She said that Kim just called in to collect Bella and then they went round to a friend's. Any idea who it might be?"

Wayne shook his head. "News to me." He got up again and walked to the back door. "Shouldn't you be on your way? You know what Old Bill is like if you're late." There was nothing he could say about his sister's latest deception.

"Don't remind me." If there was one fact of her life about which Bev never needed reminding, it was Bill Hamilton. The last thing she wanted to do now was call him and say that she was going to be late in, and she couldn't say how late. Nevertheless, she called the office, told the receptionist she needed to speak to him and waited to be transferred.

"This is very inconvenient," he said.

In the moment it took her to process his words, she lost it with him, and instinct trampled all over common sense.

"How 'inconvenient' do you think it is for me that my daughter has gone missing? I'll make sure the first thing I tell her when I find her is how you have been 'inconvenienced'."

"Do not take that tone with me, Mrs Ford. There are plenty of others who want your job if you don't."

Yes, and how many will put up with your wandering hands and 'you work for me 24/7 whatever your contract says' attitude? she wondered, as she thumbed across the red button on her phone, taking deep breaths to calm down. Yes, she probably shouldn't have said it, but he had to understand children were important to people, more important than jobs. Just because he couldn't have any, didn't mean everyone had to be obsessed with work. She enjoyed her work, and was good at it, despite Bill Hamilton, not because of him. It wouldn't be easy to find another one, but a job was all it was. He'd made her think of looking for another one anyway. He hadn't pushed her beyond her limits before. Well, he had now.

She sat down at the kitchen table, the nails on her right hand scratching at her left palm, craving a cigarette more than anything as she tried to prioritise what she had to do. The first thing was to go to Kim's school, see whether she was there.

Chapter Two

Colliers Lane High School was built years before Beverley attended and needed serious remedial work even then, having been built by a very profit-conscious builder who later became mayor. Some of that work still needed to be done, more than two decades later. Obviously new paintwork blistered on the rusting metal. Hardly a paving stone was not cracked. She felt an increasing weight of depression as she approached the gates, which were already locked against any traffic. A young teacher, who obviously wanted to be somewhere else, anywhere else, stood across the pedestrian gate, taking names from the dribs and drabs of latecomers. With her name not on the list of expected visitors, he was reluctant to allow her entry.

"Look, I'm Kimberley Ford's mother. This is important…"

A broad smile flushed over his face at her name. "Kim! Why didn't you say!"

Because you wouldn't let me, she thought.

"Just go in the main doors and go to reception. See Mrs Dainty."

He stood aside to allow her entry, stepping across the gateway behind her to bar it for two girls whose uniform skirts were too short and whose ties were nothing like the regulation knot. "Valerie," he said, "and Diane. How many times is that this week?"

Bev's unease increased as she approached the school buildings, the same unwelcoming concrete with glass curtain walls as thousands of others up and down the country. The abstract logo above the door made it seem like some office block that had to announce its identity to distinguish it from dozens of others in the area, rather than the school that had been there in one shape or another for more than a century. She had never felt so nervous going in as a student and could not understand why she should feel so as a parent.

"Don't be ridiculous," she muttered to herself as she paused and then pulled on the door handle. The door didn't move. Only then did she see the handwritten sign 'Use other door'. Opening that door, she went inside a foyer that was all polished blonde wood, high windows and noticeboards advertising the extra-curricular activities for which Colliers Lane was known. There was a door and an opening in the wall beside it, with 'Reception' in pitted silver letters above it. She strode towards it, trying to ignore the squeaky sounds her shoes made. She was reaching for the bell when a very solid woman in late middle-age, wearing a tweed skirt, cotton shirt with a silk scarf at her throat and very business-like horn-rimmed spectacles on her nose, appeared.

"It's Beverley Wright, isn't it!" the woman said, and Bev realised it was the same Mrs Dainty who had been the school secretary when she was a pupil.

"It's Beverley Ford now…" Bev began.

"And you're here to tell us about Kimberley," Mrs Dainty continued, as though Bev had not spoken. "There was no need to come in person. A phone call would have been quite sufficient to explain her absence."

Bev became aware of two young women staring at her over the top of their computer screens. They both saw her noticing them and ducked back down to do whatever it was they were supposed to be doing. Mrs Dainty hadn't needed two assistants back in the day. Of course, there were no computers then.

"That's just it. I can't explain her absence…"

More words were about to pour out when Mrs Dainty put a finger to her lips and almost imperceptibly shook her head. They dried in Bev's throat instantly, and she had to cough the debris out before she could breathe.

"Take a seat, Mrs Ford." Mrs Dainty nodded to the plastic and metal stacking chairs on the opposite side of the corridor. "I'll get Mrs Norden. She's the Deputy Head with responsibility for pastoral care."

The chairs looked most uncomfortable and proved to be so when Bev sat down. Not that she noticed as she watched Mrs Dainty make a phone call. Moments after she put down the phone, the door two along the corridor from reception opened, and a tall, slim, very elegant woman – who could have been anything between twenty-five and sixty-five years old – came out. She had dark-blonde hair piled up in a chignon on the top of her head, clear skin and bright blue eyes. She was wearing a severely tailored business suit that hid her figure but showed it off well enough to make Bev feel just a little envious.

"Good morning, Mrs Ford." Bev scrambled to her feet and took the outstretched right hand, uncomfortably aware that hers was clammy.

The woman gave no sign of having noticed. "I'm Mrs Norden. Would you come into my office, please?"

Bev recognised an instruction disguised as a request and allowed herself to be ushered into the deputy head's room. The room itself was perfectly ordered, shelves with files upright and in alphabetical order, except when they contained books, which were equally upright and alphabetized. The desk had a computer on it, a telephone with a Rolodex beside it, and two framed photographs of young girls wearing different school uniforms. Mrs Norden waited until Bev sat down on the opposite side of the desk, then sat down herself.

"I confess to being surprised to see you here, Mrs Ford, almost as surprised as I am to find that Kimberley is not." She tapped her computer and brought up the file she wanted. "Kimberley's attendance record is impeccable. And she always insists on being called 'Kimberley', doesn't she? So unlike most girls who insist on whatever diminutive they like. Her best friend, Isabella, must be called 'Bella'. I can understand why, but couldn't she choose a different book?"

Bev said nothing. She had no idea what book she was talking about, and Kim insisted on being called 'Kim' at home. Some days she wouldn't even answer to that.

"Her teachers tell me that if everyone was as cheerful as Kimberley, worked as hard, was as helpful to everyone, their lives would be a lot easier."

Bev wondered who this Kimberley creature was. It certainly didn't sound like her daughter. "Mrs Norden," she said, "I'll be blunt. Kim did not sleep at home last night. I had to work late yesterday, it is that time of month and we are short-staffed." She paused for a moment, thinking, and they're going to be even shorter-staffed after this.

Mrs Norden shook her head, wearing what she believed was an understanding, sympathetic smile. "You don't have to explain yourself to me, Mrs Ford."

"Ordinarily, I look in on the children before I go to bed, but yesterday I didn't get home until eleven and I went straight to bed. When I got up this morning, I found that Kim's bed had not been slept in. Wayne, that's my son..."

Mrs Norden nodded. "I know Wayne." Those three words suggested she knew Wayne rather better than he might like.

"Wayne said she had gone to a friend's house for the night. They often have sleepovers. But when I phoned, her mother said Kim hadn't been there and she thought they had spent the night at ours."

Mrs Norden's expression showed a concern it had not before. "Isabella Conway?"

"That's right."

Her fingers clattered over the keyboard again before she picked up the telephone. "Mrs Dainty, have Isabella Conway report to my office. Right away." She did not wait for an answer.

Bev recognised her voice as being one used to command, and not accepting excuses.

"I generally find that when thirteen-year-old girls conspire to deceive their parents there are boys involved. Can you think of the names of any boys Kimberley might associate with?"

Bev's dislike of the words 'conspire' and 'deceive' was swept away by the mention of boys. "She's only thirteen!" she said.

Mrs Norden shook her head slowly. "I am afraid there is no such thing as 'only thirteen' nowadays, Mrs Ford. Not when it comes to sex."

Bev thought herself a broad-minded woman, earthed and in touch with real life. The use of the 'sex' word in connection with her daughter shocked her. Yes, when she'd been thirteen, she'd gone to the Odeon to see the Bay City Rollers and screamed out to Eric that she would have his babies, but she hadn't meant it and besides, nobody would have heard her screams over all the others. They definitely hadn't been able to hear the Rollers.

"Colliers Lane has students from all over the world, some from countries where it is much more common for girls of thirteen to be wives and mothers than attend school. I can tell you, in the strictest confidence, that thirteen is not the youngest age one of our students has fallen pregnant. Thirteen is by no means too young for people to be sexually active nowadays, despite our best efforts to educate them to the dangers. We live in times when it is almost impossible to protect the innocence of our children."

Bev glanced at the photographs on the teacher's desk. Perhaps they had more in common than either might wish to acknowledge.

There was a knock on the door. "Enter," Mrs Norden ordered. Bella entered, only opening the door wide enough to slide in sideways. It sprang shut behind her.

Bella was a slight girl, well-scrubbed with no real figure to speak of yet, and waist-length blonde hair the colour of ripening wheat done up in a French plait. Her uniform was clean and pressed and her tie was done up in a thick Windsor knot that covered just the top button of her shirt. She walked to the desk and stood where Mrs Norden indicated – right in the middle, a little in front of Bev on her chair who was to the left-hand side nearest the smeared window. Bev tried to speak but Mrs Norden beat her to it.

"Now then, Isabella, I believe you are friends with Kimberley Ford."

"Besties, Mrs Norden, besties." Her voice was all but inaudible.

"Perhaps you can tell us where she is."

This time she only shook her head so violently that her plait whipped about both sides of her face.

"Oh, come on, Isabella, don't be shy. Kimberley told her brother that she was going to spend the night at your house. Slightly unusual for a school day, but nothing wrong with that, I suppose. You're both as good as model pupils."

The longer Mrs Norden went on speaking, the more uncomfortable Bella became, wringing her hands together and shifting from one foot to the other.

"Now, when Mrs Ford here" – Mrs Norden nodded towards Bev as though she was some stranger rather than someone Bella had seen most days since she and Kim had started play school together – "when she called your mother this morning to see why Kimberley had not slept in her own bed last night, your mother said that not only had she not seen Kimberley, but also that she believed *you* were spending the night at *her* house."

Bella said nothing, although her discomfort appeared to be approaching wet-knicker level.

"We know that isn't true, and nobody seems to know where Kimberley is. She isn't at school. She isn't at her home. She isn't at your home. So, where did the two of you spend last night?"

No reply came, so Mrs Norden spoke the word 'Bella' with all the promise of a devil put aside for the child unless she answered immediately, and with a satisfactory answer.

"We was going round to stay at Frankie's…"

"We *were* going round to stay at Frankie's," Mrs Norden repeated. "Who is this 'Frankie'?" She glanced at Bev with just a hint of the 'I told you so about boys' in her expression. "I don't believe we have a 'Frankie' currently enrolled at my school."

"Francesse Brady, Mrs Norden."

"I do not recognise that name."

"She goes to St Thomas's, Mrs Norden."

St Thomas the Martyr was the Catholic high school nominally in competition with Collier Lane, but with such a fierce reputation that quite a few Catholics – like Bella's mother – recalled their own education by Irish nuns with less than a rosy glow, and sent their children to Colliers Lane.

Bev leaned forward, unable to hold her tongue any longer. "So, you spent the night at this 'Frankie's'…"

"No, Mrs Norden, I went home."

"Well, you're here now. Where is Kim?"

Bella stared at her feet. "Dunno. She went off on her own, never came back. Her phone's turned off."

"Don't lie, Bella…" Bev said. Her ears might not be as attuned to the timbre of adolescent deception as Mrs Norden's, but she could remember being thirteen well enough to recognise a lie when she heard it.

"That is enough," said Mrs Norden.

Once again, Bev found herself instinctively responding to the command in her voice.

"We will not get anywhere making accusations."

Bev stared at her, wondering how she could say that.

"I think you need to report Kimberley as a missing person to the police."

Bev was perplexed. Where had that come from? "I do?"

"Time is of the essence, Mrs Ford." Mrs Norden was on her feet and ushering Bev to the door. She gave her a card with her name and several telephone numbers printed on it. "Please, let me know as soon as you discover anything." She had Bev out in the corridor and by reception before she was aware of what was happening. "Ask Mrs Dainty to call a taxi for you."

"No, no thank you, that's all right…"

Mrs Norden strode back towards her room. Before she got there, Bev heard Bella call out, "Can I go back to my class now?" and the deputy head reply, "You stay exactly where you are, young lady. I am not nearly finished with you yet." Then the door closed with the finality of a stone being rolled in front of a tomb.

Bev stood where she was, trying to arrange her thoughts and emotions before deciding that that was something she would leave for later and striding towards the doors, this time oblivious to the squeaks her shoes made.

Chapter Three

Cooper Street police station was close enough for Bev to walk there without having to find somewhere to park the car. It was built along Stalinist Eastern European lines, with armoured roller blinds above each window in case the mob finally took to the streets. Razor wire cemented into the top of every exposed wall deterred pigeons perching there. Bev's determination dribbled away as she approached, unnerved by the prospect of encountering her ex there. He was a detective constable and their relationship had ended in anger and violence. It was only when she remembered he worked out of Forth Banks that the clouds lifted, and she managed not to walk on by the steps up to the front doors, which still had a blue lantern above, as though George Dixon still patrolled peaceful streets.

The female sergeant who stood behind the front desk looked up as the door closed. She must have seen the agitation in Bev because she asked, "What can I do to help?" before Bev even got to the desk.

"It's my daughter. She's thirteen and she's gone missing. She didn't come home yesterday. I was home late from work, and I didn't know…" The words vomited out of Bev's mouth in an almost undifferentiated stream.

Before she was finished, the sergeant had come out from behind the window and was leading Bev by the arm into a room that wasn't in the official area of the station. She sat Bev down on one side of a small table and sat down herself on the other side, putting a pad of printed forms between them and taking a pen from her shirt pocket.

"I'm going to need to take some details from you. Is that okay?" Her voice was low and comforting, inviting Bev to have confidence she was on her side, whatever might have happened. Bev nodded. "First of all, I am Sergeant Heather McCloud, and I am based here at the Cooper Street station."

The sergeant held up her ID lanyard to prove she was who she claimed to be, but Bev waved it away. She was not so agitated to think she needed proof of a copper's identity.

"Can I have your name and address and telephone numbers, please?"

Bev gave the details straight away, although she had to delve into her bag for her mobile to get that number.

McLeod chuckled. "Nobody over the age of forty knows their mobile number by heart," she said, "even if they do know their landline that they changed only last week."

Bev nodded, not quite understanding what that had to do with the price of fish.

"You say your daughter has gone missing."

Bev nodded.

"I'll need her details as well, and what has happened. Then we'll see what we need to do next. Is that okay?"

Bev nodded again. What option did she have?

What seemed like an eternity later to Bev, but was closer to ten minutes, the sergeant had completed her form, and was reading through it to make sure everything was as it needed to be. Bev noticed her handwriting was very small and precise, and thought it seemed somehow out of keeping with McLeod's size and fleshy build.

"Have you got a photo?" asked the sergeant.

Bev got out her purse and produced a well-thumbed head-and-shoulders portrait of Kim taken on her eleventh birthday, when she had looked particularly angelic. It was all Bev could do not to burst into tears as she looked at it. "This is the newest I've got on me," she said, pushing it across the table. "She's two years older now; she's shot up, her hair is longer, just a bit more than shoulder-length…"

"Is she recognisable from this?"

Bev wondered. There were days even she did not recognise Kim. "Yes, yes."

McCloud picked up the photo and looked at it. "She's beautiful." She got up. "I'll go and get this onto a flyer. Won't be long. Can I get you anything, a cup of tea?"

Bev shook her head. There was no way she could keep down anything, even a cup of tea as anaemic as it was likely to be in this place. She didn't know how long she sat there, or what she thought, just that ideas she could not quite catch whirled around in her brain, making her head ache. Eventually, the sergeant returned, wearing a reassuring smile.

"Well, I have put out a missing-person bulletin. Strictly speaking, we should wait until she's been missing twenty-four hours, but seeing as Kimberley is a child and has never done anything like this before…" Her voice trailed away, turning this into a question.

Bev nodded. The action only made her headache worse.

"Now, we have your home number and your mobile number, as well as Kimberley's. We'll call you the moment we find her, and you'll call us if she turns up at home, which she probably will. Kids do things for reasons that seem really, really important to them at the time, only to realise they aren't that important at all when they get to think about it."

"I've got your numbers?" Bev asked.

The sergeant smiled and tapped the business card on the desk just in front of Bev's folded hands.

"Oh, yes, yes, thank you." Bev fumbled the card into her bag without looking at it.

"I'm sure everything will turn out all right," the sergeant reassured her as she showed her out and watched her go down the steps, seeming smaller than she had when she came into the station.

* * *

Sergeant McCloud wished there was something she could do for Beverley Ford, other than mouth empty words that did not reflect the gnawing sensation she felt in the pit of her stomach. Without knowing why, she knew this one would not end well, but there was no way she could say that to anyone, least of all that poor mother. She went back inside, leaving the door to swing closed after her. There had to be something in there to take her mind off this.

Chapter Four

Bev felt the cold air outside the station like a punch in her stomach. Had she not caught hold of the railing, she might have fallen down the steps. A lot of good that would do Kimberley, she thought, if she was rushed to A & E at the Royal Victoria Infirmary. All the adrenalin surging through her had gone, leaving her light-headed and unsure whether a gust of wind might not swirl her into the air and off to Never-Never Land. She had loved that story as a child. A Peter Pan to take command of everything now would be a blessing.

But Peter Pan was fiction, Never-Never Land an impossible dream. Kimberley was real. Newcastle could be far too real.

She had walked to Cooper Street without noticing the effort. She walked slowly to the bus stop and waited there, lost in confusion that brought tears to her eyes; tears she could blame on the chilly wind that always blew along Cooper Street, just as it seemed to always blow along every road on Tyneside.

"That's two sixty-five," the bus driver told her. Getting the money out of her purse was more effort than it should have been, and she heard a couple of old biddies in the nearest seats tut-tutting about people who didn't have their fare to hand and kept good people waiting. At least, she thought that was what they said, although the one on the outside smiled at her as she brushed past. Ordinarily she would have gone upstairs, a relic from her younger days when she smoked, ever so sophisticatedly, and smoking was permitted on public transport. Those days were long gone, and as she caught hold of the rail to go up the stairs, she realised she did not have the strength. She flopped down beside an old woman who was holding tightly to a green tartan shopping bag on wheels in front of her, and closed her eyes, hoping for the next few minutes to pass in an instant.

She felt a hand press on her arm and saw an old lady looking up at her with concern in her eyes. "I hope you don't mind me saying so, pet, but you look in a right state."

Bev stared at her, wondering if it really did show on her face, the emotional battering she had taken, and for a moment was about to tell the old dear all about it. Instead of which, she shook her head.

"I've had a bit of a shock, that's all. I'll be fine." She would be fine, sometime; she just didn't know when.

The old woman smiled and nodded. "As long as you're sure." She patted Bev's arm again. "Just take my advice, get yourself home, put your feet up and get yourself outside a cup of hot, strong tea. It works wonders, take it from me. And don't be shy about adding a drop of whatever does you good."

Bev found herself smiling and nodding, saying nothing about her first-aider training that had taught her under no circumstances should you give alcohol to someone suffering shock.

"You mind what I said," the old woman called after her when she got up for her stop.

Bev turned, smiled and nodded. Yes, of course she would do exactly that.

Between the bus stop and her house was a corner shop run by a Sikh family that stocked almost everything a superstore would and a few things it wouldn't, like mousetraps and packets of cigarettes without the excise stamp on them. Bev went straight to the counter and asked for a quarter bottle of Bell's whisky and twenty Lambert & Butler.

The matriarch of the family was a short, stocky woman whose hair was greying in stark contrast to the luminous colours of her sari and the bright sparkle in her eyes. "Why, Mrs Ford, I thought you had given up," she said.

"I had," Bev replied, holding out a twenty-pound note and feeling a little shocked by how little change she received.

At home, she draped her coat over the newel post and took her handbag into the kitchen, where she rooted around in her glory drawer for a lighter or even some matches. Finding nothing, she tossed the cigarette packet in a disgusted curve towards the bin, where it bounced off and fell onto the floor, skidding almost all the way back to her feet. She ignored it and opened a cupboard to get a glass. Unable to decide which one to choose, she closed the door and went into the front room, where she slumped on the settee and channel-hopped, until she found an inoffensive nature programme about sheep.

Winding the sound down low enough for her not to hear, she cracked open the cap on the whisky bottle and took a mouthful. It scorched as it went off her tongue and down her gullet. By the time it got to her stomach, however, it was warm and soothing. The second mouthful went down much more smoothly, and she began to idly wonder why she had chosen to deny herself this mother's little helper to carry her burden. She had just swallowed the third mouthful when her eyes closed, and she toppled over sideways, hitting her head none too gently on the thin padding on the wooden arm of the settee. She did not wake. The opened bottle fell out of her hand and onto the floor, where the Scotch poured out, fizzing and smoking and taking the varnish off the floorboards.

Chapter Five

Florence Ballard threw a ragged yellow tennis ball for her dogs, two relentlessly energetic Jack Russells – Rascal and Bouncer – to chase around Hallam Dene. It was exercise for them and for her. She was of slightly-below-average height, made to appear even more so by being sturdily built, the image of a country lady, wanting only a blackthorn walking cane. She made do with a folding black aluminium stick.

But Florence was a city girl, always had been and always would be, unless one of her daughters persuaded her to quit Newcastle and spend her remaining years of retirement from the NHS in Australia with them. Both Jo and Eddi had already asked but she had never liked their husbands and she didn't like children, never had. She loved her own, of course, but didn't like them. Australia was a long, long way from Tyneside. That was why they lived there.

Picking up the ball that Bouncer had deposited at her feet, she fitted it back into the cup at the end of the plastic throwing stick and made to throw it up the incline towards the little car park. Instead of flying forwards, it shot out of the cup backwards, down towards the bushes at the bottom of the slope. The dogs chased after it. They would bring it back in a moment or so.

Only they didn't. They stopped before the bushes and stood there, straining, barking at the tops of their voices.

"Oh, what is the matter with you?" Florence muttered, before calling, "Rascal! Bouncer!"

They ignored her, standing where they were.

Huffing in annoyance, she strode down the slope. "Do I have to remind you that dogs who do not come to heel when they are told do not get allowed off the lead the next time they go for a walk?"

The dogs did not move, but turned their heads to look at her, tongues lolling, eyes pleading with her to come and see what they had found. "Rascal! Bouncer! Come here!" There was something in her voice that convinced the dogs they had pushed this as far as they could. Their heads went down, submitting to the alpha female in the pack. She quickly clipped their leads to their collars and told them to sit, which they did. "Stay." They obeyed, waiting as she went forward to peer under the bushes and see what had attracted their attention.

It looked like a small, pale human hand. She bent forward and discovered it *was* a small, pale human hand.

She staggered backwards as she processed what she had seen, making the dogs whimper as she almost stood on them. Those sounds brought her back to herself, feeling her heart pound in her chest as she commanded it to slow down. "It's just a dead body," she told herself. "You were a nurse for more than forty years. How many dead bodies have you seen?" She squatted down to fuss the dogs until they, too, were calm. She took the reels their leads fed into and pushed her stick through the handles before laying them on the ground.

"Stay," she said, and turned towards the bushes before seeing whether they obeyed. They did.

Lifting the branches of the bush with the throwing stick, she saw that the hand belonged to a child, a girl who was naked and dirty and, from the blood and bruises all over her, had obviously taken a terrible beating. She let the bushes fall and stepped backward. This was not the first murder victim she had seen, not the first child sacrificed on the altar of some savage's selfish lust. She remembered a group of nurses discussing her first child victim, or maybe it was her second. To a woman, that gathering of decent women had resolved that if they were ever left alone for five minutes with a man who had done something like that, they would show the man suffering.

Sitting on the ground, she took her mobile out and dialled 999. "I need the police and an ambulance," she said. "I have found the victim of a murder." Moments later, having given the operator the details, she agreed that she would stay where she was until the officers arrived.

"Don't go there," she told a young couple with a golden retriever bouncing at the end of a long lead.

The man glared at her, silently asking 'why?'

Florence repeated herself, and her tone convinced him to ask only whether there was anything they could do.

"You'll hear all about it on tomorrow's news."

He moved as though he was going down there, but the woman caught hold of his arm and pulled him away. Florence watched them walk away and wondered how long the police were going to be. She wished she had brought her husband's hip flask with her, the one he secretly took with him when he went golfing. A tot of whisky would do her good. She wondered where the flask was. In the attic with his golf clubs, most likely.

Chapter Six

Florence heard a car pull up in the parking space at the top of the slope. Glancing in that direction she saw two cars, her dark blue Peugeot and a white Vauxhall with orange and yellow stripes along the side and blue lights on the roof. Two officers got out, both wearing fluorescent jackets, and came towards her. She got to her feet as they approached. Rascal and Bouncer hid behind her.

"Did you call the police?" asked the older constable, his voice as rich and round as might be expected from a man of his build. She saw the name 'Winter' on a flash on his jacket.

"I did," she said. "You'll find the poor little thing under those bushes." She pointed without turning in that direction.

The younger officer, whose name appeared to be Collins, spoke to his colleague. "Should I call an ambulance?"

"She's past needing an ambulance, young man."

Collins turned towards her. "An expert, are you, missus?"

Florence bit down on the first reply that rose to her lips and counted to ten, while fixing her gaze on Winter.

"A nurse with more than forty years' experience," she said. "I've have seen a lot more corpses than you have… sonny boy."

He shuddered. Rascal and Bouncer growled at him.

She stood there glaring at him, her lips compressed into a thin line, her heart thumping in her chest. It didn't matter how many bodies you'd seen in the past, the latest one was still a blow.

"I'm sorry, Mrs Ballard. I didn't mean to offend you."

Oh yes you did, she thought, you thought I was a just another civilian. "None taken, Constable."

* * *

Winter stood for a moment before shaking his head briefly and turning to walk down the slope to where Collins waited for him just before the bushes.

"She's a bit of a battle axe." Collins chuckled as he joined Winter. The joviality went out of him as he saw his colleague's thunderous face.

"She's right, you twat," Winter said.

Collins stiffened at his use of that word. The police canteen was just as much a place of profanity as anywhere men gathered together to get some respite from the demands of their job, but Barry Winter was not a 'fuck this', 'fuck that' type. In civilian life, he was a lay reader, something Collins could not begin to understand. For Winter to have called him a 'twat' meant he had transgressed some unseen boundary. Collins' first reaction was to snarl back, attack being his preferred form of defence, but there was something about the set of the older man, the way both his feet were planted very firmly on the ground, that made him change his mind. They weren't there to argue.

Winter lifted the shrubbery and stepped inside, holding it up for Collins to follow before he let it fall. The younger man stared at the battered, bloodied corpse for a long, long moment before turning and barging through the shrubs to the fence beyond the clearing.

"Make sure you're right at the far side…" Winter called after him, his last couple of words drowned out by the sound of Collins retching, spitting and cursing.

The child lay on her back, arms and legs spread; eyes still open staring up into the sky. Winter found himself wanting to close those eyes, so he did not have to see their bewildered, clouded expression, but he knew better than to touch her. As he looked at the corpse, he tried to work out how old she was. Her hips were straight, almost but not quite boyish, and she had only a suggestion of a waist and breasts. There was absolutely nothing of the 'jello on springs' about her. Twelve, he guessed, maybe her early teens. She hadn't lived long enough to discover what life was about, much less squeeze the juice out of it. Sadness and futility poured down over him. This was the sort of obscenity he existed, as a policeman, to prevent. He was a failure.

Collins returned to the scene, wiping his mouth on a handful of tissues he stuffed into his jacket pocket.

"There's some wipes in the car if you need 'em," Winter said, "in the glovebox."

Collins nodded, pale-faced and ashamed.

"At least you managed to get right away from the crime scene, lad," Winter reassured him. "You know what McCreavie would say if you contaminated it."

The younger man did not seem at all reassured by this.

"Right, I think we've done enough sightseeing. You go and fetch some bollards and tape from the car, get a perimeter set up. I'll get this called in."

Collins ducked under the shrubbery and all but ran up the hill, ignoring Rascal and Bouncer yapping at him as he went. Winter stayed where he was until he had finished reporting to Control. Only then did he emerge and walk slowly towards Mrs Ballard, his notebook in his hand.

"You'll understand this is a serious matter," he began.

"None more serious," she said, getting unsteadily to her feet.

He almost made to help her, but her glare told him she was perfectly capable of standing upright with just the help of her stick.

"The detectives will want to take a full statement from you," he said, "but if you can just give me a quick run-through of what happened, maybe we can get you home before they put you through that this evening."

She nodded her approval of that idea and talked him through what had happened, even though she was growing increasingly unsure she would ever know untroubled sleep again.

Chapter Seven

Detective Inspector Pen Darling sat back in her chair, savouring the meal he had cooked for her, eyeing the white wine with desire. Just because she wasn't at the station did not mean she wasn't still on duty, and she did not drink on duty.

Paul Reid, her recently re-found lover, had restricted himself to just the one glass too, an old-fashioned wine glass rather than the glass bucket you needed two hands to lift, which was how wine came in bars nowadays.

The sun was just touching the tops of the Durham hills she could see in the distance. The light it cast in the valleys was magical. While his house was not that big, no bigger than her own with three bedrooms, it was detached and far better decorated. The garden had been the subject of loving attention by someone with green fingers. It even had a strange, abstract metal sculpture they had never discussed.

Paul came out of the kitchen with a cafetière, two small cups and a jug of cream.

"No sugar?" she observed.

"Ever the detective!" He laughed. "You don't take it. Neither do I, now."

Back when they had known each other for the first time, he had taken his coffee the way most coppers did, with enough sugar to stand up a spoon.

He said nothing but poured the coffee and handed her a cup. She could help herself to cream.

"On the other hand, I don't remember you being interested in any food that didn't either come with ketchup or fries, preferably both."

He laughed and took a sip of his coffee. "A man needs a hobby."

"I was trying to work out the mortgage you must be paying on this place."

He shook his head. "Never had a mortgage."

"God! What on earth rent must you be paying?"

Once again, he shook his head. "I bought it after I had a run of luck at Ascot. Almost went through the card on an accumulator and bought this with the winnings. Cost a bit to get it back in shape, but I think it was worth it. It is a negotiable asset if everything goes pear-shaped."

She took another sip of her coffee. The approximate value of the house floated through her mind. "I didn't think you could make so much money gambling."

He chuckled. "You win some, you lose some. It all depends on how much you're prepared to lose. I'm a 'professional' gambler. I keep records of everything. I declare it all to the taxman, and I pay my taxes. I even pay my National Insurance contributions." He looked out over the countryside in the distance. "The big wins don't come along too often. Fortunately, neither do the big losses. I've always made a strict rule of not betting anything I can't afford to lose. That's why I'm a professional gambler, not a gambling addict."

They were silent for a moment, remembering people gripped by that addiction.

"You don't have to explain yourself to me," she said.

He raised a questioning eyebrow. "Maybe I want to."

She looked away. She had no intention of telling him about her father gambling money he could not afford to lose and the years of long frigid silences between her parents after he lost the family home. To her, gambling was understandable but too dangerous, like drinking and smoking, or taking recreational drugs. If this made her a puritan in some eyes, she was happy to wear the hairshirt.

"Any trouble at the station about… me?" he asked.

She snorted. Everyone at the station knew better than to make any comment on her personal life. Only Deputy Chief Constable Pattison had very diffidently broached the subject with her, although, for that unreconstructed male chauvinist pig who would have been considered hidebound in the nineteenth century, diffidence equated to the approach of a rhino with toothache. And he had found her equally blunt.

"My private life is exactly that. Private. I am not associating with a criminal…" *Unlike some*, she could have reasonably added, but didn't.

She sighed. "I need a holiday. I think we should go somewhere I can lay in the sun and ripen, like a vegetable."

"That's all very well for you. I can't lie around in the sun, not with my complexion."

"Your complexion... oh, I forgot, you only come out at night."

He looked west and put his hands in front of his face. "The sun, it burns, it burns..."

They both laughed at that.

"I like the idea. Let's have a look when I get back," he said.

Her brow lowered just a little as she looked at him. "I didn't know you were going anywhere."

"Yeah, Atlantic City, tomorrow. The World Championship of Poker."

"Doesn't it cost thousands of dollars to enter that?"

The entry fee was actually two hundred and fifty thousand dollars, but this was not the time for pedantry. He had the money. It was his working capital. He had to speculate to accumulate. If he won, he would never have to work again.

"You don't mind me going?"

"What?" She laughed. "Not as long as you let me help you spend your winnings."

He joined in her laughter.

She liked the way he could make her laugh. It was a long time since there had been anything like enough laughter in her life.

The laughter was interrupted by the buzzing demand of her work phone. She raised her finger as she answered it but was getting to her feet even as she listened.

"Gotta go!" She plucked her jacket from the back of her chair. "I'll do the washing-up some other time."

He went on smiling, liking the idea of there being another time. "What's up?"

"A child's been murdered."

He grimaced and his stomach muscles clenched as though he had been kicked. He put his hands over his ears. "Don't tell me anything. I'll read all about it when I get back."

She took hold of his hands, pulled them down and kissed him quickly on the lips. Then, she was gone without another word.

Chapter Eight

Detective Inspector Pen Darling parked the car halfway between the car park and the entrance into Hallam Dene, behind the last police vehicle in the line. She got out and looked towards the refreshment van that was one of the first police vehicles to arrive. She shook her head. It was there. That was all that mattered. This promised to be a long night and keeping everyone on their toes with tea and bacon sandwiches was something very much to be desired.

Darling paused at the top of the slope as Detective Sergeant Peter Morton carried on down in the direction of Winter and an elderly woman at whose feet curled two unhappy dogs. She had never been one for pets but even she could tell how disconsolate they were. There was a polystyrene cup in the woman's hand. She had to be the civilian who had reported the find. Standing there, she took in what there was to see, the topography of the small park – a grassy slope that ran down to some bushes, with trees and the woods of the real Dene beyond them. Beside the bollards and tape dividing off the crime scene was the medical examiner's anonymous black van. Darling was mildly irritated he had got there before her.

Past the car park were more tall trees obscuring the houses behind. She made a note to get those houses canvassed, even if it would probably wait until tomorrow.

It was all but dark now, which was why she could see a couple of SOCO technicians setting up some lights beside the white tent already erected by the body. As she looked around, she took in that the area was secluded, pretty much hidden from the sight of anyone outside the park, with the woods marking the perimeter. The track that led to the park was little more than a hundred yards long, all between trees. This was just about a perfect place to commit a murder or dump a body. It was one of the few places on Tyneside not overlooked by CCTV. She made another mental note to have the CCTV on the main road checked, to see what vehicles turned down there, especially at night.

The moment of professionalism did nothing to dispel the weight of depression pressing her down into the grass. That anyone should be murdered she had only recently stopped taking as a personal affront, and that this victim was a child brought that back into stark relief. The waste of all that potential and the devastation it would inflict on her family and friends was a black shadow on the world. The years had not changed that, any more than they had changed her anger. Killing people was wrong. Everybody knew that. Anyone who did not believe the commandment applied to them was irretrievably damaged goods. That anger fuelled her determination to get any homicide puzzle resolved as quickly as possible, the murderer apprehended.

Her experience was that most murders were solved easily enough. Murderers weren't master criminals, cleverer than the police searching for them. Most might as well have sat in a chair in their local with an illuminated 'Here I Am!' sign above their heads. Just as most murders were domestic, most murderers were stupid. That was what Joe Milburn had told her on the first homicide she had been involved in investigating, and she had only encountered a couple of murderers who had suggested the observation was incorrect.

She walked slowly down to where Winter stood with the civilian.

He turned to see her, and saluted, which still embarrassed her. "Inspector."

"Constable." She turned towards the woman. "And this is?"

"I'm Florence Ballard. I discovered the body and called you lot."

Darling took the woman's hand and squeezed it in both of hers. It was a very cold hand. "I'm Detective Inspector Darling. Thank you for everything you've done."

Florence coloured in embarrassment. "I didn't do anything anyone wouldn't do."

Darling kept herself from chuckling at the innocence. "You might be surprised, Mrs Ballard. Have you given anyone your details, so we can take a formal statement later?"

Winter coughed his answer.

Darling nodded. "Of course. Now I don't think we need to detain you here any longer; it is getting chilly, after all."

The sun had now vanished, and the temperature had dropped. Florence, on the other hand, was dressed to withstand a winter cold snap.

"Can I get the constable to give you a lift home?"

"I have my own car in the car park."

"Someone will follow you home, make sure you get there, okay? You have had a shock, after all."

Florence was opening her mouth to tell Darling exactly what she had told Winter, that it would take a lot more even than the naked corpse of a murdered child to shock her, but before she could speak, Winter took her free arm and began to lead her up the slope, Rascal and Bouncer slouching along behind. It was after their teatime, and when it came to feeding time, they were as bad as cats.

Darling watched them for a moment, then shivered and buttoned up her coat. She went and stood by the tape barrier around the white tent, next to the van.

Not long afterwards, a man in his late fifties emerged from the tent, gone to fat with ginger hair and looking ill at ease in his white coveralls. Ordinarily, he was all bluster and high colour, evidence of the high living he had pursued despite his medical knowledge and his conviction that the accident of his birth better fitted him to rule the world than anyone. The bright lights revealed a sheen on his face, which was almost as white as his suit.

Darling had as little time for him as a man, but she could not help but be concerned about his appearance.

"Dr Wolstenholme… Henry… are you all right?"

He turned towards the direction of the voice; his eyes did not focus on her initially. If anything, his appearance suddenly worsened. "Good evening, Inspector… Penelope…"

Wolstenholme was one of two people who called Darling by her full first name, which she hated. Neither he nor her mother had much of a regard for her opinion on the subject.

"I am decidedly not 'all right'," he said, shivering where he stood.

For a moment, Darling thought he was about to burst into tears.

"I have examined more murder victims than I can remember, or care to, in all honesty. I believed I had seen every injury, every indignity we savages can inflict on one another." He shook his head and looked down at the fingers of his right hand, turning them over and then back again.

Is he imagining he has a cigarette in it? she wondered. The staining on those two fingers showed he had been a heavy smoker.

"I was wrong," he continued. "That is a child in there, Inspector, a child who may not have been exactly 'innocent' for quite some time, but a still a child. I haven't conducted a full autopsy, but I can tell you this. That child was beaten with fists and blunt objects everywhere on her body except her head, and this happened recently. I would put the time of death in the early hours of this morning. Once again, I should be able to give you a more accurate estimate—"

"So, she died sometime after midnight?" Darling could not prevent herself from interrupting.

Wolstenholme glared at her. "If you would allow me to conclude, Inspector?"

"Sorry," she muttered. There was a further, prickly silence as he waited for her to say more, and she refused to say anything further.

"So far as I can tell, something…" His voice died and he looked away for a while, his mouth working as though he was chewing on the words he wanted to say. When he turned back, his features were softer, and there was a defeat in his eyes. The words he did speak were low, harsh-toned and clearly cost him much to speak. "That child died in agony, unimaginable agony."

They stood for a moment in silence, Darling's reaction to what he had just told her tempered by concern for him. She had never seen him like this before. Wolstenholme was the original crusty old medic who had seen everything and come out the other side.

"Now I am going to have the body removed to my mortuary, where I shall conduct my post-mortem examination, after which I shall write my report. After that I shall go home and drink myself unconscious. If I still have any luck, I shall drink myself to death."

All Darling could do was not stare at him open-mouthed. She knew that his constant encounter with death had to have some emotional effect. He was a man, after all, even if not a very pleasant one.

His face brightened, just a little. "I may write my resignation first. I have not decided. All I know for certain is that I have had as much of the human race as I can stomach. You probably do not know that I have a grand-niece, Charlotte. She is just about the same age as that poor child. More than once, I felt I was looking into Charlotte's face. A man cannot exist like that, Inspector. He must know when he has reached the end."

He shrugged and took a breath deep enough to lift his shoulders up to his ears. Then he put his hand on her arm, which shocked her. Would he be kissing her cheek next? she wondered. Whatever the antithesis of touchy-feely was, its name was Wolstenholme.

"In the meantime, Inspector, I should be obliged if you would make me a promise."

Darling nodded. "If I can."

"When you find this monster, Inspector Darling, as I am confident you will because you are a good detective, allow me ten minutes alone with him, just him and me and my instruments. Ten minutes. Is that too much to ask?"

Of course it is. You know it is, thought Darling. "I'll do what I can," she said.

Wolstenholme nodded, turned away and stamped off up the slope towards the car park looking like he was climbing Everest without oxygen and needed to take a deep breath with every step.

Darling watched – a tight, clenching sensation in the pit of her stomach making her feel as though she had been punched, hard. Whether this was because of what Wolstenholme had said or the way he had said it was very much the question. She was used to having to deal with people in various states of high emotion, but she had never had to deal with anything like that. Her feet were on solid ground, nevertheless she felt unsteady.

Wolstenholme's assistants emerged from the tent with a stretcher between them, carrying it because the ground was too uneven for a trolley. The body was in a black, heavy neoprene body bag, looking hideously small. Darling found breathing more difficult than it had been a moment before. They stopped beside her, and the technician at the back – she thought his name was Dunn, although she wasn't sure – nodded down towards the bag, inviting her to take a look. She shook her head. She did not like looking at murder victims. She was a real-life police officer, not some telecop who could march into the mortuary, glance at the corpse and see something no one had noticed before that was vital to breaking the case. Investigations relied on everyone doing their job. She was never going to catch anything that Wolstenholme might have missed, or the SOCO team overlooked. They did not expect to do her job either.

She watched as they took the stretcher to the ambulance, opened the back doors and slid it inside. They then drove it slowly towards the entrance to the park, their place being taken by an equally anonymous van from which emerged the SOCO team in white Tyvek coveralls and pale-blue plastic bootees. They carried metal equipment cases and tried to pull cotton masks over their mouths as they went. By the time they had finished covering themselves, all that was visible was an inch or so of forehead above their goggles, and Darling knew they would tuck their hoods into their goggles, erasing even this small indication of humanity, before they set to work.

Darling reached out to the first, stocky female figure. "Mind if I look inside?"

"Don't you go touching anything," Sergeant Rose McCreavie said. "It's bad enough Wolstenholme and his elephants have been stamping around in there."

"I won't," said Darling, and leaned forward over the tape, peering through the door McCreavie held open for her. She stared intently, without looking at anything specific, just trying to take in the whole scene. "Thanks."

McCreavie stepped inside and let the door fall after her.

Darling walked back up to the car park and took a cup of tea. The tea was foul, just hot enough to scorch the roof of her mouth. It didn't matter. All she could really feel was that thumping pain at the back of her head, where her spine joined her skull. She had some painkillers in her bag, but she ignored them. The only cure for this pain, which she knew was psychosomatic, was to catch whoever was causing it. She believed she would do that. The problem was that, just at the minute, she had no idea exactly how.

Chapter Nine

Darling woke next morning before her alarm sounded, as usual. She wanted to go back to sleep but knew she wouldn't, couldn't. The nightmare that had her tormented was forgotten, the hair stuck to her forehead and neck the only evidence she had not slept soundly. She didn't have to remember the images to know what they represented, the promise of an investigation that would gut her, emotionally. That, she could not allow. She could not afford such self-indulgence. A dead child and her family deserved the very best she could do.

At eight o'clock she walked into the Forth Banks office, stopped to pick up the single file that was on her desk and walked upstairs to knock on the superintendent's door.

"Come in, Inspector," she heard, and did as she was told, walking in, putting the file she had read on the way up on his desk and then sitting down on the opposite side.

Detective Superintendent Joe Milburn was a big man only gone slightly to fat since being kicked upstairs. Most people would still want him on their side if an argument got physical. He was an old-school copper who believed in wearing out shoe leather talking to people and listening to what they had to say, but he reluctantly accepted using modern techniques if they got the job done. He had been a copper on Tyneside for four decades and the bad lads who had made his acquaintance wished they hadn't. He had the air of a copper who would take a miscreant out behind the bike shed and show them the error of their ways with a truncheon that was anything but standard issue. That sort of street coppering had still sometimes happened when he joined his father in the force, although nothing like as it had when Joseph Milburn Senior was a constable. 'Whatever works' was the motto Joe took from his dad and then instilled in successive generations of CID officers. Even so, he was the most thorough, painstaking of coppers, who believed that dotting every *i* and crossing every *t* was the best way of ensuring that righteous cases were not chucked out of court just because some smart-arse lawyer found a nit to pick. All lawyers were smart-arses to Joe Milburn.

He closed the file that contained Dr Wolstenholme's post-mortem report.

Darling could not remember seeing him look so grim.

"I heard the good doctor was thinking of calling it a day," he said.

Darling wondered where he might have heard that snippet but said nothing and nodded her head. Milburn shook his.

"I suppose there is only so much of this filth any man can take." He flipped the file open again, then closed it. "You have read this, I take it." When she did not reply immediately, he shook his head again. "Stupid question," he said. He took a deep breath and closed his eyes, making her wonder what announcement he might be about to make. "You know me, Pen."

He was one of the very few in Forth Banks who got to call her by her preferred diminutive. In a formal situation she was called 'Inspector'. In the canteen they called her 'The Ice Maiden', but only in her absence.

"I was born a copper. I'll die a copper. I'm a copper 'cos I'm better at it than I am at anything else, better at it than just about anyone else, false modesty to one side." He tapped the file. "This is one of the few times in my career I wish I'd been a sparks, or a grave digger, maybe even a traffic warden."

By Milburn's standards, this was a speech approaching the lengths of Shakespearean soliloquy.

"I'm sure I don't need to tell you, but I'll tell you anyway," he continued. "I want this fucker caught. I want him caught now. You'll have every asset I can find to help you catch him."

Unlike most coppers, Milburn was not careless with his expletives, only using them when there were no other words to express himself.

She got to her feet and picked up the file. "I understand, sir. I'll go and brief the team, get started."

"You do that, Inspector."

She walked towards the door. Just as she was taking hold of the door handle, he spoke again. "Make sure you keep me informed."

She did not turn around. "Of course, sir."

Chapter Ten

Darling walked downstairs, into the conference room and between the desks to the front, took a quick look at the team she had for the investigation, CID and uniforms, and felt a sharp pang of mixed anger and disappointment that this was the most manpower that could be spared for the case. There had been nearly double in her first murder investigation, and even more for sensitive cases like this. She wondered whether all the bean counters and politicians in London, who believed it was possible to cut and cut and cut again when it came to manpower while somehow magically maintaining service levels, would understand it if it was one of theirs whose justice was delayed or even not delivered because of staff shortages. She put the thought aside. No righteous indignation would put a single extra body in that room. Besides, she had confidence in every officer there. They would do what she charged them to do, to the very best of their abilities. They were good people, trained and diligent, determined. That was what she asked of them, to do their best, not to be perfect.

She hoped she was up to the task of leading them. Most of the time, she was as confident as she appeared. Her moments of doubt were kept secret.

"Good morning, everyone." She stood in front of the glass wall at the far end of the room that would be used for photos and timelines and the like. As they muttered their greetings to her, she caught a momentary glimpse of her reflection – that of a tall, strongly built woman in her late thirties with long, dark hair drawn tightly back from a face, she did not care whether it was beautiful or not. It had been a long time since she had cared, since the day she had kicked her waster of a husband out of the door and had the locks changed.

"What we have is the murder of a child, a particularly horrific murder of a child. You've all got a file with the outline of what we know already." She pressed the top corners of the post-mortem photo of the child into the very centre of the wall.

It was an ugly photograph. Darling heard indrawn breaths all around the room, even from the 'been there, done that' old lags.

She tapped the wall beside the photograph. "Apart from the post-mortem report and a few bits and bobs concerning the finding of the body, this" – she tapped the glass beside the photo with – "this is just about the sum of our present knowledge of the victim. Which is not a situation we can allow to continue much longer. Someone, somewhere, is missing her and we need to find out who she is as soon as we possibly can…"

"Boss, I think I can answer that question." A tall, slender young Asian woman sitting in the front row nursing an armful of files got to her feet. She was not in uniform, but the dark-blue business suit she wore with a grey cashmere scarf covering her head and tucked into the collar of her jacket was a near-enough facsimile of the uniform she had stopped wearing not so very long before.

"Shan?" Darling wondered why she was not surprised DC Shan Abdullah was the first with something to offer. As an ambitious woman herself, she knew she had to be at least twice as good as any of her male colleagues. She was accustomed to feeling those male colleagues looking daggers into her back. What she could only guess was the effort required to overcome all that hostility and be a Muslim as well.

Abdullah handed Darling a copy of the missing person's report Beverly Ford had completed less than twenty-four hours before. "The photo isn't up to date, boss, but…"

One glance was all Darling needed to know that there was no 'but' about it at all. She held the report alongside the post-mortem photograph. It was the same child. Darling lifted the report to read it, squinting a little, reminding herself she really did need to get her eyes checked. "Kimberley Anne Ford. Aged thirteen years and two months. Home address: 22 Woodley Street."

The remainder of the briefing passed in a blur as she quickly assigned duties around the room and sent them all on their way. "Keep in touch!" she instructed as the chairs creaked on the floor. Reaching out, she tapped Abdullah on the arm.

"DC Abdullah, if you please…"

Abdullah sat down again until the room was clear and the door closed.

"Right, Shan," Darling said, gathering up the file she had brought with her. "Let's go and visit Mrs Ford."

Chapter Eleven

Darling drove in virtual silence to Woodley Street. She rarely had any inclination to talk while she was driving, preferring to concentrate on what was for her – even now – a demanding occupation. She might not have minded if that concentration made her a better driver, but it didn't. 'Competent' was the highest compliment she was prepared to pay herself in that regard. Shan Abdullah sat silent in the passenger seat, seemingly content to watch and learn.

"How did the exams go?" Darling asked out of the blue.

"Exams?"

"Your sergeant's exams. How did they go?"

"I think I did… you never can tell, can you? I'll get the results in a few days."

"You'll have done fine."

Abdullah hoped she was right.

Woodley Street was one of the many post-war streets of semis on the steep slopes above the river to the west of the city. When they stopped outside Number 22 and got out, they could just hear the traffic rumble from the Western Bypass. The houses looked comfortable but ordinary; all featured slight variations on the theme of uPVC replacement windows, with occasional extensions to the sides, and a garage, where space permitted. Front gardens had been turned into hard standing where there was no space. Here and there, solar panels could be seen on south-facing roofs, with the universal satellite-TV dish – sometimes more than one of them where residents wanted to watch Italian soap operas or Spanish football.

Darling led the way up the concrete steps to the front door of Number 22 and used the knocker above the letter box to rap smartly on it. She was about to use it again when the door was opened by a youth who looked about seventeen, dressed in dark trousers and the black sweatshirt with a silver castle crest of the local sixth-form college. Darling wondered, briefly, why he was not in college as it was past nine o'clock, but instead introduced herself and Abdullah.

"Can I speak to Mrs Ford, please?"

The colour fled from the youth's face, taking half a dozen years with it. "You've found Kim?" He had to cough twice to moisten his mouth sufficiently to allow the words out.

"Can we come in, please? This isn't something to be discussed on the doorstep."

The youth stood aside, and Darling walked straight past him. As Abdullah went past, she looked into his face, saw his eyes glistening with unshed tears and noticed he was trembling, behind his manly exterior. Without thinking, she reached out and took his hand, briefly, squeezing it gently.

He looked down at her hand, then up into her face, and a weak smile appeared.

"I'm Shan," she told him. "Shan Abdullah. I'm a detective constable." She saw a darkness pass over his face. He knew why they were there, a detective inspector and a detective constable, to talk about Kim. They couldn't be the bearers of good news.

"I'm Wayne," he said, then coughed to clear his throat. "Wayne Ford, Kim's brother."

"You're Wayne," she insisted, gently. "She's your sister. And it's okay to cry, even if you are the man of the house." She knew instinctively that this lad was going to need to be strong in the face of what lay ahead for this family.

He looked into her eyes as she wondered where she had found those words, and were they the right ones, then he nodded, turned and went to the sitting room door.

"Mum's in there," he said. "She hasn't been to bed all night." He hesitated. "I think she's been drinking again," he muttered.

"Who's that?" Bev called from inside the room.

"It's the police, Mum."

"Show 'em in."

Wayne opened the door and stepped inside, into the gloom.

"What are you doing here anyway? You're supposed to be at school!" said Bev.

He shook his head. "We agreed I'd stay off to look after you. Remember?"

Darling stepped past Wayne and went over to the sofa, where Bev was reclining.

She looked distinctly the worse for wear, clothes wrinkled as though she had slept in them, which she probably had; hair, a bird's nest; make-up smeared over her face by tears and an idle hand.

The inspector sat down on the edge of the easy chair that had matched the sofa when they were bought but now was entirely covered by a throw from a market somewhere showing Tretchikoff's Green Lady, only she was blue. Knees together, she leaned forward, hands clasped, only just on the chair but as close as she could get to Bev.

"Mrs Ford, I'm Detective Inspector Darling, and my colleague is Detective Constable Abdullah." She motioned towards Abdullah with her clasped hands, who nodded and smiled at Bev. Neither gesture appeared to reassure the woman anyway. "I understand you reported your daughter, Kimberley, as missing yesterday."

"You've found her, haven't you?" Bev's voice was low and hoarse, barely audible, and her face was just as dull, her eyes focused somewhere nobody else could see. "You've found her and she's dead. You wouldn't be here if she was alive, not a detective inspector."

Darling remained silent. That was a very logical thing to say, but most civilians wouldn't think of that. She reached out to put her hand on Bev's, but the woman pulled her hands away before there was any contact, and Darling withdrew hers. "Mrs Ford, I have to tell you that we have found a body—"

"Where? Where did you find her?"

Darling swallowed. "Hallam Dene—"

"That's miles from here! What would Kim be doing in Hallam Dene?" She shook her head, violently. "It's not her. Kim wouldn't go to Hallam Dene. She didn't even know where it is…"

Darling reached out and took her hand. "Mrs Ford, we do not know for certain whether it is Kimberley. We need someone to come and make an identification."

"I'll do it," declared Wayne from the doorway.

"You're too young," said Abdullah, as kindly as she could.

"I'm seventeen," he said. "I'm old enough to join the army. I'm old enough to die for my country. I know what my sister looks like as well as anyone does."

Bev got to her feet, brushing her hands through the hair on her temples, straightening her rumpled clothes. "We'll do it together. That's the way this family does things, together." She walked to the doorway, where she stood beside her son and looked into his eyes before reaching out and brushing tears away from beneath his eyes with her fingers. She nodded at him, just the once, as though answering a question only she had heard asked. She turned back to the officers. "Just give me a couple of minutes to chuck some clean clothes on, make myself look presentable."

"Take as much time as you need, Mrs Ford. There's no rush."

She gave Darling a smile that was so wan yet so courageous that Abdullah thought she could feel her heart breaking.

"I'm Bev, Inspector, Bev."

Darling nodded.

43

"And there is a rush. If it isn't Kimberley, then you've got to find the other poor family who have lost a daughter."

Chapter Twelve

Dr Wolstenholme's mortuary was a grim, sterile, inhuman place. Every surface had been created with just one intention, that of being cleaned of the detritus of human beings as quickly and thoroughly as possible. Every colour was designed to emphasise the inhumanity of the place; dull black on the floor, white porcelain on the dissection tables, metallic silver on the freezer doors and immovable instruments, dun walls and, overwhelming everything, the savage glare of the overhead lights that leached everything of subtlety, leaving merely illumination and impenetrable shadow.

Wolstenholme himself was not present. The same assistant she saw at Hallam Dene told Darling that he'd done the post-mortem and report last evening but not come in that morning. They had prepared everything for this visit, nonetheless. He gestured towards the black body bag on the trolley in front of the freezer doors, a sheen of condensation testimony to it having only recently been brought out of the freezer. Darling took hold of Bev's arm and led her towards the trolley, only for Bev to shake herself free when they got there and reach out for Wayne's hand instead.

Her son stood beside her and slightly behind, reaching in front with his right hand to hold hers, his left arm around her waist without touching it.

Darling went around to the other side of the trolley, nodding to Abdullah to stand behind Bev, just in case. It was as well to be prepared for every possible reaction. "Mrs Ford, I'm going to unzip this bag now. If you can, I want you to look at the... person inside... you can look for as long as you wish, or as little, I just need you to be able to tell me whether this is your daughter, Kimberley Anne Ford."

Bev nodded and squeezed Wayne's hand. Darling took hold of the heavy-duty tag on the zip and drew it open. It was surprisingly easy to use and silent. She opened the bag and then drew apart the gauze that covered the face inside. She didn't look at the girl's face. The post-mortem photograph would be imprinted on her memory for life. Instead, she concentrated on Bev's face as she looked down at the body. For a long time, there was no reaction to be seen until, without any warning, her eyes rolled up inside her head.

She would have collapsed to the floor had Wayne and Abdullah not caught hold of her, supporting her as though she weighed nothing at all.

Darling was aware of the youth staring at her.

"That's my sister," he hissed.

She could see the muscles in his throat, about his mouth and around his eyes working to keep him from screaming and crying and venting the outrage of emotions that had erupted in him. "That's Kim!"

Darling hurried round the table, waving to the mortuary assistant to get the body bag out of sight.

"Let's get Bev out of here, somewhere she can recover." Only as she spoke the words did she realise there was a very bad chance that Bev would never recover from the shock she had just experienced. They helped the woman out of the cold examination room and into the foyer, sitting her down in one of the uncomfortable plastic chairs. Darling made sure Bev sat upright, tapping her cheeks gently to revive her, not knowing whether it was appropriate. Wayne stood back, staring at his mother, his face as colourless as the gauze that had covered his sister. Abdullah hurried off to fetch help.

After what felt like a long, long while to Darling, Bev's eyelids flickered open, although they only showed the whites of her eyes. Taken aback by this, Darling continued tapping her cheeks until the woman batted her hand away.

"Will you stop that? I'm fine."

She closed her eyes and then opened them with a faint sound that made Darling wonder whether they had somehow stuck together. It had happened to her before, and it had always given her a moment of panic.

"You fainted," she said.

"Tell me something I don't know." The woman used her hands to hold on to the base of the chair and wiggle herself upright. "Anyone got a cigarette?"

Darling glanced at the 'No Smoking' signs on all four walls.

"Mam, you don't smoke," Wayne said, as though talking to a small child.

"I stopped drinking as well," she snarled, making Wayne take half a step backwards and almost bump into the paramedic hurrying through the door with Abdullah in tow. Abdullah had a plastic cup of water in her hand, holding it out to Bev.

The paramedic pushed both Abdullah and Darling out of the way and knelt to examine her, taking her pulse, listening to her chest, shining a light in her eyes. After a while, she got to her feet, bent forward and spoke into Bev's ear, before tapping her on the shoulder.

"No sign of anything major. Shock, I expect. Be sure to eat properly and get some rest." She left as Bev started to get up.

"Is there anyone you can go to?" Darling asked. "Anyone who can come and look after you?"

"My son is all the help I need!"

Wayne stopped towards his mother and took hold of her arm, nodding.

"Have you told Kim's father about this yet?" Darling asked.

Bev glared at her, venom suddenly red in her eyes. "Tell him yourself!"

"I'm sorry, I don't understand."

"That bastard is one of yours."

"Ours? He's a policeman?"

"If he wasn't, he'd be in jail for what he did to me!"

Darling's forehead wrinkled in a question.

"Ford's my granny's name. I got shot of the Langley as soon as I could."

Darling was taken aback. Langley had been one of the officers in the briefing that morning. "Yeah, got that," she said. "Shan, you get Mrs Ford and Wayne back home." She took a business card from her pocket. "You can call me any time, day or night."

She watched them walk away, a broken woman on the arm of a son who was having to bear a much heavier weight than he thought he could carry. It was always like that, the survivors, the ones left behind, having to deal with horrors even though the 'victims' were beyond all horror. Coppers often talked about their job being to get 'justice' for the victims. She thought it was much more about getting some sort of release for the survivors, and she was never confident she could do that.

Taking out her phone, she called Morton. "Pete, I want Brian Langley off this case right now." She could hear his questions unspoken on the other end of the phone. "Beverley Ford's married name, before her divorce, was Langley."

"He's Kim's dad?"

She didn't reply.

"The stupid f…" The last word died away. "He knows the rules!"

"You just make sure he does, Sergeant. You just make sure he does."

Chapter Thirteen

The frustration of a first day in which they didn't make anything like the sort of progress she would have liked meant Darling walked into the evening round-up session with a familiar thump of an ache where her skull met her neck. Everyone was there except for Langley. Had Morton already passed the word along or had he responded to his loss by climbing inside a bottle? She walked to the glass wall, which was empty except for a photo of Kimberley and her name. She tapped the photo.

"This is just about the sum of what we know. Her name is Kimberley Anne Ford, although her father's name is Brian Langley." That got the reaction she was expecting. "Yes, *that* Brian Langley. None of you will discuss this investigation in any way, shape or form with Brian." She looked around the room and saw the weight of her tone being met by some distress. He was one of them. They all felt for him. She disregarded that.

"She was found in Hallam Dene just before five on Tuesday. The initial examination found she was murdered. Our job is to catch the bastard who did it." Her obscenity also got a reaction. If she was swearing, it was serious.

"We know she was at home in Woodley Street early on Monday evening," she continued, "after which she went round to a school friend's house on Halton Crescent; then they may both have gone round to another friend's house. Things get opaque until the body is found. We need to know where she was and who she was with after about seven on Monday evening when she was presumably killed. So, Sergeant Morton and I will go to the school and have a chat with this friend. Constable Abdullah, you seemed to get on well with the Fords. You and...

Constable Cox go around there and see what you can find out about Kim, about her friends, what she did out of school, anything and everything. Have a search of her room, see if there's anything that might give us a clue, boyfriends, that sort of thing."

Even as she spoke, Darling wanted to take the words back. The child was thirteen. Boyfriends, at that age. How old had she been when she had her first boyfriend, what was his name, Adrian? Fifteen, was it? Was thirteen today any younger than fifteen had been in her generation?

"The rest of you, house-to-house around Hallam Dene, see if anyone saw anything early Tuesday morning." She looked around the room and was greeted by the sound of chairs scraping backwards. They obviously wanted to be out and doing whatever they could to find this killer before he did it again.

She had no idea where that thought came from. Multiple murderers were rare as hen's teeth in this neck of the woods, yet there was something nagging at the back of her skull saying this might be the exception, that catching him was not just about getting justice for his first victim but more importantly saving the life of his next one.

* * *

Darling and Morton were ushered straight into Mrs Norden's room when they arrived at the school. They shook her cold and slightly damp hand and took a seat where it was offered. Mrs Norden sat behind her desk and arranged herself as though expecting to be photographed for a new school brochure. Something about the woman's attitude made the hairs rise on the back of Darling's neck. As a copper, she was accustomed to people putting on a performance for her but surely this woman had nothing to hide. Before the deputy head teacher could say anything, Darling got in first.

"Mrs Norden, I am here about one of your pupils."

"Kimberley Ford…" the woman whispered, the careful set of her face crumbling away in an instant. "Her mother came yesterday to say there might be something amiss." She hesitated. "It's bad news, isn't it?"

Darling nodded. "I'm afraid so. She has been found, murdered."

The woman turned away from them, a tissue appearing from her sleeve, which she lifted to her face, dabbing quickly at her eyes. When she looked back, her make-up seemed untouched. "I'm sorry," she began, shaking her head.

"Nothing for you to be sorry about," Darling said, trying to reassure her.

"I knew," Norden continued, ignoring her. "I knew from the moment her mother was here; deep inside, I knew. Kimberley wasn't that sort of girl."

Darling leaned forward. "That sort of girl," she repeated. "What do you mean by that?" She knew exactly what the teacher meant, that Kim was a sweet child, a model pupil, friendly and popular, not the sort of girl who got into trouble, not the sort of girl you could imagine anything this ghastly happening to, not the sort of girl who might deserve it.

She caught hold of her imagination, sternly telling herself she had no reason to think things like that, other than some instinctive dislike of the woman. She was a detective. She needed more than that before jumping to conclusions, even if she probably had a bit more experience than the teacher of predators who liked little girls. So far as she had found, the sweeter and more innocent the better, as far as they were concerned. Mrs Norden said nothing in reply, and Darling was about to ask her again, when Morton intervened, using that slow, heavy, received-pronunciation alpha-male voice he adopted when the thought things weren't going the way they should.

"Mrs Ford mentioned a friend of Kimberley's, the one she told Wayne she was going to spend the night with."

The teacher looked startled. "Isabella Conway? Is that the girl you mean?"

Morton nodded.

"We need to speak to her," Darling said.

Mrs Norden reached for her phone, then let her hand fall onto her desk. "That won't be possible."

Both officers stiffened. Neither liked being told they couldn't speak to whoever it was they wanted to interview. The teacher shook her head.

"The class is on an educational trip today. Kielder Forest. It has been arranged a long time... and nobody knew about Kimberley." Her voice trailed away until it was scarcely audible.

They both knew there was no mobile-phone reception out there. Either they could go out themselves or wait until the class got back. Darling looked up.

"Mrs Ford told us about another girl they may have visited–"

"Francesse Brady? Frankie, I think she called her," Mrs Norden finished, shaking her head with a thin smile on her lips. "She isn't one of my students."

My students, Darling thought. What made the woman think the pupils belonged to her rather than the school.

"So, you've got no contact details?" Morton said.

The deputy head shook her head, looking at the clock above the door, making no bones about believing she had more important things to do.

Darling took out a business card and slid it across the desk to Mrs Norden, then got to her feet, Morton following her lead. "I'll leave you to pass the news on to your students," she said, and felt an unpleasant momentary satisfaction, as realisation flickered across Mrs Norden's features. "I can arrange for community relations officers to attend, help with the students. Some will respond more intensely than others, Kimberley's friends."

She almost felt sorry for the teacher as she spoke. She, after all, had experience of these things. "We shall probably need to speak individually to Kimberley's friends. See to it, Sergeant," she said as she walked to the door, not turning to look at Morton, displaying absolute confidence he would do what needed to be done.

Darling opened the door and left without another word, striding towards the main entrance, conscious of eyes seen and unseen following her. As a police officer, she was used to the attention. As a senior police officer, it made her smile, inwardly, even if she kept her expression carved from stone.

Chapter Fourteen

Abdullah almost walked to the driver's side as she approached the car with David Cox but went to the passenger side instead. She didn't know him well enough to take the initiative, even though she'd passed the Advanced Driving Test and didn't think he had.

"Where are we going?" he asked as he turned out of the station.

She only just kept herself from turning to stare at him. How could he not know where the victim lived? "Woodley Street. It's off—"

"I know where it is. I just forgot is all."

He drove as though he'd been reliably informed the world would end if he took more than five minutes to get there: too fast, getting too close to people and sounding the horn every thirty seconds. She wanted to tell him to slow down, to get there in one piece, but she knew what the lads were like about their driving – good enough for Formula One, each of them – and they wouldn't take kindly to advice from the likes of her, so she held her peace and tried to hold on without him seeing. He lost five hundred miles off the tyres screeching to a smoking halt outside the Ford house. He didn't get straight out of the car, however.

"What d'you think the Ice Maiden is playing at, kicking Brian Langley off the case?"

This time she did turn to stare at him. Did he imagine she had some insight into DI Darling's mental processes because they were both women? "I neither know nor care. It's above my pay grade."

"So, you think it's fair, do you, that he shouldn't have anything to do with finding the killer of his own daughter?"

What did 'fair' have to do with anything? she wondered. "What I think is that it would have been professional of him to take one look at that photograph and say, 'That's my daughter,' and let the DI deal with that."

"You think you can lecture me about 'professionalism'?"

She saw the colour building in his cheeks as his eyes opened a little wider.

"How long you have been a detective?" he asked.

"Not as long as you, but long enough to trust the inspector more than a drunk who's been a detective constable a lot longer than the both of us put together."

His mouth opened as though he wanted to reply but he said nothing. She knew she would be forever fixed in his opinion as a pushy, brown-nosing bitch, but she'd learned within days of putting on the uniform that opinions like that came with the territory of being assertive and that she would never get anywhere close to attaining her ambitions if she was not assertive. The opinion of a DC with his nose out of joint was nothing like as important to her as the opinion of her DI who wanted results.

"He's not a drunk…" Cox began, but even he couldn't run with that. Langley's love affair with the bottle was no secret. "He needs–"

"He needs all of us to do our jobs without having to worry about him," she snapped, and walked up the worn, patched concrete steps towards the front door without looking back at him. She hadn't got to the top step when the door was opened, and Wayne appeared in the doorway.

"Morning, Wayne," she greeted him. "How are you?" She could tell from the tinge of grey in his complexion and the pink in his eyes that he was no better than could be expected, and that his 'I'm fine' was nothing like the truth, but she didn't mention that. "We'd like a bit of a chat, if that's okay."

He stood aside to let them enter. "Mam's asleep. Dr Pearce gave her something to help her."

"That's perfectly understandable," she reassured him. "We don't want to disturb her. This is my colleague, Detective Constable Cox, by the way."

Cox produced his warrant card as Wayne held out his hand, and they stared at each other for an uncomfortable moment before Wayne nodded.

"What we'd like to do is for my colleague to have a look through Kimberley's room while you and I have a talk."

"Fine by me," said Wayne, turning towards the kitchen. "I'll put the kettle on."

"Why do I have to look through a girl's room?" hissed Cox. "Who said you decided who does what?"

"Because I have already established a relationship with the lad, but he doesn't look as though he'd give you the time of day."

Cox deflated slightly. "What am I searching for?"

You're the one who's been the detective longest, she thought. "Anything that will help – photos, her diary. Use your experience," she said, and left him to it. Then she went into the kitchen, where she found Wayne looking through the cupboards.

"I can't find the coffee," he said without looking at her.

"That's fine," she told him, seeing the jar next to the kettle along with three packets of tea. "I'll get it."

He closed the cupboard doors, smiled at her diffidently and sat down opposite her. "What can I tell you?"

"Your mum said that Kimberley went round to a friend's on Monday night."

"Bella Conway, yeah, they're best friends, live in each other's back pockets, always on the phone."

"Did she sleep over there often?"

His eyes lost focus for a moment as he searched his memory. "Yeah, quite often. Bella slept here too. When I say 'slept' I mean chattered all night long."

Abdullah smiled and nodded. "I have younger sisters. I know." Not that she saw them very often nowadays. "Did they do it often on a school night?"

He took a deep breath, then shook his head. "Mam's strict about school. Never on a school night."

"Why this Monday?"

Once again, he hesitated, then took another deep breath and stared at the table. "Mam wasn't home when Kim left, hadn't got back from work, and I didn't think to tell her when she got in." He looked up at her, appealing. How could he be expected to keep his baby sister in line? "I was tired myself."

"That can't be helped, Wayne. I'm sure you did what you thought was the right thing."

His eyes asked how she could be sure of that, and she knew he would torture himself with that question for the rest of his life. "What about their friend, the one Bella says they went round to see?"

"Friend? What friend was that?"

She fumbled her notebook out of her bag. "Francesse Brady?"

The colour drained out of his face as though someone had pulled out a stopper. He shook his head. "I don't know any Francesse Brady." His voice was harsh.

Her hand slid across the table, almost touching his. "But you know *of* her," she whispered. "Don't you?"

He nodded. "Not someone I want to know." He shook his head. "I don't want to speak ill of someone I don't know, Mam wouldn't like that…"

What his mam thought about things was more important to Wayne Ford than it was to most lads of his age, she thought. "But?"

"But she's known as a right bitch…" He gasped, as though realising he had used a word he shouldn't. "Sorry about that."

She smiled and shook her head. "Don't fash yourself. I've heard a lot worse than that, been called a lot worse. Anyway, it's much easier for us coppers if you tell it the way it is rather than go around the houses."

He shook his head. "If I'd known she was going there I'd have stopped her, somehow. There would have been a screaming match… well, she'd have screamed… but at least… at least…" His voice petered out and he stared down at the table as though he just wanted the ground to swallow him.

Abdullah reached further and put her hand on his. "You can't think like that, Wayne. You are in no way responsible for any of this—"

She was interrupted by raised voices from upstairs. They both leapt to their feet and hurried into the hall, where they were greeted by the sight of Cox rushing down the stairs with a dishevelled Bev Ford standing at the top, waving one hand after him while holding a purple quilted dressing gown closed with the other.

"It's just the police, Mam," called Wayne, barging past Cox and heading up the stairs.

"What's he doing in our Kimberley's room?" she shrieked.

"What did you do?" Abdullah whispered.

"Nothing, nothing. I was just standing there and the next thing she was raising the roof."

"What're you doing at home?" Bev demanded. "It's a school day, isn't it…" Then her voice faded into silence as her son hurried up the stairs, took her into his arms and coaxed her back into her bedroom. The wail that followed him shutting the door told them she had remembered why there might be police in her house searching Kimberley's room.

"Did you find anything?" Abdullah asked.

Cox shook his head. She knew she should have done the search herself, that it was more likely she would see anything that was out of place. They would have to search the room again. Darling wouldn't be pleased at them not having done it right in the first place, at the entire visit having been a waste of time… Except it hadn't been a waste of time. Wayne disapproved of Francesse Brady. They hadn't known that before.

Wayne came downstairs. "I got her settled. I think she was confused, whatever the doctor gave her–"

"That's quite all right, Wayne. We understand."

"I think you should leave now," he said, uncertainly.

Abdullah nodded, smiling. "We'll almost certainly need to come back but we'll give you a call next time, let you know we're coming." She nudged Cox towards and out of the door, which closed behind them before they could go down the first step.

"Since when did we call ahead to let people know we're coming?" Cox sneered. "We want to have them off their guard."

"When their daughter, their sister has just been murdered. It's called diplomacy, public relations. They're victims, not suspects."

"Everyone's a suspect!"

"And they're Brian Langley's ex-wife and his son. How do you think he'll react if we go heavy-handed on them?"

Cox had no answer for that, and it was a silent drive back to the station. He went off towards the canteen when they went in. She didn't mention it but went into the office, sat down and called up a list of secondary schools in Newcastle. This Francesse Brady had to attend one of them.

"Good morning, this is Detective Constable Abdullah of the Northumbria Police. I hope you can help us. We're trying to trace a girl we think may be one of your students, a Francesse Brady."

The first three schools could tell her nothing, but the fourth – St Thomas the Martyr High School – agreed she was one of their students but were unwilling to give her any contact details.

"We can't give that sort of information to anyone who calls and says they're a detective constable."

Abdullah swallowed her annoyance. Would the woman be so reticent if Morton had called, Cox even? "Of course, of course. That's perfectly understandable. We all have to be careful about data protection, don't we?" Her understanding smile went down the connection. "Could I ask you, please, to call the station and give the details to the officer who answers? Ask them to pass it on to the Kimberley Ford team…" She thought she heard a sharp intake of breath at the other end of the line. "Thank you very much. This really is important."

She put down the phone and thought of calling up a city directory, searching for Bradys in the appropriate areas. Instead, she followed Cox's example and went to the canteen. He wasn't to be seen, which didn't bother her in the slightest. She took her cappuccino and a sneaked Danish pastry back to her desk and set to work.

Chapter Fifteen

Morton and Abdullah stood outside the Conway house, waiting for someone to answer his press on the bell. Eventually, a woman in her early forties answered the door. She was medium height, with dyed blonde hair cut spikily short in a fashion that did not match the pale-blue onesie she wore with fluffy slippers.

"Who are you," she demanded, "coming round people's houses at this time of night?"

Morton produced his warrant card and held it up so she could see it. "I am Detective Sergeant Morton of the Northumbria Police. My colleague is Detective Constable Abdullah."

Abdullah produced her card as well, but Mrs Conway appeared unwilling to look at it.

"We are making inquiries about a murder, Mrs Conway."

"Well, I don't know anything about any murder."

"Not you, Mrs Conway; your daughter, Isabella."

Mrs Conway's eyes started wide open while her right hand clutched her throat. "Bella..."

Morton climbed up on the next step, where he stood a lot closer and a lot taller than Mrs Conway. "We can come in and discuss this where nobody else can hear us, or we can stay out here and your neighbours hear everything we say."

She hesitated for a moment, then turned inside, leaving the officers to follow her. As Abdullah pulled the front door shut, Mrs Conway yelled up the stairs, "Bella, get yourself down here. There's people to see you. They're policemen!" She turned into the front room and sat herself down in a leather recliner that was obviously her usual perch for watching the television. The screen that was mounted on the wall above the fireplace was showing some programme that appeared to be about people eating a meal. She pressed the mute button, and their Estuarine accents became silent, just in time for what sounded like a baby elephant to be heard thundering down the stairs.

They were both surprised to see quite a slight child appear in the doorway, wearing tiger-striped pyjamas and a towel wrapped around her head with straggles of wet blonde hair escaping. The aroma of steam and moisturiser wafted from her. Abdullah identified it as an expensive brand, one she might use were she going on a night out but not after a Wednesday-evening shower.

Morton identified them and invited Bella to sit on the sofa, while he and Abdullah sat in the matching armchairs.

"You are Isabella Conway, aren't you?"

Bella nodded, her high spirits evaporating as she realised they were real police officers, and they really did want to talk to her.

"We are here to talk to you about your friend, Kimberley Ford."

"You don't say one word to my daughter without me here!" Mrs Conway sat upright on her chair, which was still in the reclining position.

"We would very much rather that you are here, Mrs Conway. We are here on very serious business and Isabella is still a minor. We cannot ask her anything unless there is her parent or another responsible adult present."

"I thought that was only if you was going to charge her."

Morton glanced at Abdullah. People watched box sets of TV detective shows and thought that made them experts on police procedure. He shook his head. "There is no evidence that Isabella has done anything wrong. However, we are investigating the murder of Kimberley Anne Ford."

Bella screamed, burst into tears, and went on screaming until she choked on her tears. Abdullah went to try to calm her down, and then there were two women in the room screaming.

"Leave her alone!" Mrs Conway yelled. "My Bella's done nothing. You keep your filthy hands off her, you dirty black—"

"Mother!" The new voice belonged to a young woman standing in the doorway. She was very obviously Bella's older sister, dressed in tight black jeans and a Motorhead

T-shirt, with dyed-black hair tied in a loose ponytail on her neck. "Don't you talk to her like that. She's only doing her job."

Mrs Conway shrank back onto her chair. The girl leaned against the door jamb and nodded to the police officers.

Morton glanced from one woman to the other and then back again, before devoting his attention to Bella. When he spoke, his voice was soft but still heavy, reassuring the child while threatening her at the same time.

"Isabella, nobody believes you had anything to do with Kimberley's death, but we know the pair of you told lies about where you were Monday night. Kimberley said she was here and you said you were round at hers, which isn't true, is it?" He stared at the girl, willing an answer out of her. "I need to know exactly where you were."

"You don't have to tell them anything!" her mother interrupted.

"Mum, Kim's dead. She's been murdered," she said, staring at her mother, as though unable to comprehend her reaction. "We were round at Frankie's—"

"Who?" Her mother shook her head.

"Frankie Brady... Francesse."

"I never heard of any Francesse!"

"She's a friend."

Morton shook his head and waved his notebook to regain control.

"You went round to this Francesse's. Why?"

Bella shrugged. "To have a laugh."

Morton nodded. "She's a comedian, is she, this Francesse Brady?"

Bella's puzzled expression said she did not understand, but Morton carried on regardless. "So, you went round to Francesse's, had a bit of a laugh and then came straight home. Right?"

Bella nodded, suspicion clouding her eyes.

"About what time would that have been?" Morton asked.

Bella shrugged. "Dunno. Just after midnight, I guess."

Her mother erupted from her chair, eyes blazing, spittle flying from her lips. "That is enough! Enough. You are grounded, young lady, grounded for a month. I give you an inch and you take a mile. After midnight on a school day! And you can forget about ever seeing Miss Francesse Brady again, believe you me." She stood before Bella with her fists planted on her hips, trembling as though she was about to spontaneously combust.

Abdullah got to her feet and took half a step towards them, as though anticipating having to intervene physically.

Morton motioned downwards with his hand a couple of times, instructing her to back off. He got to his feet as mother and daughter stood there confronting each other. He didn't imagine it was the first time, and he didn't like the way Mrs Conway's fists were clenching and unclenching.

Then the sister moved between them, putting her arm around Bella's shoulders, who promptly collapsed into tears, sobbing and coughing. The sister looked from Morton to Abdullah and back, taking a pack of tissues from her jeans pocket and giving them to her sister, who buried her face in them. "I think we're done here, for now," the sister said.

Morton hesitated. There was a lot more he wanted to find out here, but it wouldn't be easy if the child was hysterical and the mother hostile. "We'll be on our way, then," he said, resignedly. "But I promise you we'll be back, in the morning."

"She has to go to school!" Mrs Conway wailed.

"I doubt she'll miss a morning's lessons," the sister said. "I know I never did."

"I'll just take Francesse's number first, if you don't mind."

Bella managed to say it between hiccoughing sobs. He wrote it down in his notebook, closed it and put it back in his pocket before he smiled. "Thank you for that." He took a business card and hesitated, before giving it to the elder sister. "Call any time, if you think of anything else we should know." Then he marched out of the house without a backward glance.

Abdullah followed, smiling what she hoped would be taken as apologies for Morton's brusqueness. She caught up with him just as he sat behind the steering wheel.

"They're lying, aren't they?" she asked.

"Assume everyone is lying to you because you're a copper and you won't go far wrong." He chuckled, looking straight ahead through the windscreen. "But yes, both of them are lying. Especially the girl."

"You're an expert on teenage girls, are you?"

"I have two teenage daughters and I can always tell when they're lying to me, or at least trying to pull the wool over my eyes."

"Oh, how's that?" Abdullah leaned forward, eager for his reply.

"Their lips are moving. They get it from their mother."

As he said this he turned away from Abdullah, his expression crumbling just long enough for her to intuit he regretted saying that about his wife, and a memory came forward in her mind, that his wife wasn't well, although she couldn't remember why.

She looked at him for a long moment, wondering whether she should ask if he was okay but bit down gently on her tongue. He would tell her if anything was wrong. "You think the mother is lying too?"

He chuckled. "There's not a mother in this town whose teenage daughter could get in late and her not knowing to the second when she got in. Unless the mother was somewhere else herself, or so far into La La Land that a bus coming through the front door wouldn't wake her up."

Abdullah stopped and wondered why she hadn't thought of that herself. Morton turned, looked at her and laughed.

"I know you don't touch the stuff and I don't blame you for that, but the mother was half-cut, which was why the sister came downstairs to run interference, and if you'd looked through into the kitchen as we went in, you'd have seen a half-empty bottle of Lambrini on the kitchen table before she shut the door."

Abdullah shook her head. "I've got a lot to learn."

Morton chuckled. "At least you know that, Constable. There's some in that squad room know no more now than they did the first time they went in, and they all think they know more than a doddering old fool like me. Which is why they're still constables and I'm a sergeant."

Before he started the car, Morton called Darling. "The Conway girl is taking it badly. We won't get anything else useful out of her tonight… I thought I'd go straight round to Brady's address, strike while the iron is hot."

Chapter Sixteen

Morton drove to the Brady house without using satnav. He prided himself on knowing his city better than any taxi driver, and spent time familiarising himself with all the new developments. Torville Street was a dozen detached houses on either side of a cul-de-sac, all gated and hidden behind shrubbery and trees that had probably cost more than the first flat he bought after marrying Pam, not that she'd ever shown the least desire to live somewhere like this, and it was too late now even if she had. At least the gates were opened, not like the really expensive houses you had to play for the Toon or deal drugs or represent those that did in court to be able to afford. The drive led to a double garage at the side of a double-fronted mock-Georgian house with inappropriate bow windows and leaded lights. The lawn and rose garden to the front of the house looked as though they had been manicured within an inch of their lives, and a dark-blue BMW sports car in front of the garage suggested it wanted to be the Batmobile when it grew up. Morton parked his car directly behind it and went to the front door with Abdullah. There he rang the bell, and then rang it again when there was no reply.

He raised his hand to ring again when the door opened, and a woman stood there. She could have been any age from her early thirties onwards, her make-up having taken at least an hour to apply. Her dress and shoes cost more than the sergeant earned in a month.

"Fuck off, the pair of you, whoever you are. I'm not buying."

Morton chuckled and produced his warrant card, thrusting it out in front of her face. "Good thing I'm not selling, then. I'm Detective Sergeant Morton of the Northumbria Police." He turned towards Abdullah, who held out her own card. "This is Detective Constable Abdullah." He took half a step forward, invading her personal space. "We are investigating a murder."

The woman took a step backward, putting her right hand up to her throat. "I don't know nothing about a murder!" Her voice had gone up an octave and her eyes opened very wide.

Morton recognised fear when he saw it, and wondered what it was she feared.

"It is your daughter, Francesse, we think may have some evidence," he said.

She shook her head. "No, no, you can't talk to her. Just fuck off. She doesn't know nothing about any murder."

Morton leaned forward, almost touching her, not so much invading, as annexing her personal space. "Mrs Brady, you don't know everything your daughter knows." He took a deep breath, inflating his chest and occupying even more of her personal space. "I repeat, I am investigating a murder and I need to ask your daughter some questions. We can do this the nice way, here, with you present. Or I can do this the unpleasant way, down at Forth Banks with someone from Social Services pretending she's her 'responsible adult'. Which is it going to be?" He smiled at her, an expression devoid of affability and charm.

Mrs Brady stepped aside, allowing them to enter the house, the furnishings of which demonstrated that money did not necessarily buy taste. Everything was brilliant white, which looked good in an IKEA catalogue but was too much when the only leavening of colour was a profusion of gold touches. She showed them into a lounge with one wall given over to a TV.

This was the biggest plasma screen Abdullah had ever seen, and she had relatives who were not shy about flaunting what they had. A football team could have sat on the white-leather three-piece suite and the white shagpile rug was deep enough to make her fear it might wrap around her calves and drag her down into it, never to be seen again.

Mrs Brady sat on what was obviously her throne, nodding them towards the sofa while rescuing a mobile from her handbag.

"Francesse, get down here now, there's coppers who want to ask you about some murder."

They waited for the girl. Francesse was short, just over five feet tall, still with baby fat on her arms and face, as heavily made-up as her mother, which contrasted with the puff-sleeved, ice-blue Disney princess dress she wore.

"Thank you for talking to us, Francesse," Morton said, leaning forward as though trying to make his bulk seem less threatening to her. "I have some questions about Monday night."

Francesse's gaze flickered towards her mother, then back to him.

"We have heard that Kim and Bella were here."

"You've heard wrong." Francesse shook her head. "Bella was here, not Kim. She was never here. Who told you she was?"

"What did you and Bella do?" Morton asked.

"What do you think? We watched a DVD, gossiped, that sort of thing."

"What DVD did you watch?"

"What sort of question is that?" Mrs Brady demanded.

Morton turned towards her, his expression opaque. "A question I think is relevant to my investigation, which is into the murder of a child I was told was in this house a short time before her death."

"You were told wrong!" Mrs Brady snapped. "That Bella is a lying little madam."

He ignored her, turning back to Francesse. "Which DVD was it?"

The girl glanced towards her mother, who looked away. "I don't remember."

Morton muttered as he wrote in his notebook. "Francesse and Bella watched a DVD—"

"And some YouTube!" Francesse added.

He wrote some more. "But you can't remember what you watched?" He looked intently at the child, who could not hold his gaze. "And Kim was not here?"

"I told you that," Francesse shrilled.

"When did Bella leave?"

Francesse looked up to the ceiling, as though the answer was there. "About midnight."

"Isn't that a bit late for a school day?" Abdullah asked.

Mother and daughter glared at her as though they had just smelled a fart coming from her direction.

"I decide what is appropriate for my daughter," snapped Mrs Brady.

"Still, isn't that a bit late for a child to be walking home alone?" Morton said.

"She didn't walk!" Mrs Brady snapped. "I drove her."

Morton made a few more notes, chewing his bottom lip, then glanced at Abdullah, inviting her to ask her questions, but the constable shook her head. He glanced at his notebook.

"Let me just make sure I've got this straight," he said. "Isabella Conway was here on Monday evening, and you – Mrs Brady – drove her home at about midnight. Is that correct?"

Mother and daughter nodded.

"And Kimberley Ford was never here."

"I keep telling you that. Why do you keep asking?" Mrs Brady shuffled on her chair, her skirt riding up to reveal rather scrawny-looking legs.

"We have information that she was here," Morton insisted.

"And I'll tell you again, that Bella Conway is a right lying little bitch!"

"How do you know Isabella?" Abdullah asked Francesse, hoping the change of tack might reveal something useful.

"Sunday school."

"Sunday school?" Abdullah could not keep the surprise out of her voice.

Mrs Brady turned to her. "You people aren't the only ones who want to raise their children in the faith, I'll have you know."

Abdullah did not respond to this. She had already wasted too much of her life justifying madrasas. "Which Sunday school?" she asked Francesse.

"St Thomas the Martyr."

The church with the same name as the high school Francesse attended. "So, the Conways are Catholic as well," she said.

"What's that got to do with anything?" Mrs Brady demanded. "Why are you obsessed with religion?"

Abdullah said nothing but made a mental note to find out why Francesse attended the Catholic high school and her friends attended Colliers Lane with Kim. It might be significant.

Morton got to his feet. "Thank you for your time. You've been very helpful. If you think of anything else, please give me a call." He tried to give Mrs Brady a card, but she ignored it and he put it back in his pocket. "We'll see ourselves out."

* * *

As they got into the car, Abdullah said, "She's lying, isn't she?"

"Which one?"

"Both. They both looked at you but when you mentioned Kim they looked away, down and to their left."

Morton chuckled. "Been reading *Detecting for Dummies*, have you?"

Abdullah opened her mouth, only to realise he was almost laughing.

"Only kidding. Yeah, that tic is a dead giveaway. Thank you for reminding me. They're definitely lying."

"So why didn't you pin them down?"

"I don't know why they're lying. I can guess but I don't know. The trick of interrogation is, never ask a question before you know the answer, but not at this stage of an investigation. We're gathering evidence, that's all. Conclusions come later, a lot later. When we know more, we'll let the boss loose on them."

"She's that good, is she?"

Morton leaned back in the driver's seat and turned to study her. "Put it like this, Detective Constable Abdullah, if I had something I wanted to keep secret, the last person I'd want questioning me is Detective Inspector Pen Darling. Just don't tell her I said so."

Abdullah nodded, and resolved to observe the inspector even more closely than she already did. When she looked up, she noticed he hadn't yet switched on the engine. "Something the matter?"

He took a deep breath, drumming his fingers on the steering wheel. "I know that woman. I know her from somewhere, sometime in my past; I just can't remember for the moment. She wasn't called Brady then, I'm sure of that."

Morton's memory for people whose collar he had felt in his time bordered on the legendary. He thumped the steering wheel. "I just can't place her!" He shook his head. "It'll come to me, eventually."

"When you least expect it," Abdullah muttered.

"Damn right!" He chuckled, and switched on the engine.

Chapter Seventeen

It was beginning to spit with rain as Darling and Milburn emerged onto the steps where press briefings were customarily held. Umbrellas were being lifted over the television cameras while their attendants raised the hoods on their expensive, shiny puffa jackets, and the other journalists gave thanks they used Dictaphones nowadays rather than notebooks and pens. Joe Milburn glanced up at the sky. "At least that'll keep their questions brief."

Darling made no reply, she just stopped on the bottom step and waited as Milburn stepped to the microphone, wishing she wore a gilet under her raincoat. It might be fashionably reminiscent of the coat Bogie wore at the end of *Casablanca*, but Newcastle in the rain was a lot colder than North Africa in the early morning mist. The thought almost made her laugh. If there was one feature so far absent from this investigation, it was usual suspects.

"In case any of you don't know who I am," Milburn began, "I am Detective Superintendent Joe Milburn." His voice filled the courtyard without the benefit of the microphone. "I am here to appeal to the public for information regarding the murder of the thirteen-year-old girl, Kimberley Anne Ford, of Woodley Street in Benwell." He paused, as though expecting a reaction. There wasn't one.

All the journalists there fancied they had seen it all before. Darling knew they hadn't, at least not as close up as she had.

"We believe she left Woodley Street somewhere between seven and eight in the evening on Monday. She was found in Hallam Dene just after five in the afternoon on Tuesday. We want to know if anyone saw her between those times. You will have a photograph in the press packs you've all been given. As I say, she was thirteen years of age, five feet four inches tall – that's one hundred and sixty-four centimetres to those of you who do modern metrics – slim build and with shoulder-length, straight blonde hair. When she left home, she was wearing black jeggings with a black top, a padded black jacket and white ankle-height trainers."

Even as he spoke, Darling knew the description would apply to God only knew how many thirteen-year-old girls on Tyneside. They all wore their hair long and straight, like it was the sixties all over again, and the skintight leggings or jeans with a crop top was a uniform more strictly enforced than anything a school might have; tight whether or not they had a figure to flaunt.

"As I say," Milburn continued, "we need to know about any sighting, anywhere and at any time. There is a contact number in the press pack. It will be manned twenty-four hours a day as long as it is needed."

This came as a surprise to Darling. Maybe she could expect a few more bodies to join the team.

The rain began to fall a little more heavily. "Superintendent, can you tell us how the investigation is proceeding?"

Darling couldn't tell exactly who it was hiding inside the hood, but the voice sounded like Joanna King of *The Journal* to her. She and Ms King had history.

"I'll answer that," she said, stepping down and putting herself between Milburn and the microphone. She could see the questioner was, indeed, Joanna King. She smiled at her. The greeting was not returned. "I am Detective Inspector Pen Darling, and I am in charge of the day-to-day investigation. The answer to your question, Joanna, is that the investigation is still at a very early stage, and we are very busy gathering evidence. What I will say is that we are following up several promising lines of inquiry–"

"What might they be?" Joanna King interrupted.

"I'm sure you can't expect me to share them with you at this time. We don't want to give the murderer any more advantage than he already has–"

"So, you know the murderer of a young girl is a man!" Joanna King was a strident member of the 'All men are evil and dangerous' faction, and while Darling was certain their murderer was dangerous and probably evil – however you defined 'evil' – hysteria never helped a police investigation. That phone line would be deluged once the number was known, and the vast majority would be of no relevance to the case, but all would have to be investigated just so the one or two that were valuable would not be missed.

"I can't divulge any details yet about the actual cause of death, but I am prepared to say that, yes, we do believe the murderer is a man."

As she spoke, she was aware that her words probably guaranteed a deluge of social media speculation, but she couldn't control that. She would do whatever she could to prevent the grisly, ghastly details of how Kim was murdered from becoming public knowledge, for no other reason than protecting her family and friends from what they really did not need to know.

"Which reminds me, we must ask that the privacy of Kim's family and friends be respected at this time. They have all suffered a traumatic shock and it is in no one's interest if they are not allowed to come to terms with that in private." She had no qualms about staring directly at Joanna King as she spoke.

The silence that followed was shattered by a flash of lightning some distance away and a heavy roll of thunder about five seconds later, after which the heavens opened.

"I think that is all for now," Milburn announced, taking hold of Darling's arm to go back up the steps.

The journalists were in full flight for shelter, leaving an already bedraggled member of the public relations department to recover the microphone. As he allowed the door to close behind them, Milburn asked, "What are these promising lines of inquiry?"

Darling shook her head, feeling a cold drop of rain fall from her hair onto her neck, making her shiver. "I'll tell you when we find them."

* * *

In the room he sometimes used when working for his boss, at his home-cum-office in Darras Hall, the young man who drove a black VW Golf relaxed in his chair watching the press conference. He smiled and took a sip of coffee. The filth were so fucking dumb, he thought. They had no idea how far off they were, no fucking idea at all.

Chapter Eighteen

Georgy Lupoff came to the bottom of the stairs, yawned, stretched his arms backwards until the sinews in his shoulders cracked, and then went through into the kitchen, where Marta sat with her hands around a large mug of coffee and her attention on the TV. Her face was ashen. Georgy went to her, bent over and kissed her just where her neck joined her shoulders. She waved him away.

"You need a shave," she said.

Of course, he did. He'd only just got out of bed. He hadn't had time for washing yet. "What's the matter?" he asked, sitting down across the table from her and reaching for the mug of coffee she had already poured for him, even though it would be some time before it was cool enough to risk a sip. He didn't have the asbestos tongue she did.

Marta said nothing, just nodded at the screen. Georgy brought his spectacles down from the top of his head where he'd parked them before kissing her, and the image came into focus. His insides knotted as though someone had reached in, grabbed hold of his guts and twisted hard. The picture was of a young girl with blonde hair and a mischievous smile. The legend at the bottom of the screen read 'Schoolgirl found murdered in park'.

"I know her," he whispered.

"What?" The distress behind her eyes made him start. "How do you know her?"

"She was in my cab."

Marta swivelled around, glaring at him with tear-reddened eyes that bored through him like hot needles. "When? When was she in your taxi?"

"Monday night."

She got to her feet, hurried into the hallway and returned with the jacket he wore for work and his car keys. The one she thrust into his chest, where he managed to clutch it to himself, the others she threw, rattling and skidding on the table in front of him. "That child is dead, murdered on Monday night. You could be the one who last saw her while she was alive. Go to the police now and tell them everything you know. Do not waste a second."

Georgy opened his mouth to tell her how impossible that was. Even though his resident status was assured – all the paperwork said it was – his upbringing in Romania said you gave nothing but cash to anyone in uniform. His awe of Marta's fury, however, was stronger. She knew where he slept in those early hours of the morning when he returned from driving fares around Newcastle. His decision was made when he glanced at the photographs blu-tacked to the fridge, photographs of their twin daughters, Alicia and Frankova, taken at the party for their twelfth birthday three weeks before. He got to his feet, shrugged his jacket on and picked up the keys. "Right away," he said.

* * *

Georgy walked past the entrance to the police station in the rain four times before he shook his head, cursed himself in fluent Romanian, and walked up the steps. The young man standing behind the chest-high desk that blocked the way into the building looked him appraisingly up and down as he hesitated, two metres away.

"Can I help you, sir?" the sergeant asked.

Georgy knew he was a sergeant from the chevrons on the epaulettes of his pale-blue shirt.

"The girl," he stammered, "the girl on the television, I have some information."

The policeman frowned before realisation dawned as to which girl the man meant. He reached for the telephone. "Take a seat, sir. Someone will see you shortly."

Georgy wanted to turn and run out of the station, go on running until he got home. He sat down because Marta would never speak to him again if he did not tell the police what he knew. Worse than that, she might never stop talking to him about it. The women in her family had razor blades for tongues.

Chapter Nineteen

Monsignor Adrian Lee groaned when he heard Mrs Grace Morgan knocking on his door. He had woken at five thirty, as he did every day, slipped out of bed onto his knees and spent an hour and a half at his devotions, which he did every day. The devout had spent their lives for two millennia exploring the mysteries of the divine so he could put his mind to the demands of the modern day rather than reinventing the wheel. At seven, he had got to his feet, creaking here and there because he was not as young as he had been when he gave his life to the church, and lain back down on his bed, luxuriating in the feel of the chenille bedspread through the flannel of his pyjamas. He might be a monsignor but that didn't mean he had to deny himself all the pleasures of the flesh. Why else had God created pleasures if his people were not to enjoy them?

"Come in, Mrs Morgan," he called, more cheerily than he felt, wrapping himself in the bedspread so she would not be subjected to the sight of him in his pyjamas, although he had occasionally wondered whose modesty he was protecting.

Mrs Morgan was a widow with four children. She could not, therefore, be a complete stranger to the male form, even if only on Saturday night after closing time with the lights very definitely off.

"Good morning, Monsignor," she trilled, as always, ignoring him and stamping to the bay window where she swept aside the heavy maroon-velvet curtains and allowing in the damp, moist light of a dreary morning. "To be sure, it is a glorious day the Lord has given us."

Not for the first time, the monsignor wondered whether her relentless devout cheerfulness was, in fact, some sort of joke directed at him that he just lacked the wit to understand.

"Breakfast will be on the table at seven thirty prompt," she announced, as she did every day, without fail. In the doorway she hesitated, a divergence from her routine, and turned back. "Have you seen the news, Monsignor?"

He hadn't, and there was no way that he could have heard any news since retiring at ten the previous evening. "No, Mrs Morgan."

"There's been a young girl found killed at Hallam Dene, horribly murdered."

Monsignor Lee was at a loss to understand how a murder could be anything other than horrible, especially the murder of a child, no matter how commonplace such foulness might appear today. "That's dreadful, Mrs Morgan, dreadful," he said.

He heard the door close quietly behind her and lay back on his pillows, closing his eyes in the futile hope of turning back the sudden, engulfing desire he had to just bury his head beneath the counterpane and pretend the world outside did not exist. Instead of which, he leapt out of bed, washed and dressed, and got down to the kitchen just in time to sit down as Mrs Morgan put a plate of fried bacon, sausage and egg in front of him for his breakfast. He didn't want to eat, or at least nothing more than a slice of dry toast and a glass of water, but he ploughed his way through it, having to chew every mouthful, because it would be wasteful to spurn it, and rude. Mrs Morgan had firm views about wastefulness and rudeness, and he did not want to knock against the opinion she had of him as a walking saint. That wouldn't do either of them any good.

He was just washing down the last mouthful of toast and marmalade with the last of his second pint-cup of Mrs Morgan's breakfast tea – strong enough to make any man ready for the day to come – when the television screen came to life and the familiar, friendly face of the local early-morning news presenter appeared. This morning, she looked grim, and a photograph of a young girl appeared in the bottom left-hand corner of the screen. Lee felt the colour drain out of his face. Violent stomach cramps made him wonder through which end of him his breakfast would make its reappearance.

"Father, what's wrong?" Mrs Morgan asked hurrying towards him, concern exuding from her.

"It's nothing," he tried to say, although his mouth was suddenly too dry to permit any words to escape. He coughed, tapped at his chest and coughed again. "I'm fine, honestly, it's just… that poor child. That poor child."

They looked at the silent screen, him wondering what he was going to do, her thinking it was her privilege to see to the needs of such a good man.

"I'll wash the dishes," he said, getting to his feet.

"You will do no such thing," she remonstrated. "I will not hear of it."

For a moment, he thought of arguing, saying that what he needed right then was mindless activity, something that would get him through the next minute without his having to reveal the turmoil inside him, only to shake his head and walk away without giving any clue as to the reason for his distress. "I am going to the chapel," he muttered as he left the kitchen. God would understand. God understood everything, even if you did not, could not.

"Say a prayer for me, Monsignor," she called after him.

He wanted to shout at her, tell her that the whole point of prayer was saying the words for yourself, meaning them. Instead of which he grunted and left her to the housework.

Chapter Twenty

Darling studied the man sitting on the opposite side of the desk, a big, solid man with dark, curly hair and a swarthy complexion. Was he a witness, come to help her, or a possible suspect come to muddy the waters of the stream of truth? She asked herself the same question about everyone she spoke to in a formal context, and sometimes wondered what she had lost of her humanity by having 'suspicion' flow through her instead of blood.

"Mr Lupoff, I realise you have come to us with your information on a purely voluntary basis, for which I thank you. I trust you will understand the necessity for us to take your information formally, in view of the seriousness of the situation." She nodded towards the tape recorders and the notepad on the desk in front of Morton.

The man ran his finger around the inside of his shirt collar, as though it was suddenly too tight, even though it was unbuttoned. It was a sensation not uncommon in those sitting where he sat. Then he straightened up in his seat.

"My information is that I had this girl in my cab on Monday night, just before twelve o'clock."

"Kimberley Ford?"

"If that is her name, the child who was murdered."

Darling nodded. "Why?"

He frowned at her.

"Why did you have her in your cab on Monday night?"

"She was a fare. I was given her pick-up point by Control."

"What was that address?"

He shook his head again. "I do not recall exactly, not the number. It was Torville Street. When I got there, she was waiting in the street. She got in, gave the name of a street in Shiremoor. I dropped her at the end of that road."

The police officers glanced at each other when he mentioned Torville Street. That was where the Bradys lived.

Morton cleared his throat. "The name of the road in Shiremoor?"

"Lesbury Avenue."

Morton jotted down the name.

"You didn't find it unusual, taking a child from one side of the city to the other, on their own?" Darling drummed her fingers lightly on the desk.

He shook his head and shrugged. "No, no, not at all. It is something any taxi driver does every day."

"At that time of night?"

He nodded. "Any time, day or night." He took a deep breath and licked his lips, which were suddenly cracked and dry. "You learn not to wonder."

The two officers glanced at each other. There was always something to discover about their city.

"How did she pay?"

"She didn't. It was on an account."

"An account?" Morton leaned forward. "What sort of account?"

"You'll have to ask Control about that. I know nothing about anything like that. All I do is drive the passenger where they say."

"Oh, we will be asking Control." Darling chuckled. "Have no doubt on that score."

Morton waved his pen, attracting Lupoff's attention. "When you left her, what did she look like?"

Lupoff frowned, sucking on his teeth, remembering. "She looked like a teenage girl on a night out with her friends, all dressed up, oh and she was making a phone call."

"Dressed up?" Morton frowned.

"You know, tight shiny leggings, a top that would barely stay on, straps everywhere, made up like her mother wouldn't recognise her. You know the look. You see hundreds of them in the town centre every weekend, displaying themselves."

Darling got the distinct impression it was not a look he would approve of his daughters wearing, if he had any daughters. She was all for women wearing whatever they wanted but couldn't understand fashions requiring women to dress like tarts advertising their wares. Not that it mattered what either of them thought. "Did you see anything else, anyone else?"

He closed his eyes.

She fancied she could almost hear the cog wheels inside his brain turning over as he surveyed his memories.

When he opened them, it was with a shake of the head. "I saw no one." He made the words sound like the saddest he had ever spoken. "I am sorry."

"Nothing to be sorry about," Darling said with a brightness she did not feel. "You have given us information we did not have, and it should help us apprehend the murderer." She glanced towards the recorder and saw the pilot lights were not illuminated. She had not switched them on. Bugger it. They would have to go through all this again. Then she noticed that Morton's notepad was filled with the illegible scrawl only he could read. "My sergeant will turn what you have said into a formal statement for you to sign, if that's all right with you."

He nodded.

She left them to it, heading to tackle the mountain of paperwork that had to be looked at before her anticipated conversation with Mrs Brady. With a sudden thought, she executed a Columbo turn.

"Sergeant Morton, be sure to take the details of Mr Lupoff's employers."

Morton glared at her but nodded. He would have done that anyway.

Chapter Twenty-One

A knock on the door made Darling look up from the paperwork mountain she was moving from one side of her desk to the other. "Yes?"

Langley entered. He was a big man in his late thirties. His belly hung over his belt, straining at his unironed shirt. A couple of tufts of not-quite-still-black hair on his throat indicated he had not been as thorough with the razor as he should have been. 'Not as thorough as he should be' would probably appear on his next appraisal. He closed the door and sauntered to her desk, putting his hand on the chair back, as though about to sit down.

"This is not a social visit, Detective Constable!" His hand moved away as though he'd just grasped a hot coal. He straightened up, too, sucking in his gut and almost looking as though he might pass his next physical.

She glared at him silently, watching him squirm, wondering why he had been summoned, even though he had to know why. Eventually, she spoke. "Mind telling me when you were going to let us in on your secret?"

"Secret, ma'am?"

"That our murder victim is your daughter. That secret."

The colour fled his face, replaced by an expression of fleeting pain, as though he had just been punched in the belly. He stammered but closed his mouth.

"Oh, sit down, man. This isn't an execution."

He sat down heavily, sagging over the edges of the chair, making it creak.

"Did you think you could keep it a secret? Really?"

Eventually, he shook his head and Darling almost felt sorry for him. Almost.

"Your daughter has been murdered, and if we're going to get justice for her, and you, and the rest of your family, we are going to have to be as professional as we can. Tell me, Detective Constable Langley, do you think your conduct has been professional?"

He sat there, silent, staring into some space between them only he could see.

"Because I do not!" She brought the flat of her hand down hard on her desk. It stung but made a satisfying noise and got his full attention. "You know the rules and you chose to disregard them. I could ask why but it seems obvious to me. I should put you on a disciplinary."

His mouth fell open. "Ma'am."

"Do not interrupt me while I'm speaking, Detective Constable!"

His expression became that of a man hit by an IBS spasm. "Ma'am."

"Do not interrupt me!"

Even more discomfort showed. He shifted from buttock to buttock.

"Once more, and you really will be on a disciplinary."

He opened his mouth, closed it and chose to just nod instead.

"The only reason I'm not doing that is I have better things to do than get tied up in paperwork." She fell silent for a moment. "I understand why you want to be involved. I can't say I know how you feel. That would be stupid and insulting. Nobody else knows how you feel. We can only guess and be glad it is not us. But you know as well as I do that you cannot be involved."

He opened his mouth but closed it as she raised her hand.

"We will conduct this investigation by the book. Every *i* will be dotted, every *t* crossed. When we catch this bastard, he will not squeeze out from under because some jumped-up-never-come-down prat in a wig and gown says we did not obey every single rule. Which means I cannot allow you to compromise this investigation one second longer. This is for Kim's sake, for your ex's sake, for your son's sake, for your sake. Understand?"

Langley straightened up. "Yes, ma'am, and I'm sorry."

"How many times do I have to say I'm not 'ma'am'? I'm Inspector Darling, or just inspector, guv or boss. Do you get it?"

"Yes."

"Right, so go and get on with whatever you were doing before all this…" Her voice faded for a moment before she took a deep breath and straightened up in her chair. "And give it your entire attention. Leave this to us. Don't go bothering the team. It's not like they won't tell you, but anything you need to know will come from this horse's mouth."

He nodded, a brief smile suggesting he had heard a word she had not spoken.

"Go and get on with it. Keep your nose clean and this little chat will stay between the two of us."

"Thank you, ma… guv!"

He got to his feet and hurried to the door, where he paused and turned around. She thought he was going to draw himself to attention and salute, like a uniform, but he didn't, just turned his back and closed the door behind himself almost silently.

She shook her head, wondering whether she had done the right thing. Nobody higher up the command structure would criticise her if she had him suspended until the case was solved, except maybe Joe Milburn. Langley was nothing like the model of a modern copper. If Joe Milburn didn't like him, he'd have long since been shown the door. But that would not have been the right thing to do now. The simple fact was that if he was left unoccupied, he would not be able to resist sticking his nose in and compromising the investigation. No, she would have to run this case, keeping Langley's nose to the grindstone while she was about it. This policeman's lot was not a happy one.

Chapter Twenty-Two

Morton entered without knocking, put two cups of coffee on Darling's desk and sat down. "Yours is the black one," he said.

"And yours is the one with four sugars." She smiled.

"I've worked hard for my diabetes," he said, taking a sip and smacking his lips. "At least let me enjoy it while I can." He took a sip from the cup and blew on the tip of his tongue. "Was that Brian Langley I heard stamping away from here?"

She looked up and nodded.

"Guessed so. I hid round the corner so I wouldn't have to meet him, not with a cup of coffee in either hand, leastways." He pointed to the pile of thin reports on her desk. "Anything useful in there?"

She shook her head.

He took another sip of coffee. "I wouldn't expect anything from Hallam Dene. I've a feeling this bugger is fly enough to have dumped the body in the early hours when there's nobody around to see."

Darling looked up at him sharply. "What makes you think that? We hardly know anything about him, even if it is a *he*."

"Thirty years of coppering, you get a feeling for these things."

She grinned. "Ah, the good old copper's nose."

"The boss set a lot of store by a copper's nose."

"That's right. *His* copper's nose, and he's done more coppering than all of us put together, but even Joe Milburn prefers evidence nowadays."

"Maybe, but in the absence of evidence – and right now we've got the equivalent of bugger all – we have to rely on our coppers' noses, and you know I'm right."

She did. Not that she was going to admit it to him. "What we really need are people everywhere who are awake around the clock – they can do shifts if they like – just keeping an eye open and reporting in on anything they see."

"A Department of Twitching Curtains, you mean."

They both laughed. One feature that had so far been missing from this investigation were phone calls from little old ladies of all ages and sexes who spent most of their lives peering between their curtains. Suddenly, Darling stopped laughing and became serious. "We've already got one of those."

Morton raised a questioning eyebrow.

"It's called CCTV. There's hardly a square yard of this city that isn't covered, and even if it isn't, somewhere nearby will be. What we need to know is where and when to look."

"Apart from overnight anywhere near Hallam Dene, you mean."

Darling nodded. "I don't think it would do any good looking around the Fords's."

"We know where she's gone from and we know where she's supposed to have gone to."

"Do I detect a note of doubt she actually went around to the Conways'?"

Morton stared at his knuckles. "She may have gone to the Conways' and she may even have gone in. But I don't think she stayed there very long."

"Teenage girls with somewhere more exciting to be?" Darling nodded. "Bella did say they went to… where was it?"

"Francesse Brady's house. Torville Street."

"There's bound to be CCTV there. You went round there, didn't you? What did they say?"

Morton chuckled. "They both denied Kim had ever been near the place."

"And?"

"They're lying."

"How can you be sure?"

He tapped his nose. "I don't think that woman would tell a copper the truth even if it would put money in her purse." He shook his head. "I know her as well. I'm positive I do."

"Which means she was a bad lass, once upon a time."

"That's right." He shook his head, dolefully. "I know I'm not supposed to jump to conclusions, or let my prejudices get in the way."

"But once a scrubber always a scrubber, eh?"

He snorted. "She's got loadsamoney now."

"If she lives on Torville Street that goes without saying."

"It hasn't bought her any taste, that's what I'm saying. The house is all white leather, white shagpile carpets and a television that thinks it's a cinema screen, but she was dressed like a cheap tart trolling for trade in Byker twenty years ago." Suddenly he bellowed with laughter and clapped his hands, then raised them over his head. "I've got it. I remember who she is. Tina Brady is Tina Carey as was, and she really was a cheap tart in Byker twenty-odd years ago, although she'd gone upmarket when I nabbed her for the last time. Mind you, I was pulled off Vice just after, but I don't suppose it was her last time. She'll have a record as long as my arm."

"Which doesn't mean she had anything to do with Kimberley Ford being murdered."

"Of course not, but she lied to me about Kim being at her place, and I think that makes it worth sending in the heavy mob next time she gets spoken to."

"So, I'm the heavy mob, am I? I thought I'd been losing weight recently." At least, that was what Paul told her when he took an indecent delight in studying her undressed. Not that Morton would ever know that detail.

Darling drummed on the desk for a moment. "Right, I want any CCTV we can get for Torville Street and anything around Hallam Dene from midnight onwards."

Morton scribbled in his notebook.

"After that, we'll put the ladies to some serious questioning. That seem like a plan to you?" she said.

Morton nodded, looking at Darling with eyes that asked, 'Since when did you need my approval to do anything?'

"Right, then. The morning it is."

Chapter Twenty-Three

Darling ignored the telephone on her desk. Whoever it was could wait. If it was important, they could ring back. The ringing stopped. She sighed and massaged her neck. The pain didn't go away, and it would not leave her until they found the murderer.

The phone rang again. She picked it up prepared to give whoever it was a piece of her mind. "Sorry to disturb you, Inspector." It was Sergeant Fraser on the front desk. "I wouldn't call you ordinarily, but he insists on speaking to you."

Who could put the wind up Fraser enough to disturb her? "I'm on my way." At least, it would get her away from the heap of irreconcilable reports on her desk.

A tall, elegant, silver-haired figure unfolded itself from a chair as she emerged into the foyer. It wore an immaculate dark-grey suit, with a dog collar at its throat and a large, heavy silver cross on its chest. It extended a slender hand. The handshake was firm and dry, but brief. "Good of you to see me so quickly, Chief Inspector. I am…" It was a rich, dark voice, used to addressing people.

Darling shook her head. "Just a plain inspector, and I know who you are, Monsignor."

Monsignor Adrian Lee was well-known on Tyneside, a pathologically energetic priest who was always around when there was charitable giving to be received, good to be done, an ecumenical hand to be held out, a photograph to be taken for posterity. *The Journal* described him as 'classically handsome', and if he was not Darling's sort of man – she had problems with organised religion and those who made a living out of it – she was still sufficiently objective to understand that many women of a certain age would find him attractive, and quite a few men too. "How can I help you?" she asked.

For a moment, he said nothing, shifting from foot to foot.

Darling was experienced enough in the reading of people to know he was a long, long way outside his comfort zone.

"Is there somewhere we can talk in private?" he asked, eventually.

She led him inside the station and into an interview room, which was at once grim and functional.

Once they were seated on opposite sides of the table, he stared at the recorders.

She smiled. "Oh, they're not switched on," she said. "This is just a chat, not a formal interview."

He nodded and squirmed in his chair. The furniture on that side of the table had not been acquired with comfort in mind. "Oh, what is the point?" he asked himself, eventually. "I knew the girl, the girl who was murdered."

"Oh?!" Questions poured into her head, but she put them aside. There would be a time to ask them, but this was not it. This was the time to let him talk uninterrupted.

He took a deep breath while at the same time seeming to shrink in on himself, to become diminished.

"I was a customer," he said.

"Customer?" How could a monsignor be the customer of a thirteen-year-old girl, a child? she thought. The answer hit her like a boot in the solar plexus. She had believed she was beyond surprise, beyond shock. There was no depth human depravity and selfishness could not sound, no vocation that guaranteed a member would not succumb to forbidden desires, and she believed she had seen most if not all of it. Between men of his age and children of Kimberley's, the word 'customer' could have only one meaning, one sort of transaction. This wasn't the first time she had encountered it.

Even so, a monsignor admitting he used a child prostitute made her catch her breath. Darling leaned forward, hands clasped on the table to keep them from shaking, reminding herself Kimberley had not been a prostitute – even if the monsignor had paid her for her services – but an abused child.

"Monsignor, if what you have said means what I think it means…" Her voice dried up and she looked at him silently, hoping he would say something, anything, to convince her she was wrong.

He nodded; eyes fixed anywhere but on her.

She knew he understood. "…then I cannot keep this conversation on an informal basis."

He nodded again.

She saw a tear gather in his eye, from where it slid down his cheek to his mouth, where he wiped it away with the back of his hand.

"Of course, I understand, Inspector. I am here, so you can do whatever must be done. I am asking for no 'special treatment'. These tears are not for me. I know I do not deserve anyone's tears, even my own. They are for that child, and all the other children men like me have abused." He took out a folded linen handkerchief, shook it open and wiped his face. "I saw that news report, Inspector, and recognised her instantly. I knew I abused her. My first instinct was to kill myself. After all, suicide could not make me any more of an abject sinner than I already am. Who knows, maybe I still will, or maybe those men who will be my fellow prisoners will do the necessary for me. I know men guilty of my crimes are not exactly popular in prison. It would be no more than I deserve. First of all, however, I owe it to Kimberley to do whatever I can to help apprehend her murderer. I did not kill her, Inspector, but nothing I can do will earn me forgiveness for what I did do to her. I am reconciled to that. Nevertheless, I will do whatever I can."

He sat back in his chair, looking at her.

She fancied he was searching her for some response to what he had said, a response he was not going to get. She knew a rehearsed speech when she heard one. He was correct in one aspect. Nothing was going to earn him forgiveness for abusing a child.

"Monsignor, you would be well advised not to say anything more until you have a legal adviser with you. Do you understand?"

For a moment, she thought he was going to say he did not need legal advice. The expression he wore – of calm certainty – was insufferably smug, one with which she was very familiar, one she delighted in undermining.

Then, he nodded and reached into his jacket to bring out a mobile phone.

"Father O'Heir, this is Monsignor Lee. I am afraid I am in need to legal representation."

Chapter Twenty-Four

The office of All Tyne Taxis was on the third floor of a terraced building on Westgate Road that had a motorbike shop occupying the ground and first floors and a model agency that had been closed for years on the second. The stairs were rickety; the wallpaper was faded, worn and stained, peeling away wherever it could, like it wanted to escape. As she climbed the stairs, Abdullah thought that whatever the taxi company was paying for their offices, it was too much. If there was a fire on the floors below, anyone up there was dead meat, and even in the relatively short time she had been a copper, she had encountered more than a few fires set for the insurance money.

After the dingy staircase, the taxi offices were a shock – brightly lit, two modern desks with computer and telephone gear piled on top, and a huge map of Tyneside covering the entire wall between the two windows. Only one of the desks was occupied, by a young woman with dreadlocks of magenta-coloured hair tied in a thick cable that reached down her back. She wore a T-shirt emblazoned with a rock band logo Abdullah did not recognise. Her arms and throat were heavily tattooed, there were three silver earrings through each lobe, and a ring through her nose. She looked up at Abdullah, eyes wide open and bright.

"How can I help you?" she asked. Like so many Geordies, the young woman somehow had a perfect telephone voice, clearly pronounced with just a hint of the accent that she would allow to emerge when she was with friends.

"I'm Detective Constable Abdullah of the Northumbria Police," she said, holding out her warrant card for inspection. "I have a few questions about one of your drivers in connection with our investigations."

A cloud passed across the girl's face. "One of our drivers? Are you sure? Nobody has reported anything, and Mr Rowntree is strict about traffic accidents."

"Mr Rowntree?"

"The boss. He owns All Tyne Taxis. He's my uncle."

He's your uncle and you call him Mr Rowntree? wondered Abdullah. "Nothing to do with a traffic accident. It is much more serious than that. And he did give us this card." She pushed the card across the desk for it to be picked up.

"Yeah, he's one of ours," the girl said, after inspecting the card closely enough. "I don't really know Georgy. I do day shifts. He's on nights. What's he done?"

Abdullah sat down without being asked. "Nothing; nothing wrong, that is. We are interested in one of his pick-ups on Monday night."

Realisation of what Abdullah might be investigating began to dawn on the girl. She sat back in her chair, as though trying to get away from her, and almost fell out of it backwards when it tipped. She shrieked, but managed to catch hold of the desk with one hand and Abdullah's suddenly outstretched wrist with the other. Her face turned a colour close to that of her hair but faded quickly. "Thanks," she said. "I forgot I'd changed the settings on the chair. I'm Stan Calder, by the way. Call me Stan."

"I'm Shan," Abdullah said.

"Stan and Shan." Stan laughed. "I don't think I can help you. Georgy mostly just trawls for his own trade. As long as he pays for the directions we give him, we don't mind what he does the rest of the time."

"He said this trip was on an account, taking a young girl from a pick-up near Torville Street and dropping her off at Shiremoor. It wasn't the first such fare he'd taken."

Another cloud passed across Stan's face. "I think I know the account you mean."

"Well?"

"It's confidential, business information. I don't know if I can tell you."

Abdullah leaned forward across the desk. "Stan, this is a murder investigation."

What little colour the girl had in her face left it. "I'll call my dad," she said. "He runs the company when my uncle, William, is out of the country. My uncle is in Barbados at the moment."

Lucky man, Abdullah thought, then nodded and turned away as Stan hit a number on her mobile.

Stan had a brief, hushed conversation with whoever was on the other end. "Right, Dad says I have to give you the information."

She got up from behind the desk, went to the filing cabinet at the far end of the room and returned holding out a thin file to Abdullah, who took it and quickly scanned the contents. The file was labelled 'Tina Brady Account' and detailed what looked to be well over one hundred taxi journeys, most of which seemed to have been paid for. The starting point of each journey was Torville Street, but the destinations were all over the city.

"Mind if I take this?" Abdullah asked.

"I could copy it for you," Stan suggested, snatching the file from her and quickly running off a copy on the printer she had on her desk. Once it was done, she put the printouts in a clear poly pocket and handed it back to Abdullah before clipping the originals back in the company file. "Is Mrs Brady in any trouble?" she asked, her voice and expression all innocence.

Abdullah opened her mouth to say that she thought so but shook her head instead. "I couldn't possibly comment."

Stan nodded. "That bad, is it? I've only met the woman once. I don't think she liked me any more than I liked her, and that wasn't much."

"Thank you for your cooperation," Abdullah said as she got to her feet. Her gratitude was genuine. Not every business on Tyneside would have given her the information so readily.

"Any time," Stan said. "Just be careful of the stairs on your way down. They're a bit gash."

Abdullah smiled and left. She didn't exactly run back to Forth Banks, but anyone keeping up with her would have known all about it by the time she arrived.

Chapter Twenty-Five

Darling sat at her desk, nursing an almost-cold cup of coffee while she reviewed the investigation. She was waiting for Monsignor Lee's legal representation to arrive, and was startled enough to almost spill the coffee when she heard the knock on the door.

Morton stood in the doorway. "Boss, I think you should look at this." His voice was flat and level, exactly the way it was when he had exciting news.

She got to her feet and followed him to DC David Cox's desk. She did not really like Cox – he could be lazy – and thought of getting rid of him. Just about the only thing she liked about him was that everyone on the team called him 'Brian' without him having the least idea why, or whether it was the actor or the scientist whose name they were taking in vain.

Cox looked up as they approached. "I've been checking the CCTV from where he says he dropped her."

"Where who dropped whom?" asked Darling.

Cox looked at her blankly.

"You mean where Mr Lupoff, the taxi driver, dropped off Kimberley Ford. Is that what you mean?" she said.

Cox's look remained blank.

"People have names, Constable, and it is part of our job to know what those names are and use them, if only so we don't get people confused. Clarity is vital, Constable."

"Yes, ma'am... boss." He still looked as though he hadn't the first idea what she was on about. "The taxi driver, Mr..."

"Lupoff."

"Mr Lupoff, yes, dropped off Kimberley at the roundabout at the junction of the A186 and Park Lane just before midnight on Monday." Cox hit 'enter' on his keyboard and grainy CCTV footage appeared, showing Georgy Lupoff's Mercedes coming along Park Lane in Shiremoor from the direction of the A186 from Newcastle and coming to a halt opposite the chip shop at the junction of Lesbury Avenue and Park Lane.

The figure of a young girl dressed for a night on the town got out and stood at the side of the road as the taxi drove away along Park Lane. She made a phone call. The quality of the image was not good enough to positively identify her, but nobody had any doubt it was Kim. A couple of minutes later, a black VW Golf stopped beside her. The passenger door was opened and words seemed to be exchanged before she got in and the car drove off, following the Mercedes.

"Run that back," Darling instructed.

Cox managed to obey without tying his fingers in knots.

"Stop!" The Golf sat centre screen. It looked like a man driving it, a youngish man, but nobody could be sure. Darling tapped the screen in the area of the front number plate. "Can you zoom in on that?"

Cox bowed his head and worked the screen as best he could, eventually obtaining an image that showed the number plate large enough for them to have a go at reading it, had the number plate light been on. It wasn't.

"Bugger," hissed Morton.

"Shouldn't he get picked up for that?" Cox asked. "Having his number plate light out?"

Darling and Morton turned towards him for a moment as though unable to believe what they had heard. Uniforms had better things to be doing at that time of night to bother about a plate light being out.

"You know what that tells me?" Darling asked. "It tells me he knew he was going to pick her up somewhere covered by cameras, and he took the bulb out just so we wouldn't be able to see his registration when we looked. Any odds you like, he knows exactly where there is coverage, and he's got the bulb back in by now. He probably had fake plates just to put us off the track." She stopped talking, realising she was running off at the mouth and possibly giving the impression she thought this murderer was smart.

As far as she was concerned, there was no such animal as a 'smart' murderer. Smart people didn't commit murder anywhere outside of detective novels. Murderers might be cunning, one or two, but cunning wasn't the same as smart.

"Keep looking," she told Cox. "See if you can find anything useful, like where that Golf might have gone." She turned and marched towards the door before halting and turning around. "What are you waiting for, Sergeant? We've got to go and talk to Mrs Brady."

She had just reached her desk and was getting her coat when the telephone rang. It was Sergeant Fraser from the front desk. Monsignor Lee's legal representation had arrived. He didn't look like a man who liked being kept waiting.

Chapter Twenty-Six

The formal interview began with Morton sitting beside Darling on one side of the table and the diocesan solicitor, Michael Lander, sitting beside Monsignor Lee on the other. Lander was a stout, middle-aged man with receding dark hair, a decidedly expensive suit with an egg and tomato MCC tie, and an expression suggesting a belief that, if the sky had not already fallen, it would do so very soon. Darling introduced everyone for the record and then went straight to the meat of the matter.

"Monsignor, you told me you were a 'customer' of Kimberley Ford. Is that true?"

"Yes, it is true," he replied immediately, and very clearly.

"Will you please explain what you mean by that?"

Monsignor Lee was not so quick to reply this time, sighing deeply, making a steeple of his long fingers, which he stared at intently for a moment before shaking his head. "There is no point trying to sweeten it," he said. "I paid the child for sexual favours."

The admission lay on the table for all to see, steaming in silence.

"When I say 'sexual favours', I do not mean I had sexual intercourse with her. I did not. At no time did I lay a finger upon her."

Morton glared at him in.

"You could say what I did was entirely innocent." Lee appeared to think for a moment. "Yes, you could say that." It was evident he did not believe anyone would.

"And what, exactly, did you do?" Morton snarled. He was not blessed with patience at the best of times and having to deal with sexual predators who preyed on children guaranteed it was the worst of times for him.

"She would put on a confirmation dress and dance for me, in another room. I watched on closed-circuit television."

"Dance for you?" Darling asked.

Lander looked as though he was about to throw up any time now.

"Yes, dance. That is all." Lee looked from one disbelieving face to the next. "There was nothing of Salome in her dancing, nothing pornographic."

"What did you do while the child danced?" Darling asked.

"I covered myself with a blanket and masturbated."

"That seems a little unnecessary if she was in another room."

Lee looked at her with pity in his eyes, as if wondering how she could not understand. "I knew I was doing wrong, Inspector. I thought that if I could not see what I was doing, my offence might be less, might go unnoticed elsewhere. Not logical, I know."

That admission was greeted with silence too.

Darling glanced at Morton. Like most coppers, Morton had a basic-going-on-biblical attitude towards child abusers. He looked as though he wanted to take the monsignor out into the station yard and give him a good seeing-to with a truncheon, eventually using it on him as the murderer had used something similar on Kimberley.

Ordinarily, Darling would have disapproved of this impulse, disapproved thoroughly. Today, though, she might hold his coat.

"How many times did this 'dance performance' take place?" she asked.

Lee thought for a while.

Darling could see him counting in his memory.

"Six times, I think. Yes, six times in total."

Darling wondered how old Kimberley had been when she began selling herself to men.

"When was the last time?"

He looked up towards the ceiling, as though searching there for clues. "A week ago last Sunday."

Sunday? she thought. Wasn't Sunday supposed to be their holy day, a day when he refrained from acts like sexually abusing a child?

"How did you pay for these favours?" she said.

"I paid £100 by bank transfer over the internet and gave the child £50 in cash for herself."

"Not by credit card?" Morton asked.

"No, no, by bank transfer," Lee insisted, as though it was the most natural thing in the world.

Darling wondered whether perhaps it was, and she was not as up to date as she thought she was, as she needed to be. "How were these 'assignations' arranged. Monsignor?" she asked.

"I called a telephone number. They made the arrangements. The young lady called me, and I picked her up from wherever she was."

The police officers looked at each other. How simple an operation was that?

"How did you get the number you called? How did you know to call it? Who gave it to you?"

Ordinarily Darling would have asked one question at a time, waiting for an answer, but now she wanted to get the monsignor out of his comfort zone and dislodge some hopefully useful information. The case had suddenly developed the makings of a more complex investigation than that of the mere murder of a child; the investigation of a child-sex ring involving men with connections, men like Monsignor Lee. She swallowed, reminding herself not to get distracted. She could leave things like child-sex rings to Joe Milburn and even higher-ups on the food chain. In the meantime, no murder was ever 'mere', and certainly never the murder of a child.

"Someone I met in a chatroom. He called himself 'Hephaestus'. I've no idea what his real name is, any more than I know whom I phone. All I get off that is a recorded voice telling me my message has been received and someone will be in touch directly."

The room was silent for a while. Darling and Morton glanced at each other, then looked away. Lander polished his glasses on the silk lining of his tie. Monsignor Lee gazed at Darling with the eager expectation of a spaniel panting for the promised treat after performing some exceptional feat of obedience.

Darling glanced at the recorders, then at Morton, who switched them off. "Thank you, Monsignor," she said. "This has been a very informative discussion."

"Aren't you going to arrest me?" His disappointment sounded in every word.

"Arrest you?" Darling asked. "Why should I arrest you? What arrestable offence have you committed?"

He looked from Darling to Morton to Lander – who would not meet his eyes – and then back to Darling, his bewilderment evident. "I abused that poor child!"

Darling shook her head. "Monsignor, all I can see you have done is pay her for dancing for you while wearing a confirmation dress. I do not believe that qualifies as abuse." She looked at Morton, who shook his head, and then at Lander, who did and said nothing, except very obviously look like he wished he was somewhere else. "You never touched her, did you?"

The monsignor thought for a long moment, his eyes staring, his mouth opening and closing. "No, I never did touch her, not at all," he eventually said.

Morton leaned forward towards Lander. "I think you should explain to the monsignor that, while he has definitely been a bad, bad boy in the eyes of his employer, he hasn't actually committed any crime," he said.

Lander nodded, sighing, wishing he had gone for that round of golf this morning and left this ghastly mess to Philip Massey. Criminal law had never been an area of particular interest to him, other than passing the required exams at university. There wasn't enough profit in it for his tastes. He was more than happy to accept that the police knew what they were talking about.

"But I have sinned–" Lee protested.

"And you have confessed," Darling interrupted. "As I am sure you know better than I do, confession is good for the soul. What I must tell you is that the constabulary concerns itself only with crime. You have committed no crime. Your sin is a matter between you and your God. I suggest you take it up with him, or his representative on Earth." She paused for a moment as though she had just realised something, then grinned savagely. "But of course, that's you, isn't it?"

After a further period of uncomfortable silence, Lander got to his feet, closed his briefcase and announced he was leaving, if his presence was not required. "I do have other calls on my time, Monsignor Lee."

Morton raised his hand. "I don't think we are quite finished here yet."

"We aren't?" Darling asked.

Morton nodded, and looked directly into Lee's eyes. "Monsignor, you said that you paid Kimberley cash for her dancing."

"Yes, yes I did."

"You also said that you paid someone else rather more money, by bank transfer."

Lee frowned. So did Lander, seeing which way this was going.

"Who was that other person, Monsignor?"

Lee relaxed. "I don't know. I never knew. I knew their telephone number, they knew mine. The only other thing I knew about them was their bank account details."

"We shall need all the details of those transfers," Darling said, giving silent thanks that Morton had kept his wits about himself while she had forgotten hers, "to assist us in our investigations."

Lander was about to say they had no right to that information as, on their own admission, no crime had been committed, but the monsignor beat him to it.

"Of course. I have the details at home," he volunteered. "If they can be of any help to you."

Darling closed her file. "Very good. Sergeant Morton will accompany you there to collect them."

The monsignor nodded. Lander looked as though he would be very happy if the ground just opened up and swallowed him whole.

She turned to Morton. "Take DC Cox with you, he's up on the technical side. All his computer gear, all his telephones, bring them in."

Lander took hold of Monsignor Lee's arm. "I shall accompany you, just to make sure your new friends don't overstep the mark." He looked to Morton. "If that is acceptable to you?"

Morton laughed. "The more the merrier."

* * *

"Pull over!" ordered the man in the back of a black Range Rover Evoque. "Pull over!"

"Right away, boss," said the young driver, steering to the left-hand side of the road while looking around to see what had taken Dan Hegarty's notice. Ordinarily he travelled with a phone clamped to his ear or catching up on his sleep.

He saw they were opposite the police station, and walking away were four people, a woman and three men. He recognised the woman and two of the men. She was the detective he'd seen at the press conference about the Hallam Dene murder, while the tall, distinguished-looking man with the dog collar was Monsignor Lee, and the expensively dressed man with a briefcase and a worried expression was Michael Lander, the boss's solicitor. Who the other, somewhat careworn-looking man was he had no idea, but guessed he was another copper.

"Look there, boss!" he said, turning to look at Hegarty, who had already seen the little spectacle and had his forefinger raised in front of his lips.

"Shhh. I don't want to attract attention."

They both watched the little parade turn the corner, out of sight. "I wonder what that is all about?" Hegarty said.

"No idea, boss," the driver lied. The woman copper was in charge of the murder investigation; if she was looking at Monsignor Lee – Monsignor Lee, for heaven's sake – then she was definitely barking up the wrong tree, and he could relax.

"Drive on," said Hegarty, looking at the contacts on his phone.

"My pleasure, boss," murmured the driver. This day was getting better.

Chapter Twenty-Seven

Abdullah waited with Cox on Beverly Ford's doorstep, aware that dozens of eyes were fixed on them, most belonging to people who couldn't understand why they hadn't yet caught the beast who murdered little Kim. The remainder belonged to people who hoped they might witness something horrible. The detectives were used to all sorts.

Bev opened the door and looked down on them. Abdullah was shocked to see how wretched she looked – haggard, red-eyed and almost certainly hadn't changed her clothes lately. She didn't appear to have brushed her hair and there were dark rings around her eyes that resembled bruising but weren't.

"Mrs Ford, we're sorry to disturb you. As you know, I am DC Abdullah, and this is my colleague, DC Cox."

Bev didn't glance at their warrant cards. "Whadya want?" she slurred.

Abdullah thought for a moment that in Bev's situation she would probably want to get drunk, and she never touched alcohol.

"We need to take a look at Kimberley's room. There may be something there that would help us with our investigation."

Bev stood aside without a word and they stepped into the gloomy house. So far as they could tell, all the curtains were drawn shut and none of the lights were on. Cox reached out to switch on the light on the stairs but Abdullah batted his hand away.

"It's dark as a cellar," he muttered.

She shook her head and nodded to Bev stumbling towards the kitchen. "There's no need," she hissed, and his hand fell back to his side. There really was no need.

Kim's room was the third bedroom. As was usual with the houses built in their thousands at that time, it was small, little more than a box room, better suited to being a dressing room than somewhere a young girl conducted her private life. To live in there with a bed and a wardrobe, a desk and a chair, required everything to be in its place, and Kim – it appeared – was as obsessively neat as her mother usually was. There were a couple of posters on the long wall above the bed, boy bands neither copper recognised, and one over the bedhead of Ed Sheeran that was more than life-size. Abdullah had seen him at the Arena last year and wondered whether Kim had been in the audience too.

"You take the desk, I'll take the wardrobe," Abdullah said. He might have resented her take-charge attitude, but it had soon become clear she was brighter and more energetic than he was. She was going places. He was content to follow, as long as nobody was watching. Pulling on a pair of purple rubber gloves, Abdullah took a deep breath and reached out to slide back the wardrobe door. Before she did so, however, she remembered observing colleagues searching property and sometimes being appalled by how brusque, even brutal, they could be. She understood their reasons, being under pressure from higher-ups who wanted results yesterday. More often than not, it was bad lads' cribs they were tossing, dumps that looked tidier after they'd emptied everything onto the floor than before. Kimberley, however, was the victim here. She deserved their respect.

Opening the door, she looked at the dresses hanging in the wardrobe, the school trousers, the two pairs of jeans fashionably worn through at the knees. There were school blouses with long and short sleeves and a couple of others in lurid colours. Abdullah ran her hands down the outside of each garment, checking for anything that might be hidden in the pockets or elsewhere, and found nothing.

On the left-hand side of the wardrobe were shelves and three drawers, with clothing neatly arranged. At the top was underwear, white cotton bras that scarcely merited the name, and equally white cotton knickers that might not be the auntie's flannel bloomers Abdullah had worn to school but were still sensible, nothing like the thongs the adverts proposed every woman wore, even adolescent girls, even to school. Then came her T-shirts, mostly white, some printed but otherwise ordinary. In the drawers below were leggings, all black, and a variety of jumpers. At the bottom of the wardrobe, under the last of the drawers, was a sloping rack of sensible shoes and trainers, not a single one with the semblance of a heel. By the time she was finished, she had checked every item on that side of the wardrobe as thoroughly as those hanging on the rail and found nothing.

Just as she was about to stand up after checking the shoes, she caught a glimpse of something behind the rack, something fawn-coloured amongst the dark wood and the shadows. Unable to reach it, she had to remove all the shoes and lift out the rack to reveal a buff-coloured C5-sized envelope. Even before she touched it, she could tell there was something inside.

"Looks like we have something."

Cox turned towards her, watching as she lifted out the envelope and laid it on the bed. He peered over her into the wardrobe. "She didn't want anyone finding that by accident, did she?" he said.

Abdullah said nothing, taking two deep breaths to settle herself before reaching out and emptying the envelope onto the bedspread. The contents were a small notebook that might fit into a purse, held shut by two thick rubber bands of the sort postmen used, and several banknotes held together with a spring clip.

Cox picked up the notes and examined them while Abdullah unwrapped the notebook. He whistled. "There's more than a thousand pounds here," he whispered. "How does a thirteen-year-old girl get a grand in used notes?"

Abdullah knew exactly how that was possible from her brief examination of the diary, for that was what it was, a business diary. 'Fatman just wanted a wank' was one entry she read. 'The priest just wanted to watch me dance again. He's weird' was another. 'Frankie says dick tastes nice. It is horrible!' 'He wanted a threesome with Bella, but she wasn't having any of it.' 'I almost think the doctor likes me. He's got soft hands. Wonder where he got the scar on the back.' 'He would hurt me if he had the balls for it, I'm sure. Wonder why he's younger than the others. Good thing he hasn't called for me again.' She read this, which was the last entry, with a hand of ice tracing a heavy finger down her spine, and she had to swallow hard to keep from vomiting. Was 'He' the man who had done a lot more than hurt Kimberley? Did her two nieces, of Kimberley's age, keep secret diaries like that? Knowing her brother as she did, she doubted it, but that did not prevent her thinking a quick prayer.

"What's that?" Cox asked as she wrapped the bands back around the notebook.

She shook her head.

He opened his mouth to ask again but saw her expression and stood back.

She took out her phone and called DI Darling.

"Boss, it's Shan. We're at the Fords' house and we've found something, something I think you're going to need to look at here."

Abdullah caught sight of a cloud of doubt flickering across Cox's face. She did not understand the fear that some of her colleagues appeared to harbour for Darling. She'd never had anything but an agreeable working experience with her, encouragement to do the job as well as she could, to think ahead and outside of the box if needs be. To Abdullah, Pen Darling was a role model. She wanted to be sitting in her chair, and sometime soon. She put the phone back in her pocket and got out evidence bags for the notebook and money.

"The inspector will want to speak to Mrs Ford when she sees that," she said, lifting the clear bag containing the diary. "I'm just saving time." Then she remembered how Bev had looked when they had arrived. If the boss was going to talk to her any time soon, someone had better see about getting her sobered up, and double quick. There was only one candidate to be that person, seeing as she wasn't sure Cox could boil a kettle. "I'm going to make some tea. Fancy anything?"

"A pint of bitter and a whisky chaser," he said, grinning.

Abdullah grinned back. She knew he was only taking the piss. He'd probably forgotten she was Muslim. Let him. Life was too short to waste time on such unimportant matters, not when they were investigating a murder, and most definitely not when they were investigating a murder as ghastly as this one. What really concerned her was why Cox had not found the packet when he searched Kim's room the first time, and how she was going to explain that to Darling without making him look completely incompetent.

* * *

Fifteen minutes later, Abdullah had got the better part of a mug of strong black coffee into Bev. She wasn't sure it had made any difference to her condition, and the kettle was boiling in the kitchen to brew another when there was a knock at the front door. Abdullah hurried to open it, revealing Darling standing on the top step, and DS Morton on the one below. She couldn't help but notice that Darling wore an immaculate dark-blue business suit over an oyster-coloured blouse that looked as though it might be silk, whereas Morton was his normal shabby self in a scruffy suit with a plain blue tie askew at his open collar.

"She's in the kitchen, boss," Abdullah muttered as they stepped past her. "I've been trying to get her sobered up but she's still in a bit of a bad way."

"Can't say that I blame her," said Darling as the DC closed the door. "This evidence you mentioned…"

Abdullah withdrew the two clear evidence envelopes from her bag and gave them to the inspector.

Darling did not concern herself with the money, giving it straight to Morton, who briefly looked as though he wanted to say something he considered witty but thought better of it before he got the words out.

Darling broke the seal on the other bag and was about to take it out when Abdullah gasped, "Boss, gloves!"

Darling glared at the DC momentarily, then nodded her head and put on a pair of gloves from her pocket. "Thanks for the reminder, Constable," she said.

Morton looked in the opposite direction. Darling then riffled through the pages as Abdullah had done, reading the last few entries more carefully, allowing Morton to read them over her shoulder. She heard his indrawn breath, felt him step backwards.

"Where did you find this?" she asked.

Abdullah told her.

Darling whistled through her teeth, then put the notebook back in the evidence bag. "Right then, you and I will go and have a chat with Mrs Ford." She glanced up the stairs and then at Morton. "Sergeant, you go and make sure DCs Abdullah and Cox haven't missed anything else. After all, Cox missed this the first time."

Morton grinned, a little wolfishly. What these young 'uns thought was a thorough search and what he thought was a thorough search were two completely different things. He'd been taught to search by Joe Milburn – Detective Superintendent Milburn as he now was. He'd been taught by the best. And one of the other lessons he had learned was not to get too close to the sort of devastation he knew was going to be inflicted on Mrs Ford. She knew nothing about what the book contained. He'd bet his nearly thirty years' worth of pension on that.

Chapter Twenty-Eight

"I'm just on my way out," Darling said as she walked through the office. "I'm going to see a bank manager…"

"Boss, I think you should see this!" Pearson peered from behind his monitor, his hand in the air as though he was still in the fourth form.

Darling diverted to his desk and saw the photograph on his monitor. It was a photo of the great and good, displaying a large charity cheque outside the St Vincent de Paul community centre on New Bridge Street, all smiling enthusiastically for the camera. An expensively dressed woman in her young middle-age with a cloud of dark hair and what Darling suspected was real gold jewellery on her fingers and at her throat had her left hand on the cheque. Monsignor Lee held the other side. To her side was a stockily built man with his blonde hair in a mullet that was as old-fashioned as the several chains at his throat. On the far side of Lee was another priest, even taller than the monsignor. His severe expression suggested he did not exactly approve of this transaction. He wore a slightly battered black biretta on top of his wiry grey hair.

"Who are these people?" she said. "I know the monsignor, but who are the others?"

Pearson tapped the woman. "That's Amanda Stavely, she's the front woman for the PFI who've bought the Toon." He tapped the smaller man. "And that's Dan Hagerty. He owns half the pubs and bars on Tyneside and – five will get you ten – he's got something to do with the takeover, way in the background. He's probably on Mr Milburn's bucket list. As for the other priest, that's Father Francis Xavier O'Heir. He looks like what he is, strict, and he knows everything that's going on."

O'Heir? Wasn't that who Lee had called to arrange legal representation? "You seem to be an expert on the Catholic church, Constable Pearson," Darling said.

"Not the church, not the whole church, just him. He's my parish priest, has been all my life, popular with the hierarchy but people I trust have good reason not to trust Father O'Heir as far as they can throw him."

"People you trust?"

"Members of my family. They say he's got away with things he shouldn't have."

What sort of things could they be? The Catholic church didn't have an exactly spotless reputation when it came to offences against children. Perhaps they should have a closer look at Father O'Heir with regard to this offence against a child. "Thank you for that, Constable. We'll need to bear it in mind. In the meantime, I have an appointment."

* * *

Darling put her ID card back in her pocket and regarded the young man in his well-pressed Marks & Spencer suit, gleaming white shirt and dark-blue tie with the bank's logo carefully placed two inches below the symmetrical Windsor knot. Everything about him screamed 'ambition' and 'I am eager to move on to better things than this branch hundreds of miles from London'.

"M–" she leaned forward as though checking the man's name on his still-very-new and unworn photograph ID badge clipped to the breast pocket of his suit jacket "– Mr Carter, I appreciate you giving me your time, especially at such short notice. I think I must make it very clear to you what crimes I am investigating."

He looked back at her levelly, appraisingly, making a steeple of his fingers. She saw beads of sweat pop out on his forehead and wondered whether this was the first time he had ever spoken to a senior police officer in the execution of their duties. She could not remember having spoken to him before, not face to face, at least.

"Mrs Darling…" he began. He must have seen some reaction in her because he stopped immediately.

"That is Inspector Darling, Mr Carter, Detective Inspector Darling." She made no mention of not being a Mrs, and not having been one for several years. "The crimes I am investigating are murder and the associated laundering of the proceeds of crime through your bank, this branch of your bank."

More sweat appeared on his forehead, and on his neck too, between his hairline and his shirt collar. Money laundering was one of those banking services that kept ambitious young bankers awake in the early hours of the morning because it could cost them their careers.

"How can I help, Detective Inspector?" he asked brightly, running his forefinger around the inside of his suddenly too-tight collar.

She removed a file from her bag and extracted a single sheet of paper. There were three short lines of print on it, all numbers – six-figure branch identification codes, all three identical – and eight-digit account numbers, all courtesy of Monsignor Lee's records. "We need the full account records of these three accounts over the last twelve months."

Mr Carter shook his head. "That information is confidential," he said.

It was her turn to shake her head. "Not when money laundering is being investigated, Mr Carter. Not when the laundering of the proceeds of crime is being investigated, Mr Carter. Not when the murder of a child is being investigated, Mr Carter. Do you have children of your own?"

He did not make his usual joke, 'None that I know about'.

Darling did not give him the opportunity to answer at all, seeing as it was a rhetorical question, and she had no interest in any answer he might have. She leaned forward, elbows on his desk, invading his space. "Now," she said. "I know there is an officer in your regional head office to whom you must report all money laundering investigations. I believe it is still Christine Appleby." The same Christine Appleby with whom she had shared a fifteen-minute lifetime in a hotel bar in Coventry between conference presentations. "I am sure she can guide you through the formalities you must obey in this situation, if you are not familiar with them."

That was evidently a conversation the still-young and ambitious Mr Carter wished to avoid. He was, after all, proficient in the handling of such matters, and had the computer-based training certificates to prove it.

"I'll get those details for you right away." His smile was strained.

He began to type. He was a fast, fluent, ten-fingered touch-typist in a way Darling had never really had the time to spend learning to do. Everyone had talents, even young Mr Carter.

He bent over to the cupboard and came back into sight with a dozen sheets of paper in his hand. He tapped the edges on the desk to make a neat pile and pushed it towards Darling.

"Those are the details you required." His smile was relieved, but still worried.

"Thank you, Mr Carter." Darling smiled, scanning the pages, paying particular regard to the names beside the accounts from which deposits had been made, names like 'John Wayne' and 'Clark Kent', obvious *noms de crime*. She sighed. That was a disappointment, but the sort codes told them the bank and the account numbers the owner. It would be a little more work to uncover them, but not much. She folded the pages and put them in her bag. "You've been very helpful, I'm sure." What she was sure about was that young Mr Carter should have followed some internal procedures before giving her the account histories, probably involving a telephone call to Mrs Appleby. He might well get into trouble for not following those procedures, but that, she thought, was none of her concern. He really ought to know his job. "There is a possibility we shall need more assistance."

He waved his right hand and his sickly smile turned into something that might be better termed a 'cheesy grin'. "Any time, Inspector, any time. Just ask for me by name." He took a business card from a cache on his desk. "I am available most business hours."

I bet you are, Darling thought, getting to her feet. Eight till eight. She held out her hand. "Thank you for all your help."

His handshake was even more limp and moist than it had been when he greeted her. She only just kept from wiping her hand on her skirt, rather waiting until she was outside the bank premises before taking out a tissue and scrubbing at both her hands.

Chapter Twenty-Nine

Darling knocked on Milburn's door, waited for the call and then entered.

Milburn's eyes followed her across the room as she sat down on the opposite side of his desk. "Progress to report?" he growled.

"We're getting there. The more we discover about where she was, where she went—"

"Where did she go?"

"We have CCTV footage of her being dropped off from a taxi on Park Lane in Shiremoor and being picked up a little later in a black VW Golf."

"So, you're now going to speak to everyone on Tyneside who owns a black VW Golf?"

"I don't think we need to do that yet," Darling said. She hoped he didn't sense the doubt she felt.

He smiled at her, one of the least cheerful expressions she had ever seen. Milburn had worked long and hard on his intimidating routine; there were times she wondered whether it really was a routine or whether he was just an intimidating hard man.

"It's your investigation, Pen. I'm not going to tell you how to run it." The 'not unless you ask, or I have to' went unsaid. "But that's not why you've come to see me, is it?"

There had been times when she wondered whether all superintendents were psychic or just Joe Milburn. She took a deep breath.

"What we appear to have is a child-sex ring; three girls – Kimberley and a couple of her friends – turning tricks, organised by one of the girls' mothers. We have evidence, and DS Morton and I will be going to speak to the woman as soon as I leave here." She spoke more quickly than usual, letting the words spill out of her mouth, because she saw the muscles around Milburn's mouth and jaw tense.

"We've had one man come into the station and say he paid Kim to dance for him; just dance, nothing else."

"Monsignor Lee," Milburn muttered. "I heard he'd been in. Wondered why."

"I don't think there's anything we can charge him with, but a monsignor…"

"I can see why that might make you pause."

Every copper knew about the likes of Jimmy Savile and Gary Glitter, Rolf Harris and Jonathan King. Darling and Milburn were both high enough up the food chain to have heard tales of the investigations into Cyril Smith and the Dolphin Square farrago. There was even a local one, at Hunmanby Manor, that still caused Milburn sleepless nights, although it had been before Darling's time. A child-sex ring was one thing, as bad as it might be, but one that involved the rich and famous was another can of worms entirely, one in which everyone they might want to question had the chief constable on speed dial.

"I don't have any more names, not yet," said Darling.

"But you think you will have."

"We've found a diary in Kim's room that mentions a number of customers, none of them by name – I'd bet she didn't even know any of their names – but from the amount of cash we found… well, that suggests double figures if she was getting £50 from each one."

Milburn shook his head. "She was, what, thirteen?"

They had both been coppers long enough to know that some of the men who were prepared to pay for their sexual gratification liked the taste of flesh that was too young to be tasted, probably because it was too young. That did not mean they were not revolted by the reality.

"Well, Inspector, you know what I always taught you," he said. "Follow the evidence, wherever it leads. If that means you end up treading on sensitive toes, you can rely on me to be there with you, adding my weight. If you're going to make 'em shout, make 'em shout loud; that's what I say."

Darling nodded. She hadn't gone to get Milburn's backing for what she knew she was going to have to do, but she was pleased to get it all the same. "I just thought I'd put you on notice, in case you get any unexpected calls from the chief constable."

Milburn chuckled. The sound was as cheerful and reassuring as his smile. "Forewarned is forearmed, as they say."

They sat looking at each other for a few seconds before she nodded, got to her feet and went to the door.

"Have you asked your friend in the trade what she makes of all this?" he asked before she could touch the door handle.

She paused for a moment. Why hadn't she thought of that?

He'd suggested two lines of inquiry in five minutes that had not occurred to her. Perhaps that was why he was a chief superintendent and she was still an inspector. She didn't think Dorothy Bainbridge would know anything useful, but it couldn't hurt to ask, and it would give her the chance to catch up with the woman she was dangerously close to regarding as a friend.

"Not yet, sir, but it's on my to-do list," she lied without turning around, just going to open the door. "Along with tracking down the Golf."

"You don't have to be a stranger, Pen," he said. "My door is always open to you."

She turned and gave him a genuine smile. "Thank you, sir. I know that."

"Just keep me advised if you decide to go big-game hunting," he said. "Keep me in the loop, as I think they say nowadays."

"Of course." She closed the door behind herself, wondering why she was still relieved to be out of his presence, the man whose protégée she knew she was.

Chapter Thirty

That evening, Darling closed the front door behind herself and leaned back against it, relishing its support, feeling the thumping where her skull joined her spine slow down, as she closed her eyes and concentrated on breathing deeply; in for the count of ten, hold it for ten, exhale for ten, then hold it in for ten more, just to hear her heart.

Eventually, she stood upright and shook herself vigorously, like a dog fresh out of the waves having dropped a stick of sea wrack at her master's feet. Feeling these stress symptoms was ridiculous. This wasn't the first murder inquiry she had led, not even the first murder of a child. They would find the killer, and they would find him – as she'd told Joanna King, of course it was a 'him' – by diligent routine police work, by talking to anyone and everyone, by listening to them, by pursuing every lead they could snuffle up, like truffle pigs. There would be no blinding moments of inspired revelation, no flashes of genius from a maverick. Ordinary men and women would do their work as best they could for as long as it took to arrive at the correct conclusion. In the meantime, she would subject herself to some tender loving care. If she was to play her part, she needed to keep herself in good condition. Which meant no dull, incessant aches to distract her.

She went upstairs to her bedroom, left her clothes in a pile on the floor where a laundry basket might be in most homes, put on shorts and a T-shirt and then went back downstairs and out into the garage, where her car was only rarely parked. This was because, in the space where her Focus should be, there was a stationary bicycle, a rowing machine and a set of weights selected to give her a good workout.

Forty-five minutes later, she was drenched in sweat, her clothes were wringing wet, and she was just finishing her second bottle of water. That pain at the base of her skull had been drowned out by the screams for mercy of muscles she did not exercise often enough. A shower soothed their din to a mere buzz of discomfort, which she rather enjoyed, and she felt very much more like the human being she wanted to be, except for an emptiness in her stomach. A pot of Lady Grey tea, two slices of wholewheat toast lavishly buttered and eaten with Camembert and a smoked German cheese, cherry tomatoes and mixed olives, all finished off by two peaches that dribbled juice down her chin; now she felt ready for anything, as long as 'anything' involved going to bed.

She went through her nightly routine, the first act of which was to charge her mobiles. There was a message on her personal phone. How could she have missed the call? Because it was set to 'silent'. She never set it to silent, even at work.

The message was from Paul.

> Just about to board. Thinking about you. See you when I get back. Love you.

She had not thought much about him since leaving him on that Tuesday evening, after which the world had turned upside down and the sky had fallen. She had forgotten he was going to America. From the time on the message, he would probably have landed by now. For a moment, she thought of calling him just to say she had got his message, just to hear his voice. She didn't because he was over there on business and she believed he would appreciate being distracted while he was working as much as she would, which was not at all. Disturbing her concentration might cost some annoyance, some displeasure. Disturbing his concentration might cost him a lot of money.

Not that he was motivated by money. She had discovered that much about him in the relatively short time since their relationship had somehow rekindled itself after more than a decade. It was the risk that motivated him, the possibility of losing just as much as the possibility of winning, the pitting of his wits, his skills against those of his opponents. The money was just an accident, a pleasant by-product of the turn of the cards. He had told her he would be happy to play for matchsticks if that was the game in town. She believed him.

After plugging the phones into their chargers, she went around the ground floor checking locks on windows and doors, switching on the alarm and switching off the lights. At the bottom of the stairs, she shucked off her slippers and walked up barefoot on the hessian carpet – just as she had when she was a child sent off to her grandmother's house for the long summer holidays, so she would not be subject to her parents' arguments. Getting into bed, she picked up *Wuthering Heights* from the bedside table. Had she wanted to read something, for pleasure, there were other books in the pile, but Miss Brontë's prose had always sent her to sleep. No counting sheep on a Northumbrian hillside tonight. Her eyes closed before she reached the end of the first paragraph. A little later, the book toppled sideways off her lap, off the bed and onto the floor. A softback book, it did not make enough noise to wake her.

When she woke the next morning, she felt very much refreshed, not in any pain at all and only slightly perplexed by her reading bedside light still being on.

Chapter Thirty-One

Tina Brady opened her front door, saw Darling and Morton standing there and made to close the door in their faces. "You two can fuck right off!"

Morton managed to get his foot between the closing door and the door jamb.

"May I remind you, this is a murder investigation," Darling said as severely as she could. "You and your daughter have information that will assist our inquiries."

"Me?" Brady laughed. "What the fuck do I know about any murder? You're not getting in here without a warrant."

Darling looked past the woman into her house and saw her daughter in the entrance hall behind her. "Francesse," she called. "It is your friend who has been murdered. Don't you want to help us find her killer?"

Brady turned to glare at her daughter, who shrank back into the shadows within the house.

"Why don't you tell us what really happened?" Darling called.

"You will anyway," muttered Morton, "eventually."

"What bit of 'get a warrant' don't you fuckers understand?" demanded Brady, spittle flecking from the corners of her mouth, trying to slam the door shut through Morton's foot. He wore very old-fashioned thick-soled boots that had withstood a cobbler's ministrations for more than a decade. They cost him more than four hundred pounds a pair, and he thought they were worth every penny.

Oh, sod this for a lark, Darling thought, and stepped as close as she could, so she was in Brady's face. "What part of 'I don't need a warrant when I'm arresting someone' don't you understand?" There was nothing of the 'we're all sisters' in her tone, just a pressurised copper who'd had a bellyful. "Christina Mary Brady, I am arresting you on charges of child abuse, child sexual abuse and living off immoral earnings," she said in a voice loud enough to be heard even by Brady's neighbours.

"No!" shrieked Francesse from inside the house, dashing forward to be close to her mother.

"Good luck proving that, cunt!" snarled the woman.

"Oh, I already have more than enough evidence for that." Darling chuckled, then nodded to Morton, who put his shoulder to the door and forced it open, sending mother and daughter skidding deeper into the hallway, the officers following them.

The mother stood still for a moment before launching herself at Darling, screaming obscenities, fingers curled into talons. Darling ducked under her attack, caught hold of her wrist and dragged down on it, twisting it behind her back and catching the other hand too.

"Cuff her, Sergeant, and we'll add resisting arrest and assaulting a police officer to the charge street."

Morton did as he was told, leaving them with an incandescent and foul-mouthed Tina Brady craning her neck to take a bite out of the sergeant, who put to good use thirty years of experience in avoiding such attacks from drunks and druggies of all ages and sexes. He held her out at arm's length, holding tightly to the rigid link of the handcuffs.

Darling called for backup and left Morton to his entertainment of getting her into the car, ushering Francesse into the sitting room, which looked even more revolting in the daylight than it did in artificial light. Whatever else money might bring in its wake, it did not come with good taste.

"Can you arrest her just like that?" Francesse asked, once they were both sitting down.

"You saw what she did," Darling said. "She definitely assaulted me."

The girl shook her head. "She didn't touch you. *You* touched *her.*"

Darling smiled. "That's where you're wrong. She tried to strike me, she intended to strike me. That's what makes it 'assault'. If she'd actually hit me, it would be 'occasioning actual bodily harm'."

The girl shook her head. She wasn't the first to be bemused by that sliced legal hair, and she wouldn't be the last. "What did you mean about 'living off immoral earnings'?"

Darling didn't believe she didn't know what that meant but decided to let that go this time. She leaned forward, as if to emphasise her sincerity. As far as sincerity went, she believed in the old-school nostrum. If you could fake sincerity, you had it made. In all modesty she believed she was pretty good at laying on the sincere. She reached out to lay her hand on Francesse's. The child's flesh was cold as stone.

"Francesse, we know what you, Kim and Bella have been doing."

A veil came down over Francesse's eyes. "Oh, what's that then?"

Darling hesitated a long while before answering, long enough to see beads of sweat pop out on the girl's forehead.

"'Turn tricks' is how I believe they refer to it in the trade; the oldest profession in the world, turning tricks. Your mother's trade. Don't bother trying to deny it, Francesse. We have the evidence."

"I'm saying nothin'," Francesse said, a pale imitation of her mother when her invective was in full flow.

Darling supposed that, like everything else, it needed practice, and Francesse wasn't old enough to have mastered the dark art the way her mother had.

"You don't have to say anything, Francesse," she reassured her. "Nobody can make you say anything you don't want to say, certainly not me. Then there's the fact that none of you have done anything that anyone can do anything about. Yes, you've screwed men and been paid for it, but all three of you are children. By definition, you have done nothing wrong. It's the men who used you who have done wrong. You might look on it as fucking for fun and profit, but until you are sixteen, the law regards that as child abuse. Despite all the appearances, you are a child and you have been abused. Now, I know how your mother was paid for your services, I've got all the bank statements and the phone records. Did you give any of the money the men gave you to your mother?"

Francesse's eyes widened. "Why the fuck d'you think I'd do anything as stupid as that? Any money the men gave me was mine, nothing to do with her. How d'you know they gave me any money anyway?"

Darling hesitated, wondering whether the small recorder she had in her pocket was picking up all this. "We found Kim's diary," she said, "and some money. Over a thousand pounds."

Francesse slumped back in her chair, pounding the arm with her right fist. "The stupid bitch! I told her not to keep anything where someone else might find it."

Before Darling could ask any further questions, the front door closed and Abdullah walked into the room with Cox in tow. "Everything okay, boss?"

Darling nodded. "Getting there. We've got the bank accounts that show the money from Monsignor Lee going into Mrs Brady's accounts, to go with the record you got from the taxi office – of Kim being picked up from here on Monday night – and I'm sure we'll soon have confirmation from Mrs Brady's phone or her suppliers that she made that call."

"This one, you mean, boss?" asked Cox, holding up a phone that looked just like the one he'd found at Kim's.

"Leave that alone!" shrilled Francesse. "That's mine!" She reached for it, but Cox held it tantalisingly just beyond her reach.

"Give her the phone, Constable." Darling sighed, like someone who believed things were getting out of control.

Cox gave the phone to the girl.

"Now go and give Sergeant Morton a hand," Darling said. Not that Morton needed a hand but it got Cox out of her presence.

There was a knock at the door, and then another when it was not answered.

"See who that is, will you, Shan?"

Abdullah did not quite jump to attention and salute in response to the order, but left with a smart "Yes, guv," and returned accompanying the same middle-aged man who had attended the monsignor. If Darling was surprised to see him, she gave no indication; she got to her feet and held out her right hand for him to momentarily grip if not actually shake. His hand was soft but not quite moist.

"We meet again, Inspector."

"Mr Lander, pleased to see you again, I'm sure." His presence set the hairs on the back of her neck prickling. He was a partner in a firm of solicitors whose services were normally retained by those higher up the income scale than her usual clientele. As far as she was aware, he did not practice criminal law, preferring to cruise the cash-rich waters of property law and taxation advice. Yet here he was, making a house call the day after attending Monsignor Lee at the station.

"I understand you have arrested my client on some absurd charges," he said.

She supposed that when you charged as much per hour as he did, you wasted no time on idle pleasantries.

"If your client is Tina Brady and you think she has been charged with child abuse, you are correct, although I am at a loss as to how you could have found out so quickly."

"A concerned neighbour called me. They are also clients of mine," he muttered, leaving Darling to wonder who they were. She thought they had been reasonably discrete. Obviously front curtains twitched, even in upmarket streets like this.

"Constable Abdullah, could you go to my car and have Sergeant Morton bring Mrs Brady back inside, please."

Abdullah scurried off to do as instructed. When she returned, she asked whether anyone would like a cup of tea.

"I don't drink tea!" snapped Francesse.

"That's all right, Shan. Just leave things be," Darling said.

Abdullah stepped back and stood behind the sofa, waiting for whatever came next.

"Francesse, is there anything you want to tell me before your mother arrives?"

The girl opened her mouth as though there was something she wanted to say but closed it just as quickly as she heard the front door close and turned her head away. She did not look back when her mother entered.

"You took your time," Brady snarled at Lander.

Lander did not respond in any way, as though being spat at by clients was all part of a day's work. "Are they really necessary?" he asked Darling, nodding towards the handcuffs.

Darling nodded to Morton, who unlocked the restraints but kept them to hand. Brady massaged her wrists and sat down heavily, her skirt riding up her thighs.

For a moment Darling wondered why a woman of her age wore short skirts. It wasn't as though her legs were anything special to put on show.

"Mrs Brady, we have some questions for your daughter."

"Say nothing," she snapped. "Don't tell the filth anything, not a word."

Francesse shot to her feet and Darling briefly wondered whether she was going to hit her mother. "It is my friend that's been murdered, you bitch. Kim! Do you think anything you say is worth Kim's life? It could be me next!"

Brady shook her head. "You're upset. You don't know what you're talking about. You're hysterical."

"I'll show you hysterical." Francesse jumped forward, fists raised.

Abdullah jumped around the sofa and put her arms around the girl before she could strike.

"Get your hands off my daughter, you black cunt!" Brady raged, as the constable wrestled Francesse back to her chair and sat her down.

"You will keep a civil tongue in your head when you speak to my officers, Mrs Brady, if you won't want more charges added to the already long list of your offences."

"I must protest," said Lander getting to his feet.

"Shut up!" snarled Brady, glancing at him and then looking back to Darling when he subsided back into his chair.

Darling was used to being regarded with hostility, hatred even, but she'd never seen anything quite like the vehemence in her eyes. She made a mental note to have the woman tested for drugs when they got her back to the station. In the meantime, she loomed over her.

"If you think you're going to get away with pimping out your daughter and her friends now you've got so old and stringy no one wants to pay for your body anymore, just because you can afford an expensive lawyer, then you have another thing coming!"

"I must protest!" squeaked Lander, trying to get to his feet. "That is outrageous!"

"Is it?" Darling said. "Is it?" She subsided a little. "Yes, I suppose it is. Doesn't mean it isn't true, does it, Mrs Brady?"

The two women glared at each other until Darling sat down and picked up the papers Abdullah had given her.

"This is corroborated evidence that a child matching the description of Kimberley Ford was picked up by a taxi from the end of this road at 11.55 on Monday night, the call having come from a mobile phone registered in your name, Mrs Brady, using an account at the taxi firm in your name and which you pay for. We have the bank account details to prove it. The taxi dropped her off in Shiremoor. After that, she wasn't seen again until her body was found in Hallam Dene." She looked from mother to daughter and back again. "Have you anything to say to that?"

Tina Brady shrugged, and slowly crossed one leg over the other as though she believed she was Sharon Stone in *Basic Instinct*. "Nothing to do with me," she drawled. "I know nothing about any of this. Kids these days. They organised everything themselves."

"Mother!" Francesse screamed. "You lying bitch."

Brady turned to have the last word, but Darling beat her to it. "Takes one to know one, I suppose."

Lander opened his mouth to object but caught sight of Darling's expression and closed it again.

"I'm not saying I wouldn't like your confessions, both of you." She glanced from mother to daughter and back again. "But as I say, I don't need them." She turned towards Brady. "I already have enough evidence to see you convicted of child abuse. I also have the written evidence of two of the children you provided to men to abuse in return for money, to see you convicted of living off immoral earnings. I have the bank records. I know where the money is. Your accounts are already frozen." She said this with her fingers crossed, hoping nobody would see, because that was not actually true – not yet. But it would be, soon enough. "But that's all small beer. I don't give much of a toss what you do. What I do care about is a child in a refrigerated drawer in the mortuary, a child who was murdered by one of your customers in a way that makes me want to be physically sick, and I've lost count of how many murder victims I've seen." That was not strictly true either. Kim was the fifty-sixth murder victim she'd seen, and all their faces waited for her to review them whenever she let her guard down.

"As I see things," she continued, "you have a simple choice. You help me, and I'll do what I can to help you. Or you *don't* help me, and I promise I will do everything I can to get you buried so deep that when your head comes out, you'll find yourself talking to kangaroos and koala bears. Do you understand?"

Once again, Brady opened her mouth to vent defiance, but before she could say anything all the fight seemed to go out of her. Her shoulders slumped, the corners of her mouth turned down and in an instant she added twenty years to her age. "What's the point? If you know, you know, and if you don't, you'll find out soon enough. It works like this. I get a call. I'm given an address and a telephone number for the client. I call a taxi for the girl, give her the number and off she goes."

Darling sat silent for a moment. "And that's what you did for Kimberley on Monday."

Brady nodded.

Darling was silent again, then she turned to Francesse. "I thought you said Kim wasn't here on Monday night, that it was just you and Bella."

Francesse said nothing for a moment, then shrugged. "I lied."

Brady cackled. "I told you so. She's nothing but a nasty little liar!"

"Like mother, like daughter," Francesse sneered.

"Will you two stop it," Darling said. "I haven't got the time for your games. We don't have to do things like this. We're going to go down to the station and I'll interview you both separately. Okay?"

Neither mother nor daughter made any reply. Darling shook her head and turned back to Tina Brady. "Okay, the sixty-four-thousand-dollar question: what's the name of the man you sent Kim to meet?"

The woman shrugged. "Me? How should I know?"

Darling didn't believe this.

"We'll be able to trace him from his bank details," Abdullah offered.

Darling nodded. "So, he called you, gave you the address and you called your usual taxi company?"

She looked around, but said nothing.

"Which taxi company was that?" Darling asked, redundantly. She already knew which company it was, thanks to Georgy Lupoff coming forward.

"I don't recall," Brady muttered. "I use more than one. Blue Moon, possibly. Zonda?"

Darling smacked her hands on her thighs and got to her feet. "I've had enough of this. I want the telephone you use for this little enterprise, your computer and your financial records."

Lander got to his feet. "You can't just trawl like that, Inspector. You know that. You need a court order."

Darling remembered why coppers, as a rule, hated lawyers. "I would remind you, Mr Lander, that this is a murder investigation, and if the murderer escapes because of that investigation being delayed by your tactics, I will make sure the media know how the bad lad escaped and who was responsible."

"Take whatever you want," Brady said, the fight gone out of her. "You'll find it all eventually, and I want to see the bastard caught as much as anyone." She glared around at the officers and the lawyer. "He's cost me money!"

Darling was unconvinced that was true, but she allowed Tina Brady to show Morton where her phone and computer were, and put them into evidence bags. Morton took them with him when he put her in the car to go to Forth Banks, minus the handcuffs, this time. Before she went with them, Darling ordered Abdullah and Cox to search the house thoroughly.

"What are we looking for?" he asked.

"Anything that looks like it might be useful," Darling answered. "Her records, for a start." She nodded at

Francesse. "Just do it better than the search you made of Kim's room." She looked directly at Cox as she said this. Satisfied with the sheepishly guilty expression he wore, Darling left them to it and went out to the car.

Chapter Thirty-Two

Abdullah went to the sideboard behind the sofa and pulled open the drawers.

"What are you doing?" Francesse asked.

"Searching for evidence of a crime," Abdullah replied.

"What crime would that be?"

"You heard the inspector. Procuring a child for the sexual gratification of an adult," Abdullah replied, thankful for having spent all those evening hours inhaling law textbooks and being able to call up the words when she needed to impress someone.

Francesse stepped backwards putting her right hand to her throat. "That sounds horrible," she said.

Abdullah turned away from the open drawers, which appeared to be full of cutlery and napkins. "It is horrible." She shook her head. "Everybody thinks murder is the worst crime we can commit, but I don't know about that. Children are innocent, don't know what ghastliness grown-ups can get up to. They used to be innocent for a lot longer than they're allowed to be nowadays. But to have that innocence taken from you by someone who feels nothing for you, to whom you're just a piece of meat. That would give me nightmares for the rest of my life. That's worse than killing." She looked straight into the child's eyes. "What do you think?"

Francesse said nothing for a long time. Then her eyes began to fill with tears, and moments later she burst into shrill, hiccoughing weeping that convulsed her.

Abdullah hurried around the sofa and took the child in her arms, her mother's foul-mouthed hostility forgotten as she did what she had become a police officer to do – help someone who needed her help.

Cox appeared in the doorway, opening his mouth to speak only to close it when he saw Abdullah waving him away. If there was anything not needed at this moment, it was the intervention of a man.

Neither had any idea how long they embraced and dealt with the girl's tears, which took the whole packet of tissues Abdullah had in her bag. They found themselves sitting on the sofa, Francesse gazing at the police officer, red-eyed and grateful for her holding her hands so neither would see how much she was trembling.

"I don't think I ever was innocent," Francesse began, shaking her head when Abdullah tried to deny this. "Mum always made it clear that sex was a transaction, a business. She always expected to be paid for it, one way or the other."

"She doesn't believe in love, then."

Francesse snorted. "She loves what 'love' can get her, but I don't think she knows the meaning of the word. She certainly doesn't love Brodie, not in the hearts and flowers sort of way. She gave him herself and he gave her all of this in return. Since he went away, she's never been to visit him, and she's never been short of 'gentlemen friends'. I guess I just assumed I could play the same game as she does."

"But don't you like boys?"

She snorted again. "Oh, I like boys all right. I have boyfriends, lots of them, and Mum is right about them. They all want just one thing, to get my knickers off. None of them have got anywhere near that far and none of them will. They can't afford me. Their fathers can, though."

Abdullah said nothing. She couldn't pretend that the concept of intimate relationships as transactions was alien to her. Her father hadn't spoken to her for five years, since she refused to give up being a copper and marry the man from Lahore he had chosen for her. That hurt her every day. It was only since she was promoted to CID that her mother had stopped trying to persuade her to change her mind every time they secretly met, both defying her father. Nevertheless, she was proud of herself, of her achievement, of being a role model to other women of her community, showing they might make the lives they chose for themselves rather than one laid down by the traditions of another country.

If they wanted to marry men they didn't know and bear their children, that was fine by her, so long as they could make an informed choice for themselves. She had made her bed and was happy to lie in it, alone.

She'd made that choice as an adult, though. Francesse was a child, a mature-seeming child, but a child, nonetheless. If she decided to be a sex worker when she grew up, she might not get Abdullah's approval, but she'd get her respect, if she made the decision for herself and not at the behest of someone else who benefitted from the risks she took without taking any risks themselves. There were more than enough men like that in her community.

"Is there anyone you can stay with?" she asked.

"I can look after myself," Francesse assured her.

"I'd say you're wrong about that," Abdullah told her, the police officer trampling over the sympathetic sister.

"You don't think I'd be…" She shook her head. "It was all organised by Mum. She was just lying when she said we did it ourselves. She lies a lot."

Abdullah made no reply to that. She turned away from the girl, got up and returned to opening the drawers in the sideboard.

"There's nothing in there," Francesse said. "Everything I have is in my room. I'll show you, if you like."

Her room was a symphony of pink and frills, with posters of performers Abdullah did not know on all the walls, except the one opposite her bed that was occupied by the largest flat-screen TV she had ever seen – bigger even than the one downstairs – and an array of black boxes she imagined could let the girl hack into NASA if she wished, and not a book to be seen. Abdullah liked books.

Francesse knelt down beside her bed, reached under and brought out a plastic box on wheels, the sort that were sold as underbed storage for bedclothes. She lifted off the lid to show two laptop computers and several bundles of banknotes.

"This is my computer," she said, taking the smaller computer out of the box and dropping it on the bed. "This is Mum's, the one with her real records on, not the fake ones she has on her other one." She picked up a mobile phone. "This is her business phone." She held the computer and phone out to Abdullah. "Don't you want them?"

"Yes, yes, of course." Abdullah took them, her heart racing just a little at the prospect of getting at the information they held. She put them on the desk in front of the TV screen. "David!" she called. "We're going to need big evidence bags from the car!"

Cox paused in the doorway for a moment before nodding and disappearing down the stairs.

Abdullah took the chair from before the desk, turned it around, sat down and leaned towards Francesse with her notebook in her hand. "Now, why don't you tell me all about it?"

Chapter Thirty-Three

Darling had long since schooled herself against taking an instant dislike to people. She preferred to find the evidence and then dislike them. That was the way she mostly went about things. People who sat across the table from her in the interview room usually had enough in their past to earn her disapproval. For this Tina Brady, who seemed a very different person from the one Darling met at her home, she believed she was prepared to make an exception.

The woman was forty-five years old, according to the information Darling had, and sat on the far side of the table glaring at her, raising an imaginary cigarette to her lips with heavily nicotine-stained fingers and blowing invisible smoke in her face, as though she had been taken unawares at home but now she was in the station she was comfortable to play a familiar role.

What surprised Darling more than her appearance was Michael Lander, the solicitor sitting beside her, who was quite clearly uncomfortable beneath his professional veneer. Darling could scarcely credit his presence. She had never believed in coincidence, and she most assuredly did not believe in it now. There was something most assuredly not right about him being Tina Brady's legal representation after being Monsignor Lee's, but she wouldn't see the connection. Not yet, anyway.

"Mrs Brady," she began, once she and Morton had settled themselves in their chairs. "I am Detective Inspector Darling of the Northumbria Police. My colleague is Detective Sergeant Morton."

Morton glared a little more intently at the woman, who had eyes only for Darling.

"We are investigating the murder of Kimberley Anne Ford. Do you understand?"

The woman did not answer.

"This interview is being recorded, and I must ask you to speak any answer you make to any question clearly, so it will be recorded."

The woman mimed stubbing out her cigarette on the table which bore the scars of many real cigarettes that had gone exactly the same way. "Ask your questions."

Darling opened the top file of the several she had in front of her.

"What was your relationship with Kimberley?"

Morton's eyes widened slightly, and he quickly glanced at her, eyebrow raised. He was surprised she should ask such a general question straight out of the blocks. Joe Milburn had brought her up in interrogation techniques the same way he had him. Begin with a simple 'Yes/No' interlude to get the ball rolling, to convince the interviewee that your questions were easy and that telling the truth was easy too. If you made them think you knew the answer to every question before you asked it, never mind before they answered it, that was a bonus.

"Kimberley? Oh, Kim! She's a friend of my daughter's... was... poor little thing."

Darling said nothing, just looked at her with those dubious, questioning eyes of hers, inviting her to say more, to elaborate. Most of those she questioned in that place could not abide silence and would fill one with an outpouring of words, often saying things they could not possibly intend to say. Mrs Brady, though, was made of sterner stuff.

Eventually Darling said, "A friend of your daughter's? Mmmm." She looked at the woman again. "Are you sure of that?"

"I'm sure I don't know what you mean, what you're trying to get at." There was colour at the base of the woman's neck and in her ears that had not been there before.

Darling ran her forefinger along the first lines of the file she had in front of her, appearing to read through the information printed there. "According to the information we have, Kimberley was an employee of yours."

"A what? An employee?" The woman laughed and shook her head. "The child was what, fourteen?"

"Thirteen, actually."

"Thirteen, then. How could I have employed her, even if I had any employees? Which I don't. Who said I have employees?"

It was Darling's turn to laugh, an expression as devoid of mirth as Brady's had been. "In this case, by '*employee*' I do not mean that you employed her in the generally recognised sense of the word, with Kimberley having a legal contract of employment with you, or that you paid National Insurance and PAYE for her. What I mean by '*employ*' is that you acted as a conduit, putting her in touch with men who would then pay you for her... services. The way a pimp '*employs*' a prostitute. You know all about that sort of employment, don't you?"

Tina Brady glared at her for a moment, then turned towards Lander, with an expression that said 'She can't talk to me like that! Can she?' Then she turned back towards Darling. The Tina Brady from the house on Torville Street had returned.

"Jesus Christ, what fucker told you that about me? I'll have their fucking guts for garters, so help me, I will. That's outrageous. That is fucking dreadful. That makes me out like some sort of fucking monster."

"Oh, not so much a monster," muttered Morton, "just a pimp, that's all, a pimp for children."

Brady jumped to her feet, thighs thumping into the tabletop so hard she would have moved it, had the legs not been screwed to the floor. She waved her arms, eyes wide open and filled with rage and hate. Her breasts wobbled inside her blouse like blancmanges in an earthquake. "Which fucking cunt said that about me?" she stormed. "I'll have 'em, I will. I'll fucking well do for 'em, good an' fuckin' proper, just you fuckin' see if I don't."

Darling glanced at Morton, who nodded. Both thought the lady protested too much.

Lander had not said anything so far. He put his hand on Brady's arm, trying to get her back into her seat. She slapped his hand away without thinking, the crack of it echoing around the room. Only then did she realise she had hit her only ally in the room. She dropped into the seat, counting to ten, her lips forming the numbers even though no sound emerged from her mouth. Then, she crossed her right leg over her left and did her poor best to appear calm and respectable.

"I'm not saying nothing. You can't make me say anything."

"No, I can't," Darling said, "but I should have thought you might want to cooperate with us."

"Why should I cooperate with a fucking copper?" Hatred glittered in Brady's eye.

Darling shrugged. "Self-interest, I'd have thought. I am investigating one of the most horrible murders I've ever seen. And you are up to your neck in it. You arranged for Kimberley to be delivered to her murderer."

"I did no such fucking thing."

Darling smacked her hand on the table, making a loud crack that got everyone's attention. It hurt but she didn't let it show, just like the last time she'd done it for effect. She opened the file before her and tapped the papers inside. "This is the evidence proving you did exactly that. Evidence you gave us voluntarily. He phoned you and you arranged for Kimberley to be delivered to him." She looked directly at Lander. "I'd say that makes you an accessory, an accessory to murder. Am I right, Mr Lander?"

The solicitor, who could not have looked more uncomfortable and apprehensive had he been strapped inside an iron maiden and was watching the door closing, shuffled in his chair. "I am not a specialist in criminal law, Inspector, but I should expect that to be the case."

Darling nodded and looked at Brady, wearing an expression she knew intimidated people, even hardened old lags like her. "So, tell me the name."

"What name?" Brady tried to look nonchalant without really succeeding.

"The name of the man you sent Kimberley to. The man who probably is the murderer we're looking for."

The woman shrugged. "I don't know."

"Tell us the name," Morton intervened, leaning over the desk as though he wanted to take the woman warmly by the throat. "Give us his name and you might save the life of another girl. Who knows, maybe it'll be your own daughter's life."

"I don't know any names," Brady shrieked, then caught herself, and breathed deeply three times. When she spoke again, she was much more controlled. "I get a call. Nobody ever uses any names."

"How do you know who you're talking to?" Darling said.

Brady shrugged. "If they've got that number, there's only one thing they want, and I don't ask questions. Besides which, I recognise the numbers that've called before." She tapped her temple. "I've got a good memory, I have."

"So, this guy had called before?" Morton wondered.

"Yeah–"

"How many times?" Morton got in almost before she finished speaking that single word.

She shrugged. "I don't recall."

"I thought you said you've got a good memory."

"I have!"

"But you can't remember how many times one of your small number of… clients called you!" Morton was openly contemptuous.

Darling reached out and put her hand on his forearm. "That's enough for now, Sergeant."

Morton glared at her, then shrugged and sat back in his chair, his expression promising Tina Brady they were not yet done with that subject.

"And once they were done, your clients paid you by bank transfer."

"Or credit card, yes." Brady nodded. "I might belong to the oldest profession but that doesn't mean I can't use modern business methods." She looked very pleased with herself.

"So how did you know who was paying for what? From what I've seen of your bank records, there are no names attached to any of the payments into your accounts, just numbers."

"I know the numbers." She poked her tongue out at Morton. "I told you, I'm good with numbers."

Darling allowed a silence to develop. "You recognise the numbers that pay you…"

Darling glanced at the papers in the file open before her and for the first time noticed the reference on all the accounts, the name Frankimbel. Her eyes widened as she realised what it represented. Francesse, Kim and Bella. For a moment she could not breathe. How could she possibly not have noticed that? She shook her head and coughed, closing the file. "So you recognise the numbers that pay you but you have no idea about the men behind those numbers."

Brady shrugged. "You never know a John once he's paid. As long as he's paid, you don't care."

Another silence drew out. "Even if 'the John' has beaten you bloody?"

"Especially then. Beatings come with the territory."

Darling nodded. "Let me tell you about the 'beating' this particular 'John' meted out to Kimberley, who was a thirteen-year-old child, a friend of your daughter. Her ribs and arms and legs were shattered like china," she said.

Brady's face lost whatever colour it had as she listened to this.

Darling leaned forward so she was as close to Tina Brady as she could get. "In my time as a police officer I have encountered most obscenities that we can inflict on each other, and this murder breaks new ground even for me. I cannot imagine the pain and terror that engulfed that child as she died alone and without any hope of release from her torment except death. You are protecting that creature. I won't call him a monster or an animal because it is only human beings who do that sort of thing to their fellow human beings. If you don't help me find him, I promise you—"

"I don't know!" Brady sobbed. The tears streaming down her cheeks looked real enough. If they weren't, she was a better actress than Darling had imagined. "The numbers are all I have. If I knew the name, I'd tell. I– I would, I would…" Her words were drowned in her tears.

"Inspector, I think you need to call a halt to this," Lander said. His complexion was as pale as everyone else's in the room.

Darling glanced at Morton, who nodded. "Interview terminated," he said, looking up at the clock but switching off the recorders before saying anything else.

They sat in silence as Lander took his leave, his shoulders heaving, and Brady was led off to the cells, head bowed and shuffling, all the defiance gone from her.

Darling tapped the sheets with their bank details printed on them. "We must be able to put names to these accounts. If there is a name attached to her accounts – Frankimbel – there must be names attached to the others."

Morton nodded. "We got her name, didn't we? We'll get his." His dark expression and his low, bitter tone suggested his name was on the list of people who wanted five minutes alone with this bastard, when they caught him; near the top of the list.

Chapter Thirty-Four

Darling was aware of the team watching her closely as she entered the room and walked towards the glass wall that was now festooned with photographs and writing, and coloured lines connecting them. From the state of the cups and empty plates on their desks, they had obviously been waiting some time for her to arrive, even though the clock above the door showed it was not yet nine. A pang of jealousy went through her. They, at least, had breakfasted. She hadn't. A restless night and actually sleeping through her alarm to be wakened, late, by a dustbin lorry passing in the street had seen to that. Rushing to get in on time had meant she didn't have the time to shower or have anything to eat, although a quick look in the hall mirror as she left reassured her that she looked immaculate.

"Right then, let's recap what we know. Then we'll go on to what we need to know. After that, we'll get to how we're going to find that out." She tapped the photo of Kim. "Kimberley Anne Ford. Thirteen years old. Murdered horribly."

A grumble went around the room. However hard-bitten they thought themselves to be, however much they thought they'd seen everything, what had been done to the child made them want to tear something apart, starting with whoever had done it.

"We know where and when she was last seen, which was getting into a black VW Golf Park Lane in Shiremoor just before midnight on Monday. We haven't traced that vehicle yet." She looked at Cox as she said this. He looked away. "We also know why she was there. She was meeting a customer of a child abuse ring organised by this woman" – she tapped Tina Brady's photo – "Christine Brady, the mother of one of Kim's friends. She has a record for prostitution and related offences a few years ago." She paused for a moment and looked individually at each member of the team. "You'll note I use the term 'child abuse'. Kim and her friends, Isabella and Francesse, Bella and Frankie as they call themselves, are all under sixteen; children. As far as we can tell, none of them were forced to do what they did and were quite happy to take the money. That doesn't make an iota of difference. They are children, were children, and that means they cannot give consent. They weren't 'just' prostitutes, they're children. What was done to them was child abuse, and if I hear of anyone saying it wasn't, I shall come down on you so hard you'll need a JCB to dig you out. Do I make myself clear?"

The silence made it clear that she did.

"What we need to do is identify and track down all those fine, upstanding pillars of the community who abused those children. Fortunately for us, Mrs Brady did all her business by telephone and the internet. Which means there are records." She held up a sheaf of papers. "Every one of Mrs Brady's customers has paid their money into her account, which means we can trace them from their bank details. That is how we found Mrs Brady in the first place. If we can find one, we can find them all. We'll be doing twenty-first-century policing, following the money."

She saw them smile at her little joke. The team had once been Joe Milburn's and in those days, even with her as a part of it, the motto had been 'Old-Fashioned Coppering', wearing out shoe leather, knocking on doors, speaking to people who didn't want to talk to you and speaking to them again when they really didn't want to talk to you. There was nothing wrong with that sort of coppering as far as she was concerned, especially talking to people who didn't know what they'd seen. Most people only saw flashes of things happening, had no idea of the picture, what it meant if it meant anything at all. The only sense life made was when someone looked at all those glimpses and arranged them into order, like some existential jigsaw puzzle, and even then the picture didn't always make sense. Sometimes you had to look at it upside down or turn it over and look on the back. But that was the secret of all investigations. Asking the right questions. That took skill. That required experience. That was built on insight. Even then, twenty-first-century policing relied on the virtues of old-fashioned coppering to dot the i's and cross the t's.

"So, while you are tracking down the name and address of everyone who has paid money to Mrs Brady, or made a call to this telephone" – she held up the evidence bag containing the phone Francesse said was the one her mother used for business – "Shan is going to exploit the rapport she established with Francesse Brady to get a formal statement out of her. That is going to require 'a responsible adult' to be present. So don't forget." She could tell by the way Abdullah wrote in her notebook that she wouldn't forget that. "That goes for the rest of you. Everything gets done by the book. This case will attract all sorts of attention, and not just because of it involving the murder of a child. We have the name of one of Mrs Brady's customers, the monsignor who came in here to confess his sin if not his crime. He and Mrs Brady share the same very expensive solicitor, who somehow turned up at her house before we charged her."

The impossibility of that coincidence appeared to her again as she spoke the words, and she didn't know which annoyed her more, that she had not thought of that at the time – just as she had not thought of checking every black VW Golf registered in the Tyneside area before Joe Milburn mentioned it – or that someone in the room could have called Lander, or someone who had instructed the solicitor. That thought sent another rabbit dashing across the open field of her consciousness, that someone in that room knew more about Tina Brady's business than they were letting on.

She shook her head, mentally. She didn't have time to chase those rabbits. That way led to the dead end of confusion via the by-roads of suspicion and paranoia. Everything would fall out in the fullness of time. What she had to concern herself with exclusively, right now, was the gathering of evidence.

"While you're all doing that, Shan and I are going to have a conversation with Isabella Conway." She moved towards the door. All around her, chair legs scraped and conversations began. She stopped. "When anyone finds anything, I want to know straight away. Understand?"

Their mumbling assured her they understood.

"You think they'll turn up the name of the killer from those bank records?" Morton asked as everyone else was leaving.

"I very much doubt he'll have paid for this time with Kim, so we won't be able to tell who he is because his is probably one of the last bank accounts on the list. What we do know for a certainty, however, is that his will be the telephone that made a call to Tina Brady on the night of the murder."

Morton nodded, silently, making Darling wonder whether that was something that he hadn't thought of. Suddenly, she was struck by something that had not occurred to her in the uproar of the investigation.

"Pete, wasn't it today Pam was going into hospital for her radiotherapy?"

He looked at her, puzzlement in his eyes, then nodded.

"For fuck's sake, man, what are you still doing here?" she hissed.

The puzzlement became bewilderment. The boss never swore, not like that, not proper swearing.

"She needs you. We can do without you for a bit. Even *you're* not indispensable." Sometimes she thought he was, more or less, but this wasn't the time to tell him.

"We talked about it last night," he lied. "She knows what hospitals do to me. She said I should distract myself with work." At least, she might have said that, if they had discussed it. "Besides, Lily is with her. I can go in for evening visiting."

Darling wanted to press the matter, but something told her he was so scared by what the cancer was doing to his wife – what it might do to her, and then to him when it

144

was finished with Pam – that he'd just dig his heels in if she didn't let it go. Everybody had their own way of dealing with stress and she was thankful she did not have any experience of what he was suffering. She took hold of his hand. "Anything, Pete, anything you want, you need. She's more important than all of this." She's still alive, she thought, and kept it to herself.

He stared at her, then nodded, briefly, just the once, and they got on with business.

Chapter Thirty-Five

Darling and Abdullah sat at either end of the leather sofa in the Conway front room, waiting for Mrs Conway to fetch Bella down from her room. The room was like so many others they had been in, plain-walled, dominated by a huge flat-screen TV above the mantelpiece with an array of black boxes linked to it by cables. There was a matching black leather reclining chair in pride of place directly opposite the screen. In the corners were tall bookcases filled with VHS boxes that hadn't been opened in years and DVD cases that had.

Mrs Conway appeared in the doorway. She was a medium woman, in height and build, wearing a knee-length grey skirt and an almost matching blouse that looked like it came from a catalogue. While she wasn't wearing high heels in the house, the pronounced musculature of her calves told the story of what she always wore outside.

"You're not going to talk to my daughter without me being here!" she announced.

Darling adopted her best reassuring voice. "Of course not, Mrs Conway. She's a child, a minor. The law requires a responsible adult be present to prevent the possibility of any suggestion or undue pressure. There are very clear rules about interviewing children and the Northumbria force is absolutely set on those rules being followed meticulously."

"A child," Mrs Conway insisted. "You just remember that."

Darling considered telling her that they had proof Bella had been up to the sort of things no child should know about and much less do, but she doubted Mrs Conway had the slightest idea about any of that. Before she could say anything, Bella walked into the room, along with her sister. She sat down beside her mother, looking at her rather than the officers. Her sister sat on an upright wooden chair she brought in from the dining room, sitting backwards – her arms across the back of the chair; her chin resting on her arms; her expression, that of someone anticipating entertainment.

Darling leaned forward, inviting the girl's confidence. "Isabella."

The girl looked towards her with obvious reluctance.

"Isabella, I have to tell you we know what you and Kim were doing for Mrs Brady…"

Isabella squeaked. All the colour drained from her face and she began to tremble.

Mrs Conway took her in her arms and glared daggers at Darling. "What are you talking about?" she hissed.

Darling was accustomed to intense emotional responses to what she said, especially from women. She had long since ceased to be concerned. It came with the territory. "Isabella knows what I'm talking about. Don't you, Isabella?"

The girl hesitated, then nodded.

"I want to know what you're talking about!" her mother shrilled.

Darling shook her head. "In good time. Isabella?"

She turned to look at her, eyes swimming with tears.

"You are not in any trouble, not with us. Understand?" said Darling.

Mrs Conway opened her mouth, only for her other daughter to lean forward and put her hand on her shoulder. "Let the inspector speak, Mum. Let her speak."

Mother and daughter glared at each other for what seemed to Darling to be a long time before the older woman nodded, and the starch seemed to drain out of her.

"Do you understand what I'm saying?" Darling eventually continued.

Bella sniffed and nodded, just a little.

"You are a child. Nothing of this is your fault. I don't suppose anything you did caused what happened to Kim."

Bella shrieked again and instantly began to weep. Her sister moved quickly to comfort her, handkerchief in hand, while her mother glared at Darling, looking positively murderous herself.

"Bella, all we are interested in is finding Kim's murderer. He's the one who has done wrong, and the other men who used you."

Her mother shrieked. "Used? What are you talking about? Used?" Then she realised what Darling meant. Her mouth stayed open but no sounds emerged.

Bella's sister leaned over the back of the couch and put her arms around the pair of them.

"It's not that," said Bella, hiccoughing. "It was supposed to be me."

"What do you mean?"

The girl shook her head. "Tina said the man had asked for me."

"By name?" breathed Darling.

"No, no, none of them know our names. Tina said he wanted the skinny girl with the very long blonde hair."

A silence fell over the room as the four adults realised that could only be Bella. Mrs Conway's hands covered her mouth as the sudden ashen cast to her face betrayed her knowing what her daughter meant, even if she could not – would not – accept it.

"Why did Kim go, if he asked for you?" asked Darling.

"I've got my… you know…"

Darling reached forward and put her hand on Bella's knee. "That's all right, Isabella. I think that's enough for the time being." She got to her feet. "We're going to have to take a formal statement from you, Isabella, but you've been through enough. It can wait."

The girl looked up at her, red-eyed and with dried tear tracks down her cheeks.

Darling smiled and nodded, then turned to her mother. "I realise this has all come as a shock to you, Mrs Conway, what your daughter and her friends have been doing. Frankly, we're all shocked and we like to think we're hardened, seen it all. But you have to remember what you told us is true, that Bella is still a child and she's going through a lot. What she needs more than anything is your support." As she spoke she wondered where the words were coming from. If asked, she wouldn't have thought she had them in her. She looked directly at Bella's sister, who still had her arms around her. "Your unconditional support and your unconditional love."

The girl regarded her with cold, clear eyes.

"She's got it."

Chapter Thirty-Six

Darling walked into the lounge bar of The White Hart and, as she always did on walking into any room, tried to take it all in with a single glance. It was working very hard to look like a traditional country pub with dark, low beams, hunting prints and the sepia front pages of ancient newspapers on the wall. It scarcely differed from a couple of dozen other pubs owned and themed by the same chain and was distinct and individual as a pound coin. She made no judgement on this, not being the target market, lacking a family to bring along for the pub's 'celebrated' Sunday lunch. There were a dozen customers in the bar, in twos and threes at scattered tables, and Dorothy Bainbridge sitting alone at the very farthest end, in the corner, where she had her back to two walls and could see everyone else.

Darling nodded, raised a questioning eyebrow and mimed holding up a glass.

Bainbridge shook her head and nodded at the large wine glass on the table before her.

Darling bought a tonic water and walked over to join her. "Here's a health to them as loves us," she proposed after sitting down.

"And damnation to the rest." Bainbridge laughed, taking a sip of her wine.

They had met when Darling was investigating the murder of a local businessman with a shady past, Barry Dance, known as 'The Dancer'. They made an incongruous pair, the hard-eyed detective inspector and the soft-edged suburban widow and mother who just happened to have a sideline in organising very discreet escorts for anyone with enough money to pay the amount she charged. This had included the Dancer on the night he died.

Nevertheless, they had struck a spark of friendship with each other and met on an irregular basis to chatter about anything that wasn't business. Darling was Ms Cheese, Bainbridge Mrs Chalk.

They had chattered and laughed for about ten minutes when Mrs Bainbridge put down her scarcely touched wine glass, dabbed at her dry lips with an unnecessary tissue and ran her tongue over her teeth. "How can I help you, Detective Inspector Darling?"

Darling started, raising her left hand to a colouring cheek. "Am I that obvious?"

Bainbridge laughed. She had a pleasant laugh that came from her chest and went right up to her eyes. Darling liked it.

"Penny, you are transparent." She was the only person in the world Darling allowed to call her Penny, except for her mother, who wouldn't take any notice of her preferences anyway.

Darling shook her head and took a mouthful of her tonic water, feeling it fizz against the roof of her mouth. "Okay, no more games. I'm sorry to bring my business here. I guess you know which case I'm working on now."

"That poor little girl."

Darling nodded, then glanced down at the table as though she didn't really want to say it. "Looks like she was a working girl."

Bainbridge's mouth dropped open and all the colour drained from her face. "I... I..." she stuttered. She shook her head. Had anyone else said it, she would not have believed them, but she knew Penny Darling better than that. "She was thirteen years old?"

"We haven't said anything about this in public yet. If I get my way, we never will."

"I hope you don't think I have anything to do with that." Her voice was so thin, so weak, it hardly made it across the table.

Darling shook her head. "If I did, we'd be having this conversation in the station with tape recorders and cameras rolling, and your solicitor present. He isn't Michael Lander by any chance, is he?"

The woman was bewildered, shook her head. "I don't have any solicitor," she said.

Darling smiled, although the expression didn't appear to reassure her any, then reached over the table and took her hand. "Sorry, sorry, that was just my private joke, nothing to do with you. I don't mind telling you this is all getting to me, really getting to me. It doesn't normally, but this case..." Her voice drifted into silence.

Bainbridge took a gulp of her wine, big enough to make the result of any breathalyser later on problematic. "I have heard things," she said eventually. "Nothing... nothing... well, a couple of the younger women and one of my young men mentioned they had been asked if they knew anything about finding young partners, younger than... well, young." She shook her head again. "I have very strict rules, none of my... clients even look as though they might be underage. I know that might seem silly to you, but I do, and that's it." She took a sip of her wine and swallowed without tasting it. "The girls didn't seem to think it was anything serious, so I just deleted the clients they'd last been with from my database and paid no more attention. This was a couple of months ago. Nobody has said anything since. I wish I hadn't deleted the names."

"Maybe our computer guys could recover them."

Bainbridge laughed. "My late husband was a programmer. Before we had the children, I worked in program design. When I delete something, it stays deleted. The system is backed up offline every day and is purged weekly before I reboot it from an equally offline cache. The truth is, I'm better than your computer guys." She shook her head again. "I'm sorry to disappoint you."

"Perhaps I could speak to your girls, your boy..."

Bainbridge shook her head again. "Penny, we're friends. I like you, I really do, and I know what you're trying to do. If there was anything I could tell you that would help, I'd do it in an instant. I hope you know that. But I can't give you my people's names. We both know that what they do, what *I* do, is only borderline legal..." She paused for a moment, and when she spoke again, her voice scarcely had the strength to make it across the table, even though she was leaning forward, her head only a couple of feet from Darling. "Maybe not even that. You can break me if you choose to. You can come at me with a court order and I will have to give you all my records. I would do that because I think of myself as basically law-abiding. But my people won't be there for you to interview. They don't lead exactly normal, stable lives. One whisper that the police are interested, and they'll be gone. You'll have me. You'll have my records, assuming that I don't go home from here and dump everything onto a portable hard drive that you'll never find and then purge the system, reboot it back to what was supplied by the manufacturer. As I say, I can do that."

Darling looked into those clear hazel eyes and knew Bainbridge was telling her nothing but the plain facts. She could do everything she claimed. "But you won't, will you?" she whispered.

Bainbridge looked into her eyes for a long time, then looked away after a brief shake of her head.

Darling reached out and put her hand on Bainbridge's, which was shockingly cold. She squeezed it, a gesture of affection. "I'm sorry, but I did have to try, you understand."

The other woman smiled a brave smile that contradicted her trembling lips. She had to cough to clear her throat before she could speak. "Of course, I understand. I only wish I could help you more. I will call the girls, see if they can remember anything, but I'm sure you know they're not the sort of people who respond well to questions. If I do hear anything, I'll call you straight away."

"Night or day, Dorothy, night or day. This is important."

"I know that, Penny."

At that moment Darling realised something that made her feel as though someone had just kicked her in the stomach. "Your little girl," she whispered.

"Helen." Bainbridge's face could have been carved from rock for all the expression there was on it.

"She's—"

"It is her thirteenth birthday the week after next."

For a long while, Darling did not know what to do. She wanted to just take the woman in her arms and reassure her that everything was going to be all right, that she was in no danger, that her daughter was perfectly safe, that they would find the murderer soon. None of which was certain. She might not find the murderer, and even if she did, Helen was still as much in danger from the other perverts that hadn't yet crawled out from under their stones, the ones who would take his place when they caught this one.

"She's never going anywhere on her own again, I can tell you that," Bainbridge said. "As for boyfriends, forget it."

Darling had nothing to say to this. She could understand at the same time as knowing that keeping every child safe all the time was an impossible dream. That sort of regime would cause more problems than it solved, especially if Helen was the feisty young girl she could just about remember meeting. She suspected Bainbridge knew that as well. When this terrifying alarm faded from memory, normal life would be resumed. Until the next time.

"Got to get back to work," Darling said, draining her glass and getting to her feet.

Bainbridge said nothing, just went on looking out of the window.

Darling walked away, wondering whether she had ruined a promising friendship for nothing. When she got to the door, she stopped and turned around to see Bainbridge staring at her. When she saw Darling looking at her, she raised her right hand up to her head, little finger and thumb extended, the universally understood gesture 'call me'.

Darling nodded. Maybe the damage was not fatal.

Chapter Thirty-Seven

Abdullah was roused from her reverie of absorption in the data on her desk by the sound of her mobile, which had switched over to answerphone by the time she found it and flicked the answer icon. "Hello?"

"Shan, where are you?"

"Indira, what do you want?" There was a silence at the other end of the connection in which she could hear the nearest thing to a best friend she had counting to ten. "Ahhh!" she shrilled. "I forgot!"

"And I never forget when I've been let down, Shan. You know that."

Abdullah shook her head. That much was true, she knew. "I've been busy, distracted."

Indira laughed, the carefree laugh of a woman who didn't care whether anyone laughed with her. "There's an old saying. When you're at the bottom of a hole, stop digging. I know you're a busy woman, we're all busy women, which is why I'm calling you now to remind you that you're having tea with me and my cousin at five this afternoon."

"Where?"

This silence was really disapproving. "I'll see you at five." The connection was terminated.

Abdullah glanced at the time on her phone. There was just enough to go home, dress up and get to the Lahore Tea House for five o'clock. She did not want to go, not really. The investigation had left her battered and drained, and what she really wanted to do was lie back, close her eyes and forget about everything. Only she couldn't say 'no' to Indira, not after everything she had done for her.

Wearing a dove-grey business suit that differed from the suits she wore to work only in its colour with a matching headscarf, Abdullah walked into the luxurious entry of the Lahore Tea House just off Grainger Street and was immediately engulfed in her friend's embrace. "It's been so long," Indira cooed. "So long."

"Too long," she agreed with a smile that no longer needed forcing.

Indira's enthusiasm for life had that effect on her. Indira was a tall woman who wore what looked like traditional Eastern clothing cut with an eye to Western couture and make-up that was similarly founded. Only her jewellery spoke of their Pakistani roots. Indira loved gold in a way that made Saddam Hussein's obsession seem like a minor dalliance. There were rings on every finger, bracelets everywhere and a glittering throat piece where Abdullah had her headscarf tucked modestly into her collar. She'd once asked her friend why she dressed so extravagantly. Indira had laughed, saying that they – she and Imran, her husband - worked hard for their money, and what was the point of having it if you hid it away?

"Aren't you afraid of people being jealous?" she had asked.

Once again, Indira had laughed – she laughed a lot. "I'm an example," she'd replied. "There's no need to be jealous of me. Just work eighteen hours a day and you can have all this!"

Abdullah sometimes felt as though she did work eighteen hours a day and had no chance of having that sort of wealth. *Not that I want it*, she told herself.

They went upstairs in a clanking, open metalwork lift Indira told her had come from one of the old hotels of the Raj, although she couldn't remember which one, just that it cost more than she earned in a year. Indira led her to an alcove overlooking the main floor downstairs. It was lined with ornately carved wooden screens that looked as though they had come from some pasha's harem. Anyone

155

sitting there could see the other diners clearly but could not be seen themselves.

A man stood up from the table as they approached. Abdullah thought he was in his mid to late thirties, slimly built with dark hair thinning on top. He was clean-shaven, wore a three-piece suit that was the same colour as hers, with a dazzling white shirt and a plain royal-blue tie.

"This is my cousin, Afzahl, Afzahl Khan," Indira announced.

Afzahl reached out, took Abdullah's hand before she could think to resist, and bent over to kiss her knuckles. His lips did not quite touch her skin. "Charmed, I'm sure," he whispered.

Her instinct was to turn and leave as fast as she could, even run if she had to. She wore flat-heeled shoes and would have no difficulty running. Indira was up to her old matchmaking tricks again. She glared at her friend even as Afzahl helped her to her seat. His hands were at the same time soft, gentle and strong, although a long, crooked scar disfigured the back of his left hand. He ushered Indira into her seat before retaking his own.

"Afzahl, may I introduce my best friend, Shan Abdullah?"

Afzahl bowed and smiled, an expression Abdullah saw did not quite reach his eyes. "As I say, I am charmed."

You don't know me, Abdullah thought. "You are Indira's cousin?"

He smiled.

"I should think I would have met all of Indira's cousins—"

"Afzahl is a busy man," Indira interrupted. "He's a doctor."

At least he's not a lawyer, Abdullah thought. Or an accountant. "It's a pleasure to meet you, Dr Khan."

He took a sip of water. "It's *Mr* Khan, actually. I am a surgeon. I specialise in ear, nose and throat at the RVI." He took another sip of water and turned towards Indira without enquiring what Abdullah did. "What do you recommend we order, cousin? This is your establishment, after all."

Indira laughed and raised her hands above her head to clap. She had so many gold bangles around her slender exposed forearms, Abdullah was almost surprised she had the strength to lift them so high. Three waitresses appeared carrying trays of pastries and sweets enough to feed a platoon of starving soldiers, followed by an extravagantly bearded man wearing a scarlet coat braided in gold, pushing a trolley bearing all that was necessary for the proper preparation and serving of tea. The silver glittered with the patina of more than a century's use and polish, something else brought from their homeland.

Abdullah was relieved not to have to say anything as they began to make inroads on the feast. To begin with, she discovered she was a lot hungrier than she thought. Then there was the fact that Indira kept an excellent teahouse where everything was the best and tasted better than everything else. Eventually, though, even she could eat no more, and the only reason for taking another sip of tea – Jasmine flavoured, was it? – was that her mouth had dried up at the prospect of what she had to say next.

"You're not married?" she asked Dr Khan.

He looked shocked, as though he was as disconcerted as most Asian men would be when asked a direct question by a woman. "That is true," he managed to say, eventually. "Why do you ask?"

Because you're a successful man in your early middle age and you haven't got a ring on your finger, she thought. "Well, dear Indira here is an incorrigible matchmaker. I know I'm not married, so I'm assuming you're not, otherwise we wouldn't be here today."

The doctor and Indira looked at each other. He inclined his head. "I am indeed an unmarried man, although I could say that I am married to my work."

Join the club, she thought. "You must be a strong man to withstand your mother's constant demands for you to provide her with grandchildren."

He swallowed, hard, and Indira turned away. "My parents are both dead. They were in an accident on the Coast Road, just about ten years ago."

"Oh, I'm sorry about that."

He shook his head. "No need, it was a long time ago. As I say, I am married to my work."

Abdullah chuckled. "Like me."

"What do you do? I surmise from your attitude towards my marital status that you do not spend your days with your hands in the washing-up bowl and watching the afternoon soap operas."

"Shan is a policewoman," Indira said before any words could escape between her friend's clenched teeth.

"My brother is a military policeman," the doctor said. "He's a colonel in Rawalpindi."

"A colonel, in Rawalpindi?"

"He did not come with us when my parents moved to Britain. He already had his career, so he stayed."

"A successful career, by the sound of it," Abdullah said. "A colonel." So far as she knew, policing in Pakistan was closer to the military than it was on Tyneside. To her ears, a 'colonel' was someone much more attuned to firearms than made her comfortable. She didn't think a colonel would make very much of policing by consent.

"So, Constable, what are your duties?"

Abdullah's dislike of the man was suddenly complete. "Actually, it's, and at the moment my duties are the investigation of a particularly horrible murder, of a child."

Indira inhaled noisily and her hands flew up to her face, covering her wide-open mouth of distress. "I had no idea."

Abdullah shook her head. "There's no reason why you should, but I don't get any special treatment because I'm a woman. Other than the expected disadvantages of being a Muslim woman of colour in a workplace that is still

158

basically masculine and atheist, I am one of the lads, no favours, no easy duties. I am a police officer, not a woman police officer." She fixed the doctor with a glare. "And I'm proud of that."

"As you should be," he said in a placatory tone, although Abdullah thought she had made it clear she was in no mood to be placated. "What do you do in your spare time?"

"I bathe in asses' milk and then go cruising the streets of Newcastle in an open pink Cadillac with my girlfriends, looking for young men to ravish and cast aside." She saw his wide-eyed, dumbfounded expression and laughed.

After a moment, Indira joined in.

"No, no, most of my spare time I study," Abdullah added. She wished that was true. Far too much of her time away from work was spent so zoned-out on the couch, watching television, that she couldn't remember when the show finished.

"What do you study?"

She shrugged. "Criminology, sociology, psychology, the law – you know, stuff that is useful to my work." She had a Bachelor's Degree in Law, a Masters in Criminology from the Open University and was presently trying to decide whether she should try to get her doctorate before being made a sergeant or wait until she had some more miles under her shoes.

"That's impressive." The doctor nodded, almost looking sincere. "What do you do for relaxation?"

"I shoot."

His eyes opened wide again. "You shoot? I thought you couldn't…"

"Well, you think wrong. Under controlled conditions, you can shoot. It is an Olympic sport." She had once dreamed of becoming an Olympic shooter.

"That's a lot more dramatic than running like I do."

"There's nothing dramatic about it. It's very calming, very Zen." She was just about to say how a coach had once told her that the secret to good target-shooting was reducing your heart rate until it was as slow as possible, stopping it even, when her phone rang. "Sorry. I'd better answer this."

"Shan, can you get in?" It was Darling. "Wayne Ford wants to speak to you, just you. He says it's important."

"I'm on my way." She got to her feet, putting her phone back in her pocket. "Duty calls. I have to go."

The doctor got to his feet, extending his hand. "It's been a pleasure to meet you. Another time, perhaps."

She took his hand without gripping it and smiled. "Perhaps." She had no intention of meeting Mr Afzahl Khan ever again and looked forward to the day she could work up the courage to tell Indira to stop interfering in her life. If she needed a man in her life, she would find one for herself. She didn't wait for anyone to show her out. She could do things for herself, couldn't she?

Chapter Thirty-Eight

Wayne sat on the doorstep, hands clasped around his knees, gazing out at the world with eyes not focused on anything to be seen there. Neighbours watched him, some as they passed by, others from behind their curtains, thinking of approaching him, engaging him in conversation, seeing if there was anything they could do for him or his mother. After all, the family had lived there for five years and there had never been any suggestion young Wayne was anything but a decent lad. But what was there any of them could say to him? 'Eh, your little sister went and got herself murdered, didn't she?' was hardly the introduction to a warm, intimate conversation, however brief. So, they walked on by, and he did not see them.

Abdullah came out of the house and sat beside him.

Bev had gone to be looked after by her sister. Wayne hadn't gone with her. "No room for me there," he'd said when she asked. "Anyway, I've got everything I need here. I'll be okay."

Abdullah studied him, wondering whether he was really taking this tragedy as phlegmatically as he appeared to be. "Cup of tea?" she asked, offering him the mug in her right hand.

"Don't drink tea," he muttered.

"Here you are then, coffee!" She grinned, holding out the mug in her left hand. "Good thing for you I'm ambidextrous. Or is it elecufick? I never can remember." 'Elecufick' was a word her mother had used in situations where any answer might be appropriate. She didn't know whether it existed in English and didn't care.

"Thanks." He took the mug and sipped at it. He still didn't look at her.

"Wayne, I know this isn't easy for you."

He turned his head very slowly towards her, cold savagery in his eyes. "Oh, you do, do you? Exactly how do you know that?"

Some might have taken offence at this, but Abdullah chose to believe his antagonism was not directed at her but at the world in general. At the same time, she knew it didn't matter if it was directed at her. It really was nothing personal. She was the personification of a lot of things about which he knew almost nothing, except they hurt. "You've been though a huge shock, Wayne, massive, something most of us will never imagine, much less encounter. You can't bottle up your feelings. It's not healthy." He looked at her as though she had suddenly started speaking Latin. "If you have nobody to talk to, nobody to express these feelings to, you can always talk to me. If there's nobody else. They told me you'd asked for me to come, that you had something to say to me. Here I am." She sat on the step beside him, waiting for him to speak.

Wayne said nothing. Now she was here, he found there was nothing he wanted to say. All he wanted to do was put his head on somebody's shoulder and cry until he was all cried out, and then cry some more. Either that, or just go out into the back garden when it got dark and howl at the moon. That he hadn't already done that was nothing to do with his being a boy, a young man, and that boys didn't cry. It was nothing like that. He knew that was rubbish anyway. He wasn't thick. He read things, things that most of his mates didn't, or couldn't because they had words of more than two syllables and no pictures. Emotions were for expressing, not bottling up inside. If he bottled them up, they would fester and poison him. He knew all that, he really did. He had a fancy that the sleepless lethargy he felt growing inside him since they had viewed Kim's body, the fact that he hadn't slept at all, was the effect of exactly that, of keeping that upper lip good and stiff because he was needed to take care of everyone else, Mam especially, because there really was no one else now. He'd never felt close to the rest of the family, and when Auntie Karen had come to collect Mam he'd hardly recognised her. He couldn't look after Mam if he fell to pieces.

"I'm fine," he lied.

"No, you're not," replied Abdullah, sipping the tea, her lips crinkling at the taste of the three sugars she'd stirred into it. "No, Wayne, you are not fine. You can't be. Nobody could be. But that's okay. You don't have to say anything if you don't want to. Just know I'm there for you if you do want to talk."

The youth and the detective constable sat on the doorstep, sipping drinks neither wanted or needed or liked, looking out into the evening as it gathered in, saying nothing because they didn't have the words for what they needed to say. They were both too young to have that wisdom, or to know they did not have it. All she could do was offer him companionship for the moment, whether he wanted it or not.

"Do you really think you'll catch her killer?" Wayne asked, apropos of nothing that had been said but everything that had been thought.

"Of course we will," she replied, without thinking, because she believed it was true. "Yes, we will catch him."

"You're just saying that." His tone was dull, defeated, as though coming from his feet rather than his mouth.

She put her hands on his shoulders and turned him around, so he was facing her. This was a vital moment for him. If she could catch him, convince him that his suffering would be over, would fade away. But it would never truly go away and he would never have his sister back, though he would have his life, which was important, and he was strong enough to cope with that grief, to swallow it up and transform it into something vital, something useful, something productive. She knew it didn't happen every time. Some of those who were left behind inevitably went into a dark place and never fully emerged, emotionally crippled by the barbaric loss inflicted on them. Sometimes, though, they came through. It was up to her to convince him.

"No, Wayne, I am not just saying that. We *will* catch him. I believe that in here" – she tapped her head – "and in here." She tapped her heart. "I would not lie to you. I will not lie to you. You and your mam deserve better than that. You deserve the truth. Kim deserves the truth." She looked into his eyes and saw at once a lost little boy and a young man with the world at his feet. This was not the time to wonder but to seize the opportunity. "Wayne, I don't know you very well, but from what I have seen, you are a good lad, you care about things, you know you will have to work to get what you want out of this life. I respect you for that. I'm not going to say anything is going to be easy, because you know already that's rubbish. What I will say is that you must not allow what was done to Kimberley to make you think the whole world is against you, or that you did anything to make it happen because it isn't, and you didn't. You want to do something. You want to find whoever did it and tear out his heart. That's okay. That's cool. We all want that, but we both know it isn't going to happen, and we both know that one of the reasons it isn't going to happen is because Kimberley wouldn't want you to spoil your life doing something that isn't going to bring her back. She isn't coming back, but she's still here" – she touched his heart and then his head – "and she always will be, because she's your sister and she loves you the way you love her. She wants nothing but the best for you."

"You can't know that! You didn't know her."

"But I can. I know you, a bit, and I can see how you feel about her. I have two younger sisters and they drive me up the wall, but they're my sisters and I know they love me the way I love them, that they want me to feel proud of them the way they feel proud of me. There's any number of ways you can do it, Wayne, make Kimberley proud of you. Taking care of your mother is one way you can do that. You're already doing that. Another way is being the best Wayne you can be, the biggest Wayne, the most fulfilled Wayne. She would not want you to blight your whole life just on some futile gesture. Do you understand me?"

He looked at her for a long, long time, tears gathering in his eyes. She wanted to take him in her arms, give him a hug, give him a cuddle, and she had to sit on her hands to prevent herself doing that. No matter how much he needed it, no matter how much she needed it, that would be inappropriate behaviour and the last thing anyone needed now was some stupid action, no matter how well intentioned, to distract anyone from the only real business they had at hand, catching Kimberley's killer.

He nodded, a weak smile crossing his lips, and he wiped his eyes with the back of his sleeve.

"Thanks," he whispered.

"You are entirely welcome, Mr Ford. Any time at all." Relief coursed through her like a mountain stream when the snow melted. Perhaps she wasn't such a bad copper after all.

Chapter Thirty-Nine

Abdullah and Wayne had gone indoors, away from the darkness, when the car came kangarooing along the street, the driver missing gears, the engine racing and almost stalling equally. Neighbours peered, disapproving. Eventually it stopped outside Number 22, more or less at the side of the road, almost but not quite parallel parked. The driver revved the engine to its limit one last time, the way drivers used to do in the old days when cars needed chokes and suchlike, then switched it off. The ensuing silence was intense, until he broke it by slamming his door so violently the whole car rocked from side to side. The driver was a tall man in middle age, wearing a dishevelled suit with his tie hanging to one side, almost under the lapel. His hair stuck up in spikes that were not a usual style for anyone dressed that way. As he staggered around the car, he would have fallen over, had he not reached out to steady himself on the bonnet. He instantly lifted his hand off the hot metal, swearing like a stevedore. The neighbours tut-tutted. What sort of maniac drove a car while in that condition? Somebody ought to call the police. Nobody did. After all, the police were already at Number 22.

The man weaved his way up the path towards the front door. At the bottom of the steps, he stopped, looked up and then down to where he stood. Then, he began to shout. "Beverley Langley, get your fat arse out here, you idle stupid cow. Get out here and account for yourself!"

He had a loud voice. The neighbours heard every word. Who was this Beverley Langley?

When the door didn't open, he began to shout again — a stream of foul-mouthed invective — and started to climb the steps, only to miss the first one and fall forward onto his face, breaking his fall with his outstretched hands. The rough concrete ripped skin from his palms and set him to screaming still louder obscenities.

The front door opened. DC Abdullah stood in front of Wayne, staring down at him until she recognised him. "Detective Constable Langley, you are drunk!" She stepped down from the threshold onto the top step, to help him.

"You can shut your big mouth an' all, you black bitch, you. I only wanna talk to that slag of a wife of mine, the devious bitch who's got my daughter murdered."

Wayne shoved past Abdullah, almost barging her into the bushes that grew beside the steps. He was a footballer, good enough to have had trials for both Newcastle and Sunderland, before a wiser head persuaded him to continue his studies for the time being. With Langley on his hands and knees on the steps below him, his head was at exactly the right height to put his laces through the man's jaw.

"You don't talk about my mam like that!" he yelled as Langley's head shot sideways, taking his body off the steps entirely and into the flower bed. The man's eyes rolled up in his head and blood squirted from his mouth where he had bitten his tongue. His son stood above him, fists clenched, at once delighted and horrified by what he had done. He hadn't struck anyone in anger since he was six and Billy Gorman had ridden his trike without asking first. His father had leathered him good and proper about that. His father, whom he had just knocked to the ground.

It was Abdullah's turn to push past the lad and climb down to where Langley lay, snoring ever so gently, pink spittle frothing in the corners of his mouth. She leaned over him and slapped him across the cheeks, forehand and backhand, again and again until his eyelids fluttered open.

"What d'you think you're playing at, Detective Constable?" she hissed, putting as much contempt as she could muster into that last two words.

He looked up and eventually managed to focus on her. "You can fuck off, you Muslim cow," he muttered.

She shook her head. "Stay where you are." He tried to get up and she shoved him back down. "Just stay there, you hear?" An extendable metal truncheon appeared in her hand, and she laid it alongside his head. "Do as you're told, or I'll use this on you."

"Just try, bitch, just you try," he sneered, but he did not move.

She got back up onto the steps to stand beside Wayne, reaching for her radio.

"You don't fucking well think you're going to call the police on my boy," he wailed, then groaned as pain hit him. "The bastard kicked me fuckin' head in."

"He did? Funny, I didn't see that." She shook her head, seeing Wayne relax as she did. "Now I'm going to call for an ambulance because I think you hurt yourself when you fell off the steps." She spoke in a voice loud enough for the small crowd that had gathered to hear. She chivvied Wayne back up into the house. "You just go indoors and have a Coke or something. Leave this to me."

Wayne did as he was told without a word.

She called it in, asking for an ambulance for a man who had fallen over, then thought she should really call in for a patrol car to attend and make the clearly inebriated constable take a breathalyser. While she was prepared to gamble that no one would believe Wayne had kicked his father in the head, especially with her as a witness, but the paramedics were certain to smell the drink on him and she knew she would be expected to call that in.

She was sitting on the top step, wishing she had a coat to keep off the chill, and watching Langley lying there asleep, when a patrol car arrived, blue flashers ablaze, and two yellow-jacketed constables emerged. She recognised Constables Winter and Collins.

"Evening, Shan," called Winter as he came through the gate. "What's been going on here?"

She nodded towards Langley, whom Winter appeared to notice for the first time. "He turned up the worse for wear shouting the odds at Mrs Ford. When we came out, he fell off the steps, ending up where you see him now, sleeping the sleep of the well and truly bladdered." She wondered where that term for drunk had come from. It seemed somehow so appropriate.

Both the uniformed constables looked down at him and chuckled. Collins squatted down beside him, slapping him awake with one hand while he fished out his breathalyser with the other.

"I know he's a bit of a boozer–" she began.

"A bit!" guffawed Winter. "I don't suppose he's drawn a completely sober breath in fifteen years."

"What was he doing round here?" Abdullah said, and asked herself for the first time why Wayne should respond to him so violently.

"You don't know, do you?" Winter asked.

"Know what?" She shook her head.

"Him and Bev used to be married until she kicked him out seven years ago. Nobody ever knew why, and neither of them ever said anything, but my guess is he was knocking her about when he was drunk."

"And he kept his job?" No wonder Wayne hit him if he'd knocked his mother about.

"She never said anything, and he had friends in high places, still has by all accounts." Winter left her to wonder who Langley's rabbi – as the Americans put it – was, and whether they would pull strings for him after this.

The ambulance pulled up outside the house, and two paramedics, a man and a woman, hurried to investigate Langley.

Eventually Abdullah went back into the house, after the paramedics decided he was not in need of any urgent medical attention. "Drunks tend to fall soft because they are relaxed," the female paramedic told her.

Collins had packed Langley into the back of the patrol car after informing him he was going to be taken to the station and charged with being drunk in charge of a motor vehicle, being drunk and disorderly, and behaviour likely to cause a breach of the peace.

Those charges might cost him his job, but Langley only giggled.

Winter drove off in Langley's car, the driver's side window wide open to get rid of the foul smell.

Wayne sat in the front room, staring at the television, which was on mute.

"That should be the last you hear of him, for the time being," Abdullah announced.

He took no notice of her. "Just for the record, Wayne – and strictly off the record – you did not kick your father in the head. The report I shall submit tomorrow will say that you saw your father fall off the steps and, in your hurry to help him, you slipped on a worn step and fell yourself. Your foot may have accidentally hit his head, which will account for the bruise he will have tomorrow, but it was a pure accident. Do you understand?"

Wayne nodded, a grin spreading over his face. "Are all coppers as devious as you?"

"Devious? Me?" She laughed. "I have no idea what you mean." Only the good ones, she thought. She got up from the armchair and went to the doorway. "I do not know about you, but I could kill for a cup of tea. You?"

Wayne nodded, distracted, trying to follow the silent action on the TV. It was an old episode of *Frost* – they were all old episodes of *Frost* nowadays, like *Columbo*. Abdullah wished their real cases were that straightforward. This one, for a start.

"I'll have a Diet Coke," Wayne said, picking up the comic he was reading before they were disturbed.

"Right, then," said Abdullah, and left the room for the kitchen.

Chapter Forty

Darling parked in the car park outside the Boundary Mill stores at the southern end of Park Lane. To go any further would take them into Silverlink, the biggest office park in the country, half of the blocks having been empty for years because there could be only so many call centres in the world. She looked around the car park, which was half empty. It was after noon on a Sunday The place should have been rammed. She was sure it had been, on the odd occasions she had driven past in the past. Hadn't she heard of bus excursions for pensioners just to take advantage of the discounts there? Her mother was a pensioner and would sooner have thrown herself in the Tyne than shopped there. Her mother had always been a snob.

"What are we doing here?" she snorted. "Remind me again, Shan, what are we doing here?"

"Looking for a black VW Golf, boss." Abdullah was glad to be out of the office. Trying to make sense of the bank and phone data had given her a headache, largely because the offices at the banks and mobile-phone companies that had the information weren't open on a Sunday Ordinarily, the inspector would have taken Morton with her, but she'd all but shouted at him to go to his wife when he came into the office that morning, and he'd turned right around and left without even putting his cup of coffee on his desk.

Nobody else had said anything and Abdullah hadn't asked. Staffing decisions were way above her pay grade.

So, she had got her head down until the boss had asked, "Fancy a ride out?" and she had almost jumped for joy.

"And why are we looking for a black Volkswagen Golf?"

"Because Kimberley was last seen getting into a black Volkswagen Golf." She held up the all-but-indecipherable still taken from the CCTV footage, in its crumpled poly pocket folder.

"And we're looking for a black Volkswagen Golf in Shiremoor because?"

"Because it was in Shiremoor where she was picked up, having been driven here by taxi from Torville Street, which leads to the possibility that the killer lives somewhere in the Shiremoor area."

Darling nodded. "Very good, Constable." She sighed and lifted her coffee cup to her lips. It was empty, and if there'd been any coffee, it would have been cold. She jammed it back into the cup holder on her side of the central binnacle. "We've driven up and down every street in this area." She nodded to the street map Abdullah had open on her knees, with a blue tick on every street and cul-de-sac they had searched. The map was a mess of blue. No street or back alley was unmarked. "We've even had a uniform stop us because a local got suspicious." The constable had taken one look at her warrant card and beat a hasty retreat, almost saluting in his confusion. "How many black Volkswagen Golfs have we seen?"

Abdullah flicked open her notebook. "Two, and they were both a lot older models than the one in the photo."

Darling drummed on the steering wheel. "So, what does that mean?"

"Either the one we're looking for isn't actually in the area..."

"Or?"

"Or it's in a garage."

There weren't that many garages in Shiremoor. When most of the houses were built, the people who lived there couldn't afford cars and didn't need them. Their work was just a bus ride away. Now, of course, they worked all over the place, needing cars to get to even the most menial of jobs. Houses with two cars parked outside weren't rare, and there were often cars parked on the driveways of the houses with garages.

"Or?"

"Or it is somewhere else at the moment."

"Its owner works Sundays, and we might see it if we have another look tomorrow." Darling hoped she didn't sound as depressed as that idea made her feel. Retreading their footsteps in the hope something might have changed did not feel like making progress, and she couldn't escape the gnawing suspicion that they weren't making any progress, hadn't made any real progress since finding the footage of Kim being picked up.

"We could always search the garages," Abdullah asked.

Hadn't Pete Morton suggested that when they first saw the Golf? Darling thought. Her answer was the same now as it had been then. "We haven't got the manpower for that." If they were searching for Kim's body, she could have had every uniform in the force out looking, and called in colleagues from neighbouring forces if there was enough media publicity, but trying to find a car that might have something to do with her disappearance? That was a lot lower down the list of constabulary priorities. She might be able to raise it higher if she could claim it was important to prevent another kidnapping and murder, but she knew how much chance she had of that. Kimberley hadn't been kidnapped. The evidence was there for all to see, she'd got into the car of her own volition, and while she was an innocent child, there was no doubt that if – when – the details of their business got out, the old, dismissive attitude towards working girls – 'they've got to expect the rough stuff' – would rear its hoary, ugly head again. Darling wasn't sure she had the strength or the allies to fight against that in the campaign for more resources.

Besides, I'm not that desperate; not yet, she thought. Twenty-first-century policing would give her the answers, she was certain.

"Tell you what," she said. "Let's take a break and get ourselves a coffee, shall we?"

Abdullah agreed. She didn't like coffee, but she thought it was prudent to treat the inspector's words as an order rather than a suggestion. Darling obviously wanted a coffee, and she could sit with her while she drank it, pretending to drink her own. They ended up on the Rendezvous Cafe overlooking Whitley Bay Beach, with Darling buying them both large cappuccinos and blueberry and white-chocolate muffins.

They tasted as good as anything Abdullah had eaten in Indira's restaurant just the day before. In fact, it tasted so good that she even found herself drinking the coffee and relaxing in Darling's company in a way she never had before, so much so that she had no real recollection of what they talked about.

"What would you say to being a sergeant?"

That drove away her relaxation, like the wind outside was driving the high clouds down from the north.

"I… I've never really thought seriously about it."

Darling chuckled. "Oh, come on, Shan, it's obvious you think policing is your career. Becoming a sergeant is the next step. You've taken the exams, Shan. You're waiting for the results. So, what about being a sergeant?"

Abdullah had thought about her career. As she had told the doctor – what was his name? – she spent a lot of time studying with just that in mind. "I'm not certain…"

"You wouldn't necessarily have to go back into uniform. You're a good detective, with the makings in you of becoming a really good detective."

"I don't know."

"Well, I do, and I think I know what I'm talking about."

Abdullah nodded, hoping her inner glow of satisfaction wasn't showing through. She knew the inspector thought well of her work – her assessments said exactly that – but the simple fact was that she put Darling on a pedestal at the same time as she wanted to be her, to be the detective she was and was going to be.

"No false modesty, Shan. You're the best officer I have on my team, bar Pete Morton, and he's got decades of experience on you, as well as having got as far as he's going to go, as he wants to go. He likes his job, does it well and doesn't want the politics and paperwork that comes with a step up." She was silent for a moment, allowing her thought that Abdullah could cope with all of that to go unsaid. "You've got a review coming up. Part of that is about your career plans and ambitions. I want to write that you want to move on to being a sergeant as soon as possible. What do you say?"

"I'll think about it," Abdullah mumbled into her coffee cup.

"Just you do that." Darling smiled. Then her phone rang. She answered and jumped to her feet. "Come on!" she said, hurrying towards the door. "They think they may have found him!"

Chapter Forty-One

Both Darling and Abdullah ran up the stairs to the office, where they opened the door and found Morton and Cox staring at them over the top of Cox's monitor. Their excitement was clear even yards away. Darling stopped suddenly and Abdullah almost went into her back.

"Pete, what are you doing here?"

She watched the light drain out of his eyes. "Boss…"

Instinct told her that whatever he was about to say needed to be said somewhere quiet, somewhere private. "In my office, now."

He closed the door behind himself very carefully.

"Why aren't you with Pam?"

The colour went from his face as though he'd just been kicked in the balls. "Boss…"

"Wasn't my order clear enough for you? Some things are more important than finding some murderer. Like family." He still didn't answer. "Well?" She watched him shrink in on himself.

"Pam's dead. She died just after ten this morning," he whispered. "I was with her then." He raised his head and glared at her. "Makes fuck-all difference to her where I am now."

"Oh, Pete, I am so sorry." She reached out to take his hand. He flinched away.

"It's not like we weren't expecting it. Suppose she was lucky to live this long." His voice was bitter and hard-edged, even for him.

Darling could almost see the coiled-up rage, anger and sorrow boiling up inside him, ready to erupt.

"You don't have to be here."

"Yes, I do," he seethed, smashing his fist down on her desk loud enough to attract their attention in the main office. "Yes, I fucking well do need to be here. I'm no use to her now she's in a refrigerated drawer. I'm no use to the kids. There's nothing I can say to them, not that I know how to say. But I am some use here. Here I'm not 'Pete Morton, husband of a wife he couldn't save'. Here I'm 'Detective Sergeant Peter Morton, hard-assed copper and catcher of bad guys'. Here I can look at myself in the mirror without tears in my eyes. Here I can be the me I want to be, the me I need to be. I need this, boss. Whatever anyone else thinks, I need this now. Maybe I'll fall apart tomorrow and do the full, tearful, grieving husband bit, but right now I need to do what I do better than anything else."

She listened to the longest speech she'd ever heard him give, listened to him pouring out the heart she hadn't thought he possessed, something the Pete Morton she thought she knew wouldn't have done. She didn't believe that people management was that big a part of her job, but she knew that one size did not fit all, that what was right for one was utterly wrong for another. It was her job to help him find the right way for him.

"Right, Sergeant, let's get back to work."

He reached out and took hold of her wrist, something she would never normally permit, but she'd forgive him, this one time. "The last thing she said to me, the last thing before she said she loved me, was to catch this fucker. Those were her words. 'Catch this fucker.' My Pam didn't swear like that, any more than she said she loved me. Some things you're just meant to know, I suppose."

Unable to think of anything to say to that, she patted his hand a couple of times and went out of the room, never wanting to look into eyes like his ever again.

"Right, lads and lasses, what have you got?"

Cox and Abdullah's eyes opened wide for a moment, as if to wonder why she was so cheerful, all of a sudden. 'Lads and lasses' was not something she would usually say. The question disappeared as soon as it was raised.

"This last phone," Cox announced, pride sparkling from his voice. "I've got a name and address."

"How? I thought the phone companies didn't work weekends?"

"This one does. Well, it has its offices on Silverlink. I told the lad I spoke to why we wanted the information. He said he'd have a word with his managers, see if there was anything they could do seeing as it was urgent." Cox didn't say that he'd made a date with Robbie to go for a drink at The Strawberry next Friday night. "He got back to me with this." He put a printed sheet of paper on his desk.

The phone was registered to a company called 'Night Moves' at the address of Swan House, Middle Drive in Darras Hall, just about as far from Shiremoor as it could get in terms of location and property prices and still be in Tyneside. Darras Hall was where footballers lived, lawyers like Michael Lander and members of Girls Aloud.

"Night Moves?" Darling wondered aloud.

"Daniel Hegarty," Morton replied. "Owns half of the pubs and clubs on Tyneside. Everybody's friend, big donor to charity, used to get whispered about buying the Toon every six months but nothing ever happened."

Darling remembered what Milburn had said about stepping on sensitive toes. A monsignor and one of the richest and most visible men on Tyneside. How much more sensitive could those toes get?

"Come on, then, no time like the present. We'll go in two cars. While we're at it, Pete, see if you can arrange some backup. I know it is Sunday afternoon and Newcastle are playing at home." She saw the surprise in Cox and Morton's eyes. "I do pay some attention, you know." She laughed, deflated the bubble of tension. "As many as you can manage, even if they're uniforms." Some premonition she did not understand told her they were going to need all the help they could get. However much of a twenty-first-century police officer she tried to be, she still listened to her gut, one of the many lessons she had learned from Joe Milburn.

Chapter Forty-Two

Morton parked the car about fifty yards along Middle Drive from the entrance to Swan House. He could see the tall, black wrought-iron gates across the entrance to the drive. The other two cars stopped behind them.

"Sure you want to go through with this, boss?" he asked.

Darling did not reply. She never answered stupid questions.

"I know we've got circumstantial evidence—"

"We have a telephone number registered to his company as the only call to Tina Brady on the night in question that we cannot account for," said Darling. "Now, we can't say for certain it was him who picked up Kimberley after she got out of the taxi, until we find her phone or the company can give us a full list of all her calls, but I think we have enough evidence to ask Mr Hegarty some pointed questions. Mr Milburn would agree with me, I'm sure."

Morton's resistance collapsed. He might question Darling – it was his job to question her when he thought she was wrong – but he would never question Joe Milburn, or his occasional habit of charging in and making all the angels in heaven shuffle their feet, look around and say, 'After you'. He got out of the driver's seat and walked to the passenger side. "You'd better take it from here, boss."

Darling exchanged seats and drove the rest of the way before turning into the entrance and stopping with the front bumper an inch from the gates. They were decorated with gold roses the size of bin lids, as though the house belonged to a Tudor king, rather than a Tyneside mogul who had made his money out of booze and strippers before moving on to fine dining and legal gaming. The house she saw at the other end of the fifty-yard drive was a columned mock-Georgian mansion typical of the area, just bigger.

"Who are you? What do you want?" the black box on a black metal pillar squawked just outside her window.

"I am Detective Inspector Darling of the Northumbria Police," she said, leaning out, using her best talking-down-to-civilians voice. "I have some questions I must ask Mr Hegarty."

"Make an appointment with Mr Hegarty's solicitors," the voice replied.

Morton turned away when he saw the thunder clouds cross Darling's expression. When she spoke next, it was in that slow, precisely modulated way that said it was time to take cover.

"Young man, I have told you who I am and why I am here. I will also tell you that I am investigating a murder, a murder that is all over the front pages and the television. Now, if you insist, I will arrange an interview through Mr Hegarty's solicitors. That interview will take place at Forth Banks police station and Mr Hegarty's arrival will be photographed and broadcast by every newspaper and television channel our PR team know." She paused, for effect. "Have I made myself clear?"

All the reply that came from the squawk box was a click, after which the gates began to swing open.

"Did you really mean that, boss?" Morton whispered.

"That is for me to know and them to guess," she said.

The driveway to the house was perfectly raked beige gravel, and bowls could be played on the lawns. The house itself was very much in the Georgian mode, with triangular pediments over each window, and door on all three storeys. A rose had been carved into every pediment. Plain columns supported a portico in front of the main doors.

Darling parked under the portico and got out to see the other two cars pull up in the drive. Abdullah, Cox and four other plain-clothed officers got out and milled around, waiting for their instructions, looking as though they could kill for a cigarette. A young man standing in the open doorway looked suspiciously at the officers as Darling and Morton approached. He was tall, slim and perfectly groomed, in his early thirties, she estimated. The creases in his suit trousers could cut steel and the look he gave Darling oozed contempt. She showed him her warrant card.

"I am Detective Inspector Darling, and this is my colleague, Detective Sergeant Morton." Morton produced his card with the bored demeanour of a man who resented being governed by rules that prevented him using his fists to adjust the facial features of anyone who displeased him. "We are with the Northumbria Police and, as I say, I have some questions I wish to ask Mr Hegarty."

The young man literally looked her up and down, disapprovingly, as if asking, 'What makes you think you have the right to come here unasked?' "Mr Hegarty has told me to advise you that he is a close, personal friend of the chief constable."

"I do not doubt it," said Darling. "And if Mr Hegarty cares to call the chief constable, Mr Mowbray will tell him he will take it as a personal favour if he answers my questions." She looked at the young man, waiting for the reaction that did not come. "At least, that is what Mr Mowbray told me to say when we were discussing the case before I came here."

Morton looked away, teeth clamped together. Darling had not spoken with the chief constable that day, possibly ever. The chief didn't work weekends. He supposed that was something else for her to know and them to guess about.

The young man stood aside and ushered them inside the house. The hallway was black-and-white chequerboard marble, deeply polished wood, and rose to the full height of the house.

"How the over half lives, eh, boss?" muttered Morton, his eyes roving over the ostentatious display of wealth on show. "The other half percent."

"If you've got it, flaunt it," she replied, sotto voce.

For a moment, Morton did not reply. Then he burst out laughing, ending up coughing into one tissue and wiping his eyes with another.

"Hay fever," he explained to the young man.

He looked at them both with the slightly raised eyebrow of someone who did not know why he was expected to observe this meaningless spectacle that was diverting him from other, more immediate duties. With a brief shake of the head, he ushered them towards a closed door that was big enough to have been salvaged from some demolished Victorian town hall. He knocked on the door. It sounded as though he was knocking on the gates of Mordor. He opened it without waiting for an answer and stood in the doorway, filling the space between the door and the jamb.

"Mr Hegarty, there are two police officers here, a Detective Inspector Darling and a Detective Sergeant Morton. They want to speak to you. They say it is important."

"Of course it is important, Gerry…" came the voice from inside the room, a voice almost laughing. "Show them in, and don't go anywhere."

Gerry pushed the door further open and stood aside to allow them in.

Darling saw no obvious change in his expression, which remained hired-help impassive, but there was something about his posture, a stiffening around the shoulders and neck, that raised a red flag in her mind. He had something to hide, something he did not want her finding out about. That something might be nothing to do with what concerned her now but she still put it behind her ear for future reference.

There were shops she knew in the centre of Newcastle, successful, expensive shops that were smaller than Hegarty's study. Daniel Hegarty was a short, square man of an age that made him believe sunbed orange was a good colour for skin, the mullet was the finest hairstyle ever devised by a barber, and too many gold chains hanging in the open neck of his silk shirt were not enough. He was sitting behind a broad smile with his grey snakeskin cowboy boots up on a desk the size of a snooker table.

How many mahogany trees had given their lives for that desk? There were no chairs on their side of the desk.

"Mr Hegarty, I am Detective Inspector–"

"I know who you are, sweetheart," he interrupted, with a dismissive wave of his gold-ring-encrusted right hand. "Your pet monkey too."

"Detective Inspector Darling–" she tried to continue.

"How is Joe Milburn these days?" Hegarty asked. "It's been a long time since our paths crossed, although I'd bet he'd say, 'not long enough'."

"Superintendent Milburn is very well," Darling said. "He told me to be sure and tell you that he would regard your cooperation as a personal favour."

Hegarty laughed so loud he ended up hiccoughing. "The day Joe Milburn owes me a favour is the day after hell has frozen over." He wiped his eyes on a handkerchief fresh from his pocket. "Can I offer you some refreshment? Coffee, tea, me?"

A crawling sensation down her spine whispered he might not be joking.

"This isn't a social call, Mr Hegarty. As I say, I am here on serious business."

"A man must try, sweetheart... Inspector, I mean. That is all I'm saying." He raised his hand as though summoning a waiter. "Gerry, bring my guests some chairs. The comfortable ones, mind you. They're not trying to sell me anything."

Gerry brought the chairs with as bad a grace as possible, only just not dropping them on their feet, and then left as though his arse was on fire.

"Mr Hegarty," Darling began, "we are investigating the murder of a child last Monday night."

Hegarty clapped his hands and removed his boots from the desk, a huge grin on his face. "In that case, I'm not your man. Well, I knew that anyway, and I'm sure you know that as well, deep down. The fact is, I was out of the country at the time." He bent over, and they heard a drawer being opened. He came back up with a plastic pocket containing a single sheet of printed paper. "I flew to Milan on Friday afternoon and I only flew back on Tuesday. I stayed at the Four Seasons." He pushed the poly pocket across the desk. "There's my account."

The sheet drifted over the deeply polished desktop until Darling pinned it down and then picked it up. Her Italian was basic, a step up from the GCSE qualification she had from school or the average tourist trying to order two beers but a big jump down from being a proficient speaker. Even so, she could read it well enough to see the dates exactly matched what he said. She scribbled a quick note of the credit card he had used, but as far as she remembered, it was nothing like any of the ones that had been used to pay into Tina Brady's bank account for the girls' services. There was a dull ache in the pit of her stomach. She had so hoped Hegarty was the solution to the puzzle of Kimberley.

"Can I ask you a question, Inspector?" Hegarty asked.

"You can ask. I can't guarantee answering."

"Fair enough." He nodded. "Why did you think I had anything to do with a murder? Look at me. I'm obviously a lover not a fighter."

She could have risen to his bait, but she didn't, because she knew better than to wantonly make an enemy of anyone as obviously well-connected as Daniel Hegarty for no other reason than he was poking a little fun at her. Besides which, it was a reasonable question to her. She glanced towards Morton, who was very carefully looking anywhere but at her. She sighed, reluctant to share anything with a civilian that was not already in the public domain.

"Very well. I have told you what we are investigating, and I know you will give us any help you can, because you are a law-abiding citizen."

He greeted this description with a guffaw of laughter straight from his belly. "Touché, Inspector, touché!"

She contained the chuckle rising from her stomach, as did Morton, whose shoulders twitched, slightly. Hegarty had a long history of sailing very close to the law, sometimes paying the penalty for being discovered on the wrong side of that line. "As I say, we are investigating the murder of a thirteen-year-old girl last Monday night. We believe she was involved in an organised child-abuse ring."

The colour fled from his face and the skin around his mouth and eyes tightened. When he spoke, his voice could hardly escape through his clenched teeth. "And you thought I was involved... with children?"

"That is the way the evidence looked."

"What evidence could that be?"

His brow had furrowed and come down over his eyes. The colour in his cheeks had risen. He looked close to losing his temper.

"The arrangements were that the client would call the madam, give her their order. She would have a taxi deliver the girl into the client's general vicinity. The girl would then call the client, who would pick her up. The only caller to the madam that night we haven't tracked down and eliminated from our inquiries used a mobile that is registered to this address."

He nodded, his lips pressed close together.

"We also have some CCTV footage of Kimberley being picked up from the location where the taxi dropped her at almost exactly that time. Picked up by this car."

It was her turn to take a poly pocket from her bag and push it across the desk towards Hegarty. The photograph inside was in various indistinct shades of grey rather than black-and-white – the characteristic fuzzy image pulled off a traffic camera at night. While a person might struggle to recognise themselves, the photograph clearly showed Kimberley getting into the passenger seat of a black Volkswagen Golf.

Hegarty relaxed, sighing hugely. When he looked up, the laughter was back in his eyes. "Inspector, really. Do I look like the sort of man who drives a Golf?" He laughed some more. "I have a black Rolls-Royce Ghost in the garage, a powder-blue Baby Bentley, a pink Cadillac, a burnt-orange Lamborghini Aventador and two Range Rovers – one a silver Vogue, the other a white Evoque. No Golf."

"Added to which, you were in Milan at the time," Morton observed.

"Added to which, I was in Milan," Hegarty agreed.

"That is as maybe," Darling said. She tapped the image with her forefinger. "The fact remains that a mobile phone registered at this address made the call that led to Kimberley getting into that car, which is the last time anyone but the murderer saw her alive."

Hegarty reached down, opened the drawer again and brought out three mobile phones, pushing them across the desk. "My phones, Inspector. They are all registered to my company at this address. They are all business assets and are, therefore, registered to my business address, which is here." He spread his arms to encompass everything in the room. "Everything you see is a business asset, owned by my business; my clothes, my house, the furnishings in it, none of it is mine." His hand went to the chains at his throat. "Even my lovely jewellery belongs to the business."

Darling allowed this information to lie on the table, unremarked, remembering Morton's jibe about the other half and realising she had no real idea how the other half lived, or the other half percent at least. Then she did what she had been trained to do, which was push on with her investigation. "Who else might have had a phone registered to this address?"

"Your guess is as good as mine, Inspector. The business buys phones for all my employees, and they are allowed personal use just if they don't take the piss. None of them do... more than once, anyway."

"Who else lives here–" Darling began.

Morton raised his hand. "If you don't mind, boss."

She looked to him with that jerk of the head that suggested irritation. "What?"

"I think we can save some time if we use a little old-fashioned practical police work." He reached over and took the sheet that had the telephone number in question printed on it. Taking out his mobile, he carefully punched in the number, pressed the green icon and waited.

Moments later, they all heard a ringtone – a tinny version of the chorus from The Weather Girls' *It's Raining Men*. It came from the hallway. All three got to their feet as quickly as they could, heading for the door. Morton got there first and was just reaching for the small, black phone on the relatively small table when Darling called, "Stop!"

He did so and ended the call. She turned to Hegarty.

"Who else is in the house?"

He shook his head. "Nobody, just Gerry…"

As if they were all animated by some impulse they could neither see nor understand, the three turned to look at the front door. It was almost closed, as it had been after Gerry showed them in, but not quite. Morton got to the door first, with Darling on his heel and Hegarty a couple of his short steps behind. He was just in time to see a black Volkswagen Golf appear from around the far end of the house and accelerate towards the drive, spraying gravel every which way as the rear end fishtailed and the driver struggled for control. The car skidded first one way and then the other as it continued to build up speed on a surface designed to be driven over at a sedate pace. It bounced into the air as the driver's side wheels hit the grass.

"Stop him!" yelled Morton towards the officers on the far side of the portico, all of whom scrambled into their cars to make their pursuit.

Darling's mouth suddenly dried as she saw the main gates, that had closed behind them without any obvious human intervention, begin to open inwards as the Golf approached. She didn't like car chases at the best of times, particularly chases that involved her, and if anything went wrong with a chase in that vicinity the consequences would be both expensive and awkward. Important people lived there, important people who did not take at all kindly to being inconvenienced.

Hegarty leaned past her and pressed an insignificant button just beneath the sill of the window next to the door. "The override button," he explained with a grin, staring wide-eyed at the ongoing drama at the bottom of his front lawn, "closes the gates whatever command comes from the remote in the car."

Darling stared past Morton, who was running pell-mell towards the gates as though he expected to catch the car on foot. The gates stopped opening and then began to close again. The Golf picked up even more speed as though the driver believed he could get through before they closed. The engine note was still rising as the vehicle embedded itself in the all-too-solid gates. The rear wheels came up off the ground as the car attempted to rotate around the front axle, which was hard against the metal of the gate, only to fall back down almost immediately as the impossible manoeuvre failed. The car bounced a couple of times on its rear suspension as the engine note died away, the collision having torn it off its mountings and severed the electrical and petrol connections.

Darling stood where she was, closing her eyes and replaying the collision in her memory. She saw the driver's airbag inflate, and an unrestrained figure slam into it and ride up over, smashing his head against the screen. That would teach him not to forget his seat belt, she thought. As she set off towards the scene, she rather guiltily hoped he had not killed himself. He still had a lot of questions to answer.

"Call it in!" she yelled to the other officers. "I want an ambulance and a SOCO team, on the double."

With that, she followed Morton, running towards the car.

Chapter Forty-Three

Despite the amount of fresh, sticky red blood on the windscreen, Gerry was still alive when she got to the car, finding Morton struggling to get the driver's door open so he could get him out.

"Leave it!" she ordered. "Wait for the paramedics."

He should have known that was standard operational procedure. Yes, he might have a lot more experience of handling injured people than the man in the street, but he didn't have anything like a paramedic's knowledge and experience. He might damage Gerry badly simply trying to help him because he could not tell which bits of him were broken or whether he was bleeding internally. He ought to know that, and she briefly wondered whether he might have an alternative agenda. Had she been too easy on him, letting him stay after he told her of Pam's death?

"It might catch fire," Morton said.

"Then he'll burn, won't he?"

Gerry was obviously still conscious because he moaned dramatically at these words and made a feeble effort to get out of the car.

Hegarty came puffing up to them, not quite out of breath but close. "You can't leave him in there!" There was what appeared to be genuine concern on his face.

"Just watch me," muttered Darling, before she quickly explained to Hegarty the reasons why they should not try to get him out before the paramedics arrived.

Hegarty nodded, then stepped back with Darling as the other cars came down the drive and the officers began to set up a cordon around the vehicle.

"Can you come with me and answer a few questions?" she asked Hegarty. "Not about you. I don't believe you have any involvement in the case." Not unless loyal little Gerry was trying to divert attention from you, she thought. First impressions could mislead but hers suggested Gerry was loyal to no one but himself. "What is his full name?"

"Gerrard Byrne."

She wrote the name in her notebook.

"Where does he live?"

"Somewhere in Shiremoor. I'd have to look up the address."

She nodded. "Does he have any accommodation here?"

Hegarty nodded. "Sometimes his duties mean he is too tired... or has too much to drink... to get himself home. It is an expensive taxi ride from here, so I'm told. There's a room for his use."

"We'll need to search that accommodation."

"Be my guest."

"His duties, you say. What were his duties?"

Hegarty laughed, just briefly. "What *are* his duties. I haven't fired him yet, he hasn't quit, and he doesn't seem to be dead yet, so his duties are many and various. He's my personal assistant. He does everything, from wiping my arse if I'm too drunk to manage it, to making sure my important friends and business partners have everything they need. He's good at his job." He watched Darling scribble in her notebook. "Is that Pitman's, by the way?"

She nodded, still writing.

"Not many use it today. I always found it very useful, before they invented Dictaphones," he said. "That first bit was a joke, by the way. I always wipe my own arse."

"What can you tell me about his background?"

Hegarty sucked on his teeth. "It's all in his file in the office. He came highly recommended by Father O'Heir. I've known the father a long time, and he's heard my confession more times than he cares to remember. If the father speaks for someone, that's good as gold to me."

Instinct and her copper's nose told Darling that O'Heir must be a lot more to Hegarty than his parish priest for him to say that. If it was true that he actually was Hegarty's parish priest. She put a question mark beside O'Heir's name. She wasn't sure but would have put money on him being an inner-city priest. "I take it you had no idea Gerry was involved in anything like the arrangement I described."

"I know I look like I want to be Peter Stringfellow when I grow up, Inspector, and I know I made my money in businesses some people frown on, but personally I think I'm a very moral man. I don't lie. I don't cheat. I don't steal. I'm a gay man but I've always been celibate because that's what my church requires of me. Some things in life are sacred, and one of those things is the innocence of children. It's a wicked world we live in, Inspector, and children grow up into it far too soon without us weak grown-ups corrupting them. If I'd had any idea he was involved with children, I'd have put him under my arm and delivered him to your door myself."

She was taken aback by his outburst, although she tried not to show it. She wondered who Peter Stringfellow was. Before she could take it any further, however, reinforcements arrived at the gates, including an ambulance, so she went over to watch and supervise if required, which she knew it wouldn't be. She was a detective, this was a road traffic accident, even if it was off-road. She was only aware Hegarty had followed her when he leaned past her and spoke to Byrne.

"I'll bill you for this damage to my property, just see if I don't."

Then he turned around and walked back towards the house. Byrne's eyes followed him as he left, without him managing to speak a word. She called DC Cox over.

"Go with Mr Hegarty, get all the details he has about Mr Byrne here. Call Sergeant Morton when you have the address. Seems like he has a room in the house he uses when he must. Give it the once-over but don't disturb anything if possible. I'll get the SOCO team up there as soon as they arrive." She turned to Morton. "On your way, now, with DC Abdullah. Take it apart, if you have to, everything. Just because we don't know of any others doesn't mean Kim was his first."

A scream of bending metal brought her attention back to the spectacle of Byrne being extracted from the car. A couple of patrol officers had got the door open using brute strength without need of the jaws of life cutters that lay on the driveway in front of their car. The paramedics stepped in front of them to take over the business of getting him out of the wreckage, talking to him as they would the victim of any accident rather than the favourite suspect for being a child-killer. Darling admired their professionalism, their determination that nobody should hurt any more than they absolutely had to hurt. She was almost certain she could not do what they did and was sure most of her team would somehow have contrived to drop Byrne if they had got him out. They had put him on a trolley and were pushing it towards the ambulance when her phone rang. It was Cox.

"Boss, I've just walked in and found all these things in Byrne's room."

"What do you mean by 'things'?" she snapped. She was about to go on and say he was a police officer and supposed to be precise, when her brain processed the tone in his voice – the dull, shocked, tone about to become outraged. "What sort of things?" she asked in a reassuring, encouraging tone.

"Clothing, boss, a girl's clothing, and a telephone and a…" His voice faded away to nothing.

"And a what, Constable?" She tried to be encouraging and reassuring that she was a human being who had been in the position of discovering horrors – as she had – and that she understood the effect such a discovery could have on a person, but also reminding him he was a police officer, and doing his job of bringing an end to this horror.

"What else have you found, David?" Those last words were spoken to be a caress in his ear, as his mother might have said them, rather than his superior officer. Darling was discovering new depths of her ability to be manipulative.

"A baseball bat, boss, and… and…" She heard him take a deep breath and decided to let him spit it out in his own time. She counted to three. "There's what looks like dried blood on it." There were tears in his voice.

"Thank you, David," she interrupted. "Don't touch anything, just get out of the room as quick as you can, leave everything for the SOCO team. Well done, David, well done."

"Boss—"

She wiped her finger across the red 'end call' icon before he could say any more. There would be time to deal with the emotional impact this case was having on everyone, including her, when it was done and dusted, with qualified help for those who needed it. At the moment, she didn't have time for it. She made a mental note that Cox might not be the best choice of officer to despatch into a situation like that, if it arose again; not on his own, anyway. He might make a good copper, eventually, but everyone had their abilities and their weaknesses. Weaknesses didn't make them any less of an asset. It was her job, as the leader of the team, to make the best use of those assets, get them doing what they did best, if she could, and she was failing. She should have known they were likely to discover horrible things in the room. She should have sent Morton, only she'd sent Morton over to Byrne's place in Shiremoor, and right now, God only knew what they were going to discover there.

Putting all that to the back of her mind because it was done and stewing over it wouldn't make an iota of difference, she strode to the ambulance and climbed inside as the paramedics were getting everything stowed for the journey to hospital. She leaned over Byrne, so he could see her face.

"Gerrard Byrne, I am arresting you for the murder of Kimberley Anne Ford." She was aware of the paramedics' sudden attention. Perhaps they were regretting not taking the opportunity to drop him. "You do not have to say anything at this time, but anything you do say will be taken down and may be given as evidence in court."

His eyes rolled back in his head and his body went limp. For a moment, she wondered whether the shock had killed him, but then saw his chest rise and fall. He was breathing. "I'll keep the rest for later then, when you're properly awake," she said.

She turned towards the paramedics, who were suddenly very busy. "I'll need to send one of my team with you, just to be—"

"No problem, Inspector," said the paramedic securing the stretcher. He was a tall, solid man with a bristle of greying hair on his almost shaven head. With pronounced brows and a crooked nose, he had the look of a fighter about him. His knuckles were swollen and cracked in places. A street fighter, then. "No problem at all. We didn't find anything major amiss with Sonny Jim here – bumps, bruises, contusions, cuts to his head where he smacked the windscreen with it. Wouldn't be surprised if he's cracked his thick skull doing it. But nothing that's going to kill him quickly."

She thought she heard a tone in his voice that said, 'Because the bastard ought to die slowly, very slowly.'

She nodded, got out of the ambulance and beckoned to DC Pearson. Pearson was a bit of an old lag, a very experienced officer who had made it into CID quite a few more years after he thought he should have done. Detective constable was all he was ever going to be because he lacked that spark of imagination a real detective needed. He was a foot soldier who would knock on every door in a street a thousand houses long, and ask the questions in the last house with the same attention as he had in the first, and listen to the answers. She thought of him as 'the machine'. Every team needed one, at least one. "Go with him to the hospital. Make sure everything goes by the book. He's under arrest for murder. Understand?"

Pearson nodded, and she resolved to forget the look he gave Byrne. "I'll get you help as soon as I can." He put his hands together and cracked his knuckles, as though to say, 'I won't need any help'. She forgot she saw that as well.

"Keep me informed."

He nodded. "Of course, boss," he said then climbed into the ambulance. No sooner was he in it than the pugilist paramedic got out, closed the door, made sure they were locked and went around to the cab. She heard the door slam and, moments later, the ambulance drove off.

She turned back to the scene of the car. They were going to need to get it moved, even if only to get the SOCO vehicle into the grounds. She didn't want to ask them to carry their gear all the way from the gates to the house.

Chapter Forty-Four

Morton had to park a couple of doors away from Byrne's house. The terraced street was short, the houses no wider than a front door and a single front room. There was a busy road to one end of the street and a backstreet to the other, lined with garages, with an overgrown hedge behind them and a farmer's field beyond that. Morton walked to the door, turning a leather wallet of lock picks over in his hand inside his jacket pocket. He didn't suppose there were eyes behind every curtain watching them, just most, and that quite a few of the spectators would have him pinned as a copper even if they might wonder what

Abdullah was. He could always kick the door down, get rid of some of his pent-up fury. After all, Byrne could hardly have bolted the door from the inside and walked away, so he wouldn't be risking injury. On the other hand, he didn't want to give the nosey parkers round here a show.

"Here we go, then." He took the picks from his pocket and set to work. "I'm not doing this," he muttered.

"Doing what, Sarge?" asked Abdullah, looking in the opposite direction for anyone who might be watching.

He opened the door quickly and stepped up into a gloomy passageway that led to stairs straight ahead, the front room on the left – which looked to be equally gloomy behind the closed curtains – with another room behind it, and a narrow galley kitchen at the back with a door through to what Morton guessed was a downstairs toilet. He'd been in houses like this often enough.

He stepped into the front room as Abdullah closed the front door behind them. Opening the curtains revealed a closed blind at the window. Tugging on one cord opened the blind, allowing in enough light to reveal one of the most sparsely furnished rooms he had ever seen. On the wall above the empty fireplace was a big, flat-screen television with cables down to a table in front of the fire on which were a satellite box, two games consoles and another box he did not recognise. Was that all anyone did of an evening these days, watch satellite TV, play videogame shoot-'em-ups and gorge themselves on snacks? Briefly, he stood before the television and opened his arms. It was bigger than his wingspan, and he still stood more than six feet tall with arms to match. Against the opposite wall there was a black leather reclining chair, and another small table on which were an array of zappers and a couple of games controllers. Other than that, all that was in the room were two column speakers either side of the chimney breast and three tall columns of DVD boxes. Morton could not see how anyone could easily withdraw any disc from the bottom half of the pile.

"Well, I think we can see what Gerry m'lad does with his spare time," Morton muttered to himself.

Abdullah had continued down the passage and looked into what should have been the dining room, but was entirely dark, with heavy curtains drawn across the window. Only when she tried to open them did she discover they had, in fact, been sewn together up the middle and then tacked to the outside of the window frames so tightly they resisted every attempt she made to loosen them. She made her way back to the door, found the switch and turned on the lights. When she turned around, she would have fallen over, had she not caught hold of the door jamb.

"Sarge," she called, only the word didn't quite make it out of her mouth. She coughed, and then spat into a tissue. "Sergeant Morton, I think you should look at this." She heard him striding towards her.

"Look at what?" His words dried up as he saw the display of photographs on every wall in the room. All were young girls, some teenagers, some possibly even over the age of consent, but the vast majority were children, children who did not know they were being photographed, children who were very busy just being happy and playful, and innocent and entirely ignorant they were the object of a pervert's attention. There appeared to be thousands of photos stuck to the walls, all sorts of girls from all sorts of backgrounds. Their brief examination found only half a dozen faces that appeared more than once. Byrne's favourite type appeared to be the English rose, just touching on adolescence, blonde with a strawberries-and-cream complexion. There was a square of twelve photos set apart from the others, apparently all of the same girl, taken several years apart. Abdullah pointed them out to Morton.

"These remind you of anyone?"

He sucked on his teeth. "Kim?"

Abdullah shook her head. The girls were not actually Kimberley, although they were peas out of the same pod.

She would swear the girl was Bella. Hadn't she said something about the punter asking for her, only Kim had gone in her place? Could that be why he had killed Kim, out of frustration at being denied his favourite? Or would he have killed Bella anyway, because that's how far his perversion had taken him? she wondered. At that moment Abdullah wanted more than anything else to tear these photos from the walls, raging incoherently, screaming her head off. Instead, she turned around and walked to the door. "I think we should leave those alone, Sarge, get out of here. Let the SOCO team do their thing, stop contaminating their crime scene. Who knows what else he's been up to?" She was relieved she could talk coherently.

"You're right, Shan," he said, switching off the light and closing the door. "I'll call it in, you just give the rest of the house a quick once-over, see if there's anything else here to surprise us."

She was about to object in the most strenuous way only to find the outrage had quit her, leaving numbness behind. She was a police officer with a job to do, so she would do it. She had ambitions. She could not ask someone else to do what she would not do herself. Looking at the evidence of the worst human beings could do to each other was part of her job, just as much as helping Wayne through his darkness. She couldn't have one without the other. What was light without darkness?

"Anything you say, Sarge."

There were no other monstrosities for her to discover. The kitchen held a single mug and bowl on the draining board, one cereal spoon and a matching teaspoon. Everything else was as antiseptic as an operating theatre. The fridge held a two-litre plastic carton of milk, that was mostly full, a litre bottle of orange juice that was half empty. There was a tub of butter, a carton of eggs, an unopened packet of bacon and five of a pack of fruit yoghurts.

Upstairs there was a bathroom that gleamed with not a drop of water or smear anywhere, the faint smell of lilac coming from a block under the toilet rim. Both the bedrooms had single beds and single wardrobes. The only ways she could tell which his room was, and which was the spare, were the slippers under one bed, the clothes neatly arranged in that wardrobe, and the dark, almost black crucifix hanging above the bedhead. She peered at this, fascinated by the indistinct figure. Only when she got close enough to make out the features did she realise this Christ was contorted in the screaming extremes of mortal agony, a spear hanging from his torso. Who on earth could sleep with that hanging above their head?

"Have you seen the film *Lethal Weapon*?" Morton asked when she joined him. He stood outside the front door, drawing greedily on an already half-smoked cigarette.

"I don't think so," she said, and was about to add that she didn't know he had taken up smoking again, but he carried on.

"It's this cop movie, set in San Francisco. I think. Mel Gibson is this hot-shot young detective with a death wish 'cos his wife had been killed. Danny Glover is the older cop who's waiting to retire with his family. All sorts of crazy stuff happens, and Danny Glover says, 'I'm getting too old for this shit.' I've never known what he meant by that." He threw his cigarette onto the ground and stubbed it out under his heel. Then he took in a deep, sighing breath. "I do now."

Chapter Forty-Five

Grace Morgan had been housekeeper to Monsignor Lee for all the six years he had been in the post, and for both his predecessors, who had each been there more years than she cared to remember. She was tall for a woman her age, the far side of seventy, and carried herself as though she had a broomstick for a spine. There was no one she was not prepared to look directly in the eye, not even dear Pope John Paul ll years before. She was as precise, as thorough as she had always been. As a widow for the last twenty years, she lived her life on her own terms, giving as little of herself as she could when busy in the outside world. What time she had to herself she spent walking in nearby parks, remembering the walks she had taken with her late husband and their mongrel dog, Monty, not talking about the children the Lord had not sent to bless them. Otherwise, she read biographies of the great and good, eschewing autobiographies because she was not interested in what anyone thought of themselves. After all, she cared for a man she was convinced deserved to be in that number. While he might be a little too contemporary in his views on theology, the energy he put into his work in the community was undeniable in its scope and efficacy. He really did let his light shine.

There had been a time when she would have taken his breakfast up to him in his bedroom, a single time, after which he had made it clear he would eat in the dining room, or in the kitchen, should he be catering for himself as he insisted he sometimes must, over her voluble objections. He had possibly a little too much of the self-reliant monk about him, she sometimes thought. That was when she learned that arguing with the monsignor was as profitable a way of passing one's time as shouting at the north wind.

She knocked on the door, as she always did – 'shave and a haircut, two bits', which she had picked up from a cowboy film when she was a girl – and was turning to go downstairs when something made her pause. He had not answered. Even if he was still in bed, he always answered. 'Come in, Mrs Morgan,' was his usual answer. She was sure he woke with the dawn, if not earlier, and spent those quiet hours at his devotions or preparing for the innumerable calls on his time. For any man like the monsignor, there was no time of the day or night he could not be summoned by the telephone or the internet. She was wholly thankful that she had, so far, not succumbed to the incessant noise of family and friends to 'get online' or 'go mobile'. She knocked again and put her ear to the door, listening intently. Nothing. She knocked again and called loudly. "Monsignor!" Still no reply. Suddenly, her heart thumped in her chest. Her mouth dried out. She tried the handle. The door was locked. The monsignor never locked his bedroom door. He never locked any door. Given his way, he would have the cathedral doors open all the time.

Mrs Morgan did not fly down the stairs, but she felt as though she did, yelling Abraham's name. When she got to the bottom of the flight, Abraham Merritt stood in the kitchen doorway, mug of tea on one hand and a slice of toast in the other. Marmalade dripped onto the polished parquet flooring.

Abraham Merritt was the diocesan handyman. A massively built Barbadian with steel-coloured hair and a constant smile on his face. He and Mrs Morgan shared little in their attitude to life other than the sincere belief Monsignor Lee could walk on water.

"Mrs Morgan, what is the matter with you, woman, making all this noise?"

"It's the monsignor, Abraham. I think there is something wrong with him."

Putting his tea and toast on the hall sideboard, Abraham took the stairs two at a time. There had been a time he would have made three. His footsteps made the risers shudder as though they were small earthquakes. He rattled the handle with all his strength. Had the door not been locked, it would certainly have opened. "It's locked!" he yelled over his shoulder to Mrs Morgan, who was only halfway up the stairs.

"I know that!" she called back. "Use your spare key."

No light bulb became illuminated above Abraham's head, but it might as well have done. His eyes opened wide as a huge grin split his face. He brought the upraised forefinger of his left hand alongside his face, while his right hand went to the bunch of keys jangling on his right hip. Finding the right key took just a moment. Inserting it into the lock took a lot longer and eventually proved impossible.

"There must be another key on the inside!" he muttered, trying to dislodge it without success. After a short while, he dropped the keys onto the floor between his feet and took a suede pouch from his belt.

"What are you doing!" Mrs Morgan demanded, watching him fit a straight bladed bit into a small, powered screwdriver.

"Gonna take the lock off, aren't I," he grinned. "Don't worry, if I can take it off, I can put it back."

Mrs Morgan did not look reassured. The plate came off easily, four quick buzzes of the screwdriver, the handle and the internal bar as well. After a long while poking inside the mechanism with a screwdriver, Abraham cursed under his breath, stood back and kicked the door open before Mrs Morgan could realise what he was doing, much less complain. There was a scar of light wood on the frame where the tang had gouged its way through under the pressure of his barbarism.

"Don't worry. I can fix it," he assured Mrs Morgan, who took no notice of him.

Instead, she pushed past and stepped into the room, which was still dark because the heavy green velour curtains were drawn tightly shut, the way the monsignor liked it. Afraid of what she would find when she opened the curtains but determined to do the very best she could, whatever the circumstances, Mrs Morgan went to the bay window and, slowly but steadily, drew back the curtains.

Looking out of the window into the morning, she closed her eyes, crossed herself and whispered a prayer only she and the Lord would hear, then turned around.

The monsignor lay on top of the bedclothes, still fully dressed except for his slippers, which were arranged on the rug beside the bed, exactly where his feet would fall were he to sit up on the side of the bed. He looked to be at perfect peace, although he did not appear to be breathing. It was only when she stepped closer to the bed that she saw the scattered foil packaging of the half-dozen prescription medications he took, plus several empty boxes of painkillers and the half-drunk bottle of the Islay malt whisky to which he was partial.

She did not hesitate but took a deep breath and crossed herself again as she went to the bed and, reaching down, closed the monsignor's eyes. "You poor, poor man," she muttered. "What manner of sin did you believe you had committed to make you do this?"

"Do what?" asked Abraham, who still stood in the doorway, his sight of the monsignor on his bed obscured by the door itself. "Has he…"

Mrs Morgan stood in front of him, less than half an arm's length away. He might be nearly twice her bulk but there was no doubt which of them was the irresistible force. "That's what it looks like, Abraham."

He opened his mouth, but she went straight on.

"Now we are going to leave him in peace while we get on doing what needs to be done." She planted her hand in the middle of his chest and pushed, gently. He moved, and she pulled the door closed behind them. "Now you clear up out here, get yourself one of those chairs" – she nodded at the two upright chairs on the landing, upholstered with the same green velour as the monsignor's curtains – "then you sit down in front of this door until someone official comes along to take charge."

"I can't do that! What if he's only asleep? What if he wakes up?" He fetched the chair and picked up the debris of the lock even as he complained.

She reached up, put her hands on his shoulders and pushed him down onto the chair.

"He is not going to wake up."

He opened his mouth only for her to lay her finger on his lips as a mother would on a difficult child. "Abraham Merritt, now you listen to me. The monsignor is gone. He isn't coming back, and we must do the best we can for him. You will do as I tell you for the respect you have for that poor man in there, who loved and respected us all, whether we deserved it or not. Do you understand?"

He nodded.

She saw a quiver on his lips and a glistening in his eyes.

"Now he is in there explaining himself to his Lord and Maker. I believe you should say some prayers to help him do that. Can you do that?" she asked.

Abraham nodded again, as though his head weighed twice as much as it had ever weighed before. His lips began to move. Even she could lip-read the first words, 'Our Father, who art in heaven…'

Leaving him to it, she bustled down the stairs trying to decide what to do next. She knew what she should do. The monsignor had committed suicide. The first thing she should do was call the police and an ambulance, only it was the monsignor, and that would never do. The Church needed to be protected from any scandal that might attach itself to this unfortunate happening.

Calling the archbishop seemed just a little previous. He was a good man, a devout man and very intelligent. It was just that this situation seemed to require someone of a worldlier turn of mind, someone it would be best if you counted your fingers before and after shaking hands with him.

Father O'Heir! If there was anyone who would know exactly what to do in these circumstances, it was Father Francis Xavier O'Heir.

Chapter Forty-Six

Darling stood on the doorstep, took a deep breath and managed not to look around to see who was watching her, then rattled the door knocker. She was just about to reach for it again when the door opened, and Wayne stood there.

"Inspector." The greyness left his face as anticipation flickered through his eyes.

"Can I come in, please?" she asked.

He started, as though surprised by the question. She supposed boys like him weren't used to be treated respectfully by adults like her. "Of course, of course." He stood aside and allowed her to step past him before closing then door. "Mam, Mam," he bellowed, "it's that Inspector Darling to see you." He ushered her into the front room, which looked as though nobody had spent any time there in the last few days and could do with the touch of a vacuum and a lick of polish.

Darling wasn't surprised. Her front room wasn't exactly *Ideal Homes*, and she hadn't been through what they had endured, at least not the way they had been put through it.

"Can I get you anything?" he asked. "Tea—"

"No thanks." She smiled; she didn't intend to be there long enough to allow a cup of tea to cool down to drinking temperature.

Bev appeared in the doorway.

Darling thought she might be wearing the same clothes as the last time she'd seen her but wasn't sure.

She stood beside the couch, holding onto the back for support. "You've got the bastard." It wasn't a question, but her voice was as frail as the rest of her.

Darling had rehearsed a speech for this, but the sight of the woman's fear and expectation drove the words from her mind. "We have."

Bev stood where she was for a moment, not reacting, just looking at Darling. Then, without warning, her legs went beneath her, and she would have fallen, had Wayne and Darling not jumped forward to catch her. They bumped heads as they did so, but neither said anything about it, just gentling Bev around until she could sit down.

"Get her a glass of water," ordered Darling, as she stood back.

Wayne dashed off to the kitchen.

"A large Scotch would go down better."

Darling thought that in Bev's condition a large Scotch would just come straight back up again but kept that to herself. "Just sip," she said when Wayne returned.

Bev did as she was told, appearing to be restored by every sip.

"Confessed, has he?" she asked, eventually.

"Not yet, but it's him. We know it's him, we have the evidence…" As she spoke, her police officer's mind reminded her that all the evidence they had was circumstantial, that there was nothing yet to absolutely prove Byrne had murdered Kim, but they knew, and she knew the Fords did not need to hear that sort of hair-splitting legalese, not now. "We haven't been able to question him yet. He tried to escape and there was an accident. They had to cut him out of the car and get him off to A & E."

"Why?" Bev asked.

Darling raised a questioning eyebrow.

"Why take him to A & E? Why not just let him suffer like he made my Kimberley suffer?"

Darling knew that a lot of people would agree with that, most of her team, she suspected, and she could understand why they felt like that. Whatever happened to scum like Byrne was never enough, never as much as they deserved, but treating them the way they treated others made people like her as bad as the vile creatures they hunted. Byrne was being treated for his injuries because they had standards. This just wasn't the time to try to persuade Bev and Wayne of that. She shrugged.

"That's the way it is. We just follow the rules."

"If we don't follow the rules we're just as bad as animals like him," Wayne said.

Darling wanted to say that animals didn't do what Byrne had done, that only human beings behaved like that, but knew this wasn't the time to tell them that either. "I thought I should come and tell you just as soon as I knew anything."

Bev looked up at her. There was a light in her eyes that hadn't been there before, even if her face was still as haggard and drawn as a woman twenty years older, a woman whom life had treated to a good, long kicking. "Thank you. When will we be able to bury her?"

"I can't tell you, that's not my area…"

Clouds of disappointment flowed across Bev's face.

"…but I'll look into it, I promise. They won't want to keep you waiting any longer than is humanly possible." Only that wait depended upon bureaucracy having every box ticked, and there was nothing in the world less concerned with the emotional needs of human beings than bureaucracy. She moved towards the door. "I'm sorry, I can't stay any longer. I've got a lot to do at the station. You understand."

Bev looked up at her with an expression that said she understood but couldn't have cared less if she tried. "Thank you, Inspector. Thank you."

Darling nodded and looked at Wayne. "Be sure to look after your mum."

He nodded. "I'm just glad you got the fucker."

"Wayne, language!" Bev said.

"I'll let myself out," Darling said.

Darling did just that and walked back to her car feeling utterly drained. There was a lot about police work that got easier the more experience you got. Dealing with the families was not one of those. It just got harder, more demanding, more draining. As she sat down behind the wheel, she felt a tear gather in the corner of her eye. She wiped it away with her thumb and then blinked, to make sure there weren't anymore.

Chapter Forty-Seven

Darling walked in, looked around the office, and saw the team slouched at their desks, desultorily ploughing their way through the paperwork that was the inevitable consequence of any investigation, the fallout. The adrenalin had plainly worn off. If this was what a triumph did for them, she didn't want to see a failure.

"Come on, team," she called, clapping her hands as she walked to the case wall. "We got him, got him before he had chance to do it again, and I know enough about profiling to know we could expect him to do it again. It's a triumph. You've worked wonders. You should be proud of yourselves. You should be down the pub celebrating."

"You buying?" a voice she could not quite identify or place in the room asked.

"Sorry" – she grinned – "but I've got to the end of the money before the end of the month. It'll have to wait."

The chuckle that went round the room spoke of the team not expecting that day to come round any time soon. One of her divergences from old-fashioned coppering was not spending evenings down the pub socialising with people who had already spent too much time together at work. Alcohol might erode inhibitions, but she was partial to her inhibitions. She liked them. They were part of the reason she was who she was, and she'd seen enough of the effects of alcohol to believe she wouldn't like her uninhibited self. Which reminded her of something else she would have to do. "Has anyone told Brian Langley yet?"

"Yes, boss." There was that voice again.

"Thanks," she said, crossing that off her to-do list. "Look, we're all... tired..." She had been about to say 'knackered', but that wasn't a word Detective Inspector Pen Darling would use. "It's late Sunday and there's nothing here that can't wait. Get yourselves home, get some rest, take tomorrow come back in on Tuesday bright-eyed and bushy tailed."

She watched them clear their desks, pack up and leave, all but Shan Abdullah. When they were alone, she asked, "Something to tell me, Shan?"

Abdullah got to her feet and came to stand beside her. When she spoke, it was in a tone of voice that suggested they might be overheard by someone she did not want to hear what she had to say. "This list of men who abused the girls."

"Yes?"

Abdullah took a deep breath. "I presume we are going to do something about them."

Darling looked at her, wondering how anyone could doubt it, then she remembered all the stories about paedophiles with connections getting police protection from investigation. "You presume right, if I have anything to do with it."

"If you have anything to do with it?"

"Shan, I don't have to explain this to you, it's an operational matter, but I already discussed this with Superintendent Milburn, after we knew about Monsignor

Lee. He told me to follow the evidence and he would back me up if I trod on sensitive toes."

"And you believed him?"

Darling did not answer that, knowing that if Joe Milburn said he had your back, then your back was well and truly safe.

"In that case, I have to tell you I think I know one of these men."

It was Darling's turn to have her eyes open wide in astonishment. "How? We don't even know all their names yet. We won't get the telephone details until Monday."

"I found Kimberley's diary. I read it. There is an entry in it that refers to a doctor with gentle hands who has a scar right across the back of his left hand."

"Yes?" Darling encouraged.

"Yesterday I met a surgeon from the RVI who has just such a scar across the back of his left hand."

Darling shook her head. "That could just be coincidence." Then she looked hard into Abdullah's face. She was good at reading faces. She knew she was. "But you don't think it is, do you? How did you meet him?"

"Yesterday afternoon I was invited to tea by a friend of mine, Indira Iqbal. She's a businesswoman, owns restaurants and clothing firms, jewellery firms, who knows what else. I thought it was just for a catch-up; we hadn't met for months, hadn't met for so long I forgot she is an inveterate matchmaker."

"And you, being a single lady, are, by definition, in need of a husband."

Abdullah smiled. "You understand."

"My mother has a ghastly habit of trying to pair me off with suitable husbands," said Darling. "She was very fond of my husband, whereas I shall be delighted if I never see him again."

Abdullah looked down. "I didn't know you were married."

"*Was* married, Shan, was married." She raised her naked ring finger as though that was conclusive proof. "Anyway, my marital status is not important here. Yours might be."

"Indira brought along a cousin of hers for me to meet, Afzahl Khan. As I say, he is a surgeon at the RVI."

"And you didn't exactly hit it off."

Abdullah chuckled. "The only thing we had in common is that his brother is a military police officer too, a senior officer."

Darling raised an eyebrow. "Might I know him?"

With a snort, Abdullah told her he was a colonel in Rawalpindi. "I don't think he's a copper as we might understand the term."

"What about this Dr Khan…"

"Mr Khan, he's a surgeon. He was most insistent on the 'Mr'."

"And he's got a scar on his left hand?"

Abdullah nodded.

"I don't see why this couldn't have waited till Monday."

"Don't you see? If he is one of those men, I can't be part of the investigation, just the same as Brian Langley couldn't be part of this one. I know him."

Darling took a deep breath. "Thank you for mentioning this, Shan, but you don't know him. He's just a passing acquaintance. That won't keep you from being a part of any investigation I am leading. I want the best on my team. I want you on my team. I need you on my team. Understand?"

Abdullah said nothing, and Darling thought she could see a tear gathering in the corner of her eye.

"Off you go," she said. "Get a good day's rest. I've got this feeling we're in for a busy time ahead."

Abdullah smiled and did as she was told. When she was sure she was alone, Darling took her phone and called up Dorothy Bainbridge's number. "Dorothy, it's Penny here. Sorry to call you at home but it is important. Strictly off the record, those customers of yours you got rid of because of what your girls said, was one of them a Mr Afzahl Khan? … It doesn't matter how I know, just yes or no, please … As I say, sorry to bother you at home. I'll give you a bell when things quieten down here … What? … Oh yes, we've got him."

She thumbed the red icon and sat there thinking there was something else she had to do, something she had forgotten. Her landline rang.

"DI Darling, what can I do for you?"

"When were you going to tell me, Detective Inspector Darling?" It was Joe Milburn. That was what she had forgotten, telling him.

"Word gets around."

Especially when you keep your ear as close to the ground as I do, she thought, even off duty. "You were the next call on my to-do list, boss," she lied, cheerfully.

"But you've got him?"

"We've got his phone, his car, the murder weapon. We've got enough to put him inside forever."

"Has he confessed?"

"We haven't exactly had the chance to question him yet. He did a runner and smashed his car into Dan Hegarty's gatepost."

"Dan Hegarty," Milburn mused. "How is the old reprobate?"

"He sends you his best, boss."

"I bet he does, I bet. D'you think he's involved?"

Darling thought about her answer. "No, I don't. Not at the moment."

"So, when are you going to speak to the killer?"

"Just as soon as the doctors tell me he is up to answering questions."

"In a bad way, is he?"

She shrugged. "I'm a copper, boss, not a doctor."

"When is the press conference?"

Darling chuckled. "It's past five on a Sunday, boss. The PR department is closed. Giving the chief constable his photo opportunity can wait until Tuesday. Everything can wait until Tuesday I've given the team tomorrow off."

There was a pause before he replied, giving her time to wonder whether she might have gone too far.

"You're that sure you've got him?"

She took in a deep breath. "We've got him."

Chapter Forty-Eight

Darling woke early on Monday morning, feeling better and more relaxed than she had in a long time. The pain at the base of her neck had gone, for the moment. She'd slept right through from Sunday into Monday, breakfasting on what was left of a duck in plum sauce she had brought home for dinner, only to discover her appetite wasn't what she thought it was. That it tasted good after five minutes in the microwave, having spent twelve hours on the kitchen counter, might have suggested to her that there were preservatives in the carton that probably wouldn't do her any good, but so what? You only lived once.

Bathing, washing up, doing laundry and drowsing in front of the television had occupied the rest of the day before she had an early night. She looked at herself in the mirror, catching the cable of her hair in her left hand to tie on the back of her head, the way she always wore it. Something made her hesitate. Just because that was what she had done every day up until now was no reason to do it today. Letting it go, she combed it through with her hands, looking as it fell down around her shoulders. It didn't look bad at all. She smiled. Paul liked it like that, anyway. So she left it and went into the office.

She had just sat down when Pete Morton appeared in the doorway. "A word, boss?"

"Of course."

He closed the door and sat down, then looked at her. "Has something changed, boss? You look different, somehow."

"Thank you, Pete. What is it you want to tell me?"

"Byrne is dead. Seems as though he had internal injuries that got missed. By the time they realised something was wrong, it was too late."

She examined her thoughts reacting to this news. Nobody would miss him, that was for sure. They'd be spared the trial, which was always a good thing. Would his death mean Bev and Wayne and everyone else wouldn't get whatever it was they called closure these days? She didn't think they would miss going through it all in court. All in all, it wasn't bad news. At least, Wolstenholme would get his chance to cut him open, even if Byrne would be dead at the time. The way Morton sat in the chair, upright and nervous rather than the relaxed way he usually exhibited, caught her attention.

"What is it, Pete? You've got something else to say. Spit it out. It's not like you to keep something to yourself."

He shook his head and then took a deep breath. "You know what I was saying on Sunday?"

"You'll have to remind me."

"What I was saying about not wanting to be the man who'd lost his wife, how I wanted to be the tough guy who caught criminals?"

She nodded.

"I've been thinking, thinking a lot."

She'd never thought of Pete Morton as being an introspective sort of man.

He shook his head. "I was wrong. I've been that man long enough. I really am too old for this shit."

This was such a shock to her, she couldn't think of anything to say. She'd always thought Peter Morton had

'Copper' written through him like he was a stick of Scarborough rock. He would have to be carried out of the station with his boots on, hands folded on his chest holding his warrant card.

"I haven't been drinking, boss, if that's what you're thinking. I haven't had a drop in... I don't know how long."

"I wouldn't dream of thinking that, Pete, I wouldn't dream of it, just... well, I'm shocked. I had no idea."

He shook his head. "Neither had I, until a week ago, but there's only so much of this crap any of us can take; this case has rung me up 'full'. I don't want anything more to do with people like that, with having to see things like that little girl." He shook his head. There was nothing more he could find to say.

"Well, Sergeant Morton... Pete... if you've made up your mind, I'm not going to dissuade you. You've always supported me one hundred percent, and you will have the same from me."

"I appreciate that," he mumbled.

"You'll be missed, Pete, and not just because you're a good copper, a bloody good copper, which you are, but because... well, you're Pete Morton. You're a rock. I am going to miss you."

They sat looking at each other.

"And on that note, I'm going to order you back to work before we both start weeping."

He got to his feet and went to the door before he turned. "If you don't mind not telling anyone about this. I'd like to do it myself."

She nodded with a weak smile and drew her fingers across her lips, zipping them shut. He left and she sat back in her chair. Well, every day was full of surprises, and she hadn't even had her first cup of coffee.

Her phone rang. "I think you've got something to tell me, Inspector." It was Milburn.

"Yes, boss, I'll be right up." Coffee was going to have to wait.

Chapter Forty-Nine

Darling knocked on the door and went in without waiting for an answer. Milburn looked from the newspaper on his desk. "For someone who has just solved a particularly troubling murder, you look a little on the glum side, Inspector. In your place, I'd be in the pub by now, celebrating."

Darling shrugged. "Solving the murder was hardly any trouble at all. As you taught us, we followed the breadcrumbs. As for the pub, it's nine thirty on Tuesday morning. It isn't open yet, even for us."

He gestured towards the chair on the opposite side of his desk. "It might be for coffee."

"Have you ever had what they serve as coffee in there?"

He chuckled. "That, I have not. I'm an old-fashioned man. I don't go to a pub for coffee. Of course, back in the old days, there'd always be a pub open for us." He took a long look at her. "Okay, tell me all about it, what's bothering you?"

She took a deep breath, then put the file she was carrying onto his desk. It was the file with the bank and telephone details they had about the child-abuse ring. She knew there were those, even in the station, who termed them 'child prostitutes', but she would have none of that. If there was a child involved, even if they took money for what was done to them, it was child abuse. Nothing else. "It's the ring that bothers me. Yes, we got three of them, but how many more are there?"

"You've got three of them?"

"Yes, three. Shan Abdullah thinks she knows who the doctor is in Kim's diary, the one with the scar on his hand. We should be able to find the others from the bank and telephone records, but right now it is three, if you include Monsignor Lee for all the good that's done us."

"For all the good that's done him, you mean."

She looked up, startled. "What?"

"You haven't heard, have you? He's dead."

"What... no, I hadn't heard."

"Committed suicide. Took every pill he could find and washed them down with Scotch."

Darling shook her head. This was another blow. Just because he'd had nothing to do with the murder and hadn't done anything else they had a hope in hell of getting a conviction for, didn't mean she didn't want to have another serious conversation with him, on the record.

"The chief constable just had his ear chewed off by a Father O'Heir. He was saying you came down on the monsignor like a ton of bricks and that was what caused him to commit suicide. I put him right on that, told him I'd listened to the interview and it was by the book, as always—"

"Did you say O'Heir?" she gasped, realising immediately afterwards this was the first time she had ever interrupted Joe Milburn.

"That's what Mr Mowbray said, yes."

She pursed her lips and looked down at her desk. "You know the saying, 'Once is happenstance, twice is coincidence, third time it is enemy action'?"

Milburn nodded. "I know it from Ian Fleming, in *Live and Let Die*. Can't remember whether Bond says it, or Mr Big. I didn't think it was original even back then. Why do you ask?"

"That is the third time I have come across that name in connection with this case."

Milburn's questioning half-smile evolved into a frown. Darling ticked her fingers. "One, he sent Michael Lander here as Lee's legal representation. Two, Lander turned up at Tina Brady's house when we went to talk to her the first time. Lander said it was O'Heir who retained him. Lander doesn't do home visits in the evening unless someone is leaning on him. Three, Daniel Hegarty told me he hired Byrne on the specific recommendation of one 'Father O'Heir'. There's only one priest by that name on Tyneside. I checked. Three times already, and now this."

Milburn inhaled deeply, expanded his cheeks and then blew out a long stream of air whistling between his teeth. "Don't believe in coincidences, do you?"

"No, sir. No more than you do." She shook her head, allowing just a little of the frustration to vent. "This is poison, boss. It's a blight, a blight on the whole city, on everything."

He did not respond, inviting her to continue.

"I mean, as a police officer, you get used to looking at everyone and wondering what they're trying to hide. It gets so you do it without thinking. But looking at every man and wondering 'Do you get off on children?' I don't know if I can do that much more, boss. Truly, I do not know. Pete Morton has just told me he's putting in for retirement because he can't take it anymore. Pete Morton, of all people. You've got children of your own."

"They're grown-up now," he growled, "but I know what you mean."

She picked up the file and shook it. "I do not know exactly where this will lead. I have no idea if this ring is going to prove to be all there is, even if Tina Brady ever decides to cooperate. What I do know is that now we've got the murderer, I will not have the manpower to chase down every phone call made to and from her phone, every entry in every bank account, especially if there are more we don't know about."

"You think you're going to find more?"

Darling paused, took a deep breath and then looked him full in the eye. "I have a feeling that this is a lot bigger than it looks now."

"Feeling?" He slid his glasses down so they were on the tip of his nose, and he could glare at her over the top; saying nothing, he watched her grow uncomfortable as the silence drew out.

Eventually, he relented. "Pen, you don't work on feelings. You're not like me. I rely on my copper's nose, my instinct informed by forty years of experience. You work on evidence, on observation, on what people say when we interview them, all that practical, objective stuff we can take to court. It's twenty-first-century coppering, and you do it very, very well. You tell me you have a 'feeling'. What I hear is that you have some evidence from a source you don't want to tell me about, and this evidence makes you think there is more to this than meets the eye." He went on watching her squirm. "Well? You don't have to tell me who it is. We all have sources we prefer to keep up our sleeves. I trust you. I trust your judgement. You are going to have to trust me if this 'feeling' is sending you where I think you're going."

She closed her eyes and took three deep breaths. "I have this source in the… the escort trade. Actually, she's more of a friend now than a contact. I met her during the Dancer investigation."

"Dorothy Bainbridge."

"You know her?" she gasped, then remembered how he had suggested she ask her contact in the trade. "Of course you do".

He grinned. "I'm Mighty Joe Milburn. I know everything and everyone in my patch." He paused, wondering whether she was going to swallow his legend. "Actually, I have never met the lady. On the other hand, I did read the Dance file, in which you detailed what there is to know about her."

She cursed herself. Milburn read files to cure insomnia.

"Anyway, I agree with you about her and the service she provides for consenting adults. We have higher priorities than that. What did she say that set your stomach rumbling?"

"Nothing specific. She won't touch anyone under the age of twenty-one, and she won't deal with clients who are after youngsters."

"She says."

The idea of trusting a madam would be alien to most coppers. If a madam told them the sun was shining, they would go to the window and check.

"She says. I believe her. A couple of her girls, and boys, told her they had picked up whispers of someone who could cater for customers who wanted young flesh. She deleted the details of their last customers, never did any more business with them, on principle, if you like."

"If you like."

"One of the names she deleted was this Indian surgeon who has a scar on his left hand…"

"The man in Kim's diary."

"Mr Afzahl Khan, a surgeon at the RVI."

Milburn held out his hand and took the file. "I'm going to take this away with me, have a good read of it, have a little think about what we are going to do about this." He hit the word 'we' hard enough for her to have no option but to take it in. "We are going to do something about this, Pen, believe you me. We've turned a blind eye to child abuse far too many times in the past, betrayed the trust placed in us. We convinced ourselves it couldn't be true, or it was just delinquent kids. Yes, well, we've learned that lesson. Or I have. I do not want my children looking at me in twenty years' time, when it all comes out, and asking, 'Why didn't you do anything about it, Dad?' I feel a task force coming on."

Darling only just kept her mouth from falling open. If there was one thing Joe Milburn hated, it was 'task forces', special investigation units who kept to themselves, anything that divided copper from copper.

"Don't look at me like that! I may be an old gadgie, set in my ways, but have you ever known me not to use a tool if it is useful?"

She shrugged, recognising a rhetorical question when she was asked one.

"From what you've told me, we are going to be treading on some very sensitive, well-connected toes investigating this." He held up the file. "I tread a damn sight heavier than you do. Everybody suspects I know things about them they'd much rather stayed secret. Everybody knows I don't dance to political tunes, and I don't care whose toes I tread on, so I'm not bothered if O'Heir or whoever thinks they've got friends in higher places than I have. I've got no career to get blighted. I've climbed as high as I'm going to. There's nothing they can use against me that hasn't already been used. So, I'm going to go and plan our campaign. In the meantime, I suggest you get yourself back downstairs and wrap up the paperwork on Byrne. You never know what'll come through the door tomorrow."

Darling nodded. "More paperwork."

Milburn put his hand on the table in front of her. It was a big hand and it was planted very firmly. "You might think about getting one of your minions to do the paperwork for you, the way you used to do for me. You must learn to delegate. DC Abdullah strikes me as being a good choice."

"She's too good a detective to waste pushing paper."

Milburn chuckled. "So were you, Pen. So are you."

She hesitated, then decided the meeting was over. She got up and walked to the door.

"How's that boyfriend of yours?" he called after her.

"Boyfriend?"

His chuckle turned into a full-throated laugh. "You thought you'd kept Paul a secret, did you? In a cop shop, and him an ex-copper too. Give him my best next time you see him. I always liked him. He'd have made a good copper if only he'd been able to stick it out."

Then he nodded to her again and she left.

Chapter Fifty

Darling closed her front door behind her and would have fallen to the floor had she not leaned back against it and felt the doorknob sticking into her right buttock. She had never felt this drained before after a case, this battered, this convinced that – despite everything pointing to the contrary – she had failed. To be sure, the murderer had been apprehended. They had obtained justice of a sort for Kimberley, not biblical justice but the best they could manage. Even Bev and Wayne had been given something that might grow into closure. She knew it should feel like a victory, but it didn't. It tasted like defeat. Most crimes were straightforward, banal acts of stupidity and greed. Resolving them was little more demanding than sweeping up the broken glass after a noisy party, the only trick was knowing where to sweep and when.

Only very rarely was it Holmes against Moriarty, keen wits pitted against an intellectual equal or even a superior. She could not recall having been involved in a case like that. Most criminals were not nearly as clever as they believed themselves to be, and those who were tended not to get caught unless they – or more likely their associates – were careless. Even so, there was usually a degree of satisfaction to be derived from getting the rubbish off the streets, an emotional lift from going home after a job well done.

She felt nothing of that. This was the biggest case she had led, at least in terms of notoriety, and she had brought it to a speedy conclusion while it was still on the front pages. Her superiors had already informed her of their appreciation, suggesting that it would bear fruit come review time. She had tried to appear suitably grateful, but it had all done nothing to ease her conviction that she – all of them, even hard nuts like Morton – had been wading in squalor and human sewage and would never lose the stench in their nostrils of the futility of their actions.

Yes, they had prevented children being abused in the future by these perverts, but that did not erase the fact that real children had already been abused by them, horribly abused and one murdered in the foulest way imaginable. That abuse had been inflicted by men who strutted in society, portraying themselves as upright men, moral men, successful men, role models. For heaven's sake, one of them was even a minister of the church; a high-up, not just some obscure parish priest in the back of beyond. They were not depraved from birth. They had not been raised to believe there was no difference between right and wrong. They knew the rules. They helped make the rules. They just believed that those rules did not apply to them in any meaningful, personal way. They were entitled to satisfy their lusts at the cost of a child's innocence, entitled because they had the kind of cash to purchase that perversity. She was not a mother and did not intend to be one. She was not overly sentimental about children. Even so, there were some lines she believed should never be crossed, and abuse of children was way the other side of one such line. If there were societies in which it was acceptable, she was heart glad she did not live in one.

She did not bother making her customary pot of tea, rather going directly to the kitchen cupboard and the half-drunk bottles of spirit in there. Ordinarily she drank gin, and that only rarely. Tonight, she took out an unopened bottle of Talisker malt whisky and poured herself half a tumblerful of it. She did not like the taste, but she did like what it did when it hit her stomach, dissolving the chains that bound her to the past and present of the squalid world in which she lived. It opened the doors to a future that might be better than today.

Tonight, though, the drugs did not work. She felt the relaxing effect it had on her muscles but not on her mind. Even when she put on some Pink Floyd, the swirling, optimistic *Learning to Fly*, she did not feel any loosening of her ties to Earth. After a while – she had no idea how long, but it must have been some time – she found herself sitting in darkness, her glass empty, the stereo playing the song for the who-knew-how-manyth time. Rubbing her eyes – at least there was no sleep grit in them – she swung her legs over the side of the chair and stood up. At least, she tried to stand up. Her knees gave way as she tried to put her weight through them and, but for holding onto the chair, she would have fallen over.

For a moment, panic blossomed inside her. Such weakness was not usual for her, and she managed to dismiss the panic as soon as it arose. She was exhausted. It really was as easy as that. Strong drink on top of that and an empty stomach had knocked her out. That was all. Realising that, she also realised there was nothing to be more desired than to lay one's head down in one's own bed, knowing there would be no alarm clock ringing in the morning. In the meantime, she would solve the empty-stomach element of the problem.

She was sitting in the kitchen, chewing her way through a second cereal bar, when she happened to glance at the shelf where she kept her phone chargers, where both her phones should be charging right now. They weren't. She was just plugging in her personal phone when it rang. For a moment she stared at it, wondering who could possibly be calling her at this time in the morning? The thumbnail photo it revealed of the caller was Paul. Suddenly, the seduction of her bed paled beside the prospect of talking with her boyfriend.

She was just about to sweep the green 'answer' icon when she realised she had just thought of Paul as her boyfriend. The realisation gave her pause.

Her finger skimmed across the icon. "Hi, this is Pen. I find I can get to the phone after all. If you have any good news, any good news at all, I'd love to hear it."

"Up late, aren't you? Been out partying in my absence, have you?" She heard the chuckle in his voice and wanted more.

"No, nothing like that at all. I've been filling out my application for the nunnery is all. For an organisation that promises the simple life, they certainly do have the most complicated of application forms."

"If 'nun', write 'none', eh?" He laughed, and she joined in.

"More or less. You have some good news? Or do you want to hear mine first?"

"Yours first," he said. Even over three thousand miles on a mobile phone connection she could hear the excitement in his voice. "Yours will be real good news."

She closed her eyes, counted to ten and then took a mouthful of water because her tongue was suddenly stuck to the roof of her mouth. "That case, the one you told me not to tell you about. We solved it."

"*You* solved it. Not 'we', you."

"That's not true," she said.

"If you can't take a compliment when I pay you one, I'll stop it."

"I'm sorry. It's just—"

"I know what it is 'just'. Now do you want to hear my good news or not?"

"Yes, yes, yes." She laughed, and then frowned as the connection seemed to fade. When it was restored, it was not Paul speaking, it was Freddie Mercury declaring that he was the champion of the world.

"You won?"

"*We* won. We're rich."

Rich? As though she didn't have enough to think about. But that would wait, wait until Paul was back, wait until she knew whether she was coming or going. Did she really want to be rich? Riches didn't seem to have done Hegarty any good.

"Rich," she said. "I think I like the sound of that."

If you enjoyed this book, please let others know by leaving a quick review on Amazon. Also, if you spot anything untoward in the paperback, get in touch. We strive for the best quality and appreciate reader feedback.

editor@thebookfolks.com

www.thebookfolks.com

Also in this series

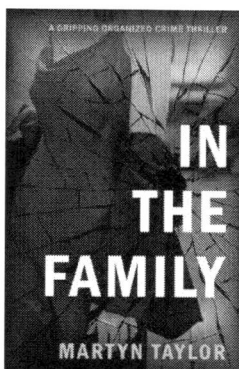

IN THE FAMILY (Book 1)

When a former gangland boss is found shot dead in his home, DI Penelope Darling knows that the investigation will take her into the nether regions of her city's criminal world. But finding the killer among the likely suspects will require keeping her eyes open to the unexpected. She'll need to have her wits about her to stop a ruthless individual from getting away with murder.

FREE with Kindle Unlimited and available in paperback!

More fiction by the author

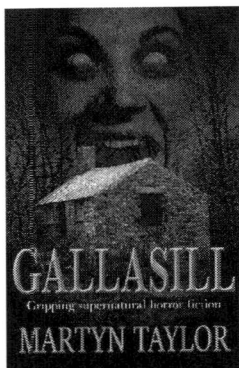

GALLASILL

The hanging of an innocent man seven generations ago
left a curse on the two feuding local families involved.
Sarah Charlton's father has hidden this family secret, but
curiosity gets the better of her. When she investigates the
story, she realises she is not the only one with a stake in
the past.

FREE with Kindle Unlimited!

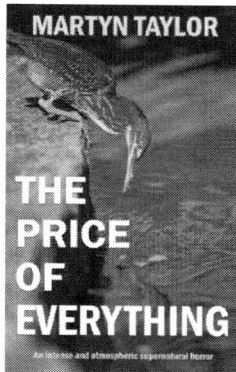

THE PRICE OF EVERYTHING

Peter Mann is a rational chap so, when his brother dies, supernatural causes are far from his mind. But when the balance of good and evil is so precarious, at what price do we not recognise the dark forces around us? That's the question that will confront Peter and his nephew Billy when a series of macabre events make them realise that true malevolence has come to town.

FREE with Kindle Unlimited!

Other titles of interest

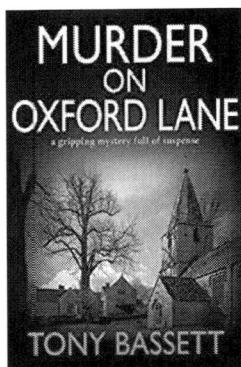

MURDER ON OXFORD LANE
by Tony Bassett

A budding chorister doesn't return home from practice
but his wife doesn't appear concerned. DS Sunita Roy
becomes convinced he has been murdered but she has her
own problems in the form of an ex-boyfriend who won't
take no for an answer. Will she keep her eye on the ball
when all expect her to fail?

FREE with Kindle Unlimited and available in paperback!

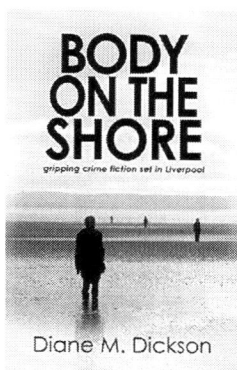

BODY ON THE SHORE
by Diane Dickson

When police retrieve a body from the flat sands of a popular beach, DI Jordan Carr is presented with his first murder case. The victim is a woman, but they know little more about her. Tracing the events that led to her death will take the detective on an uncomfortable journey into the dark side of Liverpool.

FREE with Kindle Unlimited and available in paperback!

**THE
BOOK
FOLKS**

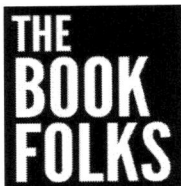

*Sign up to our mailing list to find out about new releases
and special offers!*

www.thebookfolks.com

Printed in Dunstable, United Kingdom